Now I

"It isn't often that a reader finds a volume of short stories as satisfying as THE SKY IS FAR AWAY. Each story is a polished gem…these characters touch us all. Do yourself a favor and get to know them." – Carolyn Brewer, author of: Changing The Tune; and One Song Beyond Hope.

"[These stories] are fresh, varied, startling and go deep into the human soul. Wright's characters become so real, so heart wrenching, that you linger at the end of the story, unable to let them go. I [will] recommend this book of stories to every reader I know." - Judy Ellen Crotchett, Author of: Rhody.

"The Sky is Far Away—best writing I've come across in a very long time." - Dag Scheer

NOW
I
SAY
GOODBYE
TO
YOU

Now I Say Goodbye To You

ALSO BY BROOKS WRIGHT

THE SKY IS FAR AWAY

NOW

I SAY

GOODBYE

TO

YOU

A Novel by

BROOKS WRIGHT

ARTICHOKE PRESS

BOSTON

Now I Say Goodbye To You

ARTICHOKE PRESS
BOSTON

WWW.BROOKSWRIGHT.NET

book design and photograph are by Brooks Wright

For Rita,
David, Elizabeth, and Ronoka

** ACKNOWLEDGMENTS **

I would like to thank Catherine Thibedeau for all her help with this book, Beth Luchner, and my readers, Anne and Scott Smith, Margie Talacko, Kim Fesenmeyer, Judy Ellen Crotchett, and of course Rita.

EXIT

Where's the entrance to the exit?
- Popeye the Sailor Man

One

I crouch in vacant lots to see who else is around, see no one, sprint across to backyards full of bone-dry, burnt-out Bluegrass, and make my way up to the sliding glass doors. The drapes are gone, the locks busted; the doors open easily. Then I'm in. Sometimes there are animals in the house—stray dogs, stray cats, the occasional raccoon—there have been rats on occasion; you have to be careful. And of course, there might be people—owners back for a last look before they disappear out of state, or squatters and drug addicts setting up shop. This time there are no people or rats, or squatters, either. I make my way through the downstairs, stepping lightly over the broken glass. Even though I know there is only a small chance that I have anything to fear, I am careful. I look for whatever I can find, something useful to help keep myself alive—if living is what you'd call this. Somebody's past is usually all there is, or what's left of it. They leave late at night stealing away in the dark to somewhere else and take whatever they can, but there's always a few things left behind that say something about them if you bother to look. Each house is like a story; a story revealing little items of interest. Except I keep thinking it was all a story: the house, the car, the job —everything.

It's mostly junk they leave behind. Sometimes I find books. I like books; I used to read a lot. It was real to me in a way that real things are not, and of course real things are not real at all when you think about it—not like they're supposed to be. That's Plato. He had a whole theory on this. Ideas are real; things are not. Like this house. In somebody's mind it was a home once. Now it's an empty building. But you know it was just a building before only with people in it, pretending, and loaded down with all their crap to help them do it. What was real was their idea of it. To me it's just another story to read—Story of a Home. It's my job to find out what happened, if only to amuse myself. Each room holds out a promise to be discovered. There could be anything here—food for instance, or flashlight batteries—or like most of the time, just a promise deferred. But there's almost always something I can use, even in this abandoned house. Or not, depending—that's the game.

They're mostly empty, of course, except for the stuff they left behind in their hurry to get away. Food in cans, when I can find it, is the most important. And water, of course; water's essential. I get thirsty in this heat. Once I found a whole case of beer. Hard to carry, though; and you get spoiled.

Sometimes the water hasn't been shut off, and I can fill my bottles, and if I'm lucky, take a shower, and if there's a bar of soap I wash myself. I used to try and shave. That didn't last. My hair and beard have gotten so long if I had a loin cloth and a cross you'd think I was Jesus. On my list of things to find is a pair of scissors. That way I can at least trim the beard; maybe I'll cut my hair.

This house is not too bad, messy but not awful. Some are covered in dog shit and the kitchen's got rotting garbage in the fridge, the door left open because the power's off, or there's garbage in the wastebasket that isn't covered, which fills the house with flies and a ghastly odor that sends you running when you can't take it anymore—then it's on to a new house and a new story.

I'm in the living room, now. There are notices from the mortgage company by the front door where the mail slot is. The repo guy has left his card. They come and clean the place up so the bank can sell it, trashing it out they call it, but they can't keep up, there's too many of them since the bottom fell out. That's where I come in. Officially I serve no purpose, but that doesn't stop me. I'm, in fact, no longer part of any purpose. I'm just reading my way through the neighborhood. This house is my next story. There are hundreds of them just like it. Some are still lived in so

I have to be careful, but lots of them are empty. So I make my way through, foraging and discovering what's left. I could go on like this forever.

I'm not superstitious, per se, but I have my habits. I like to check out the basements first. You get the back-story down there. In this case the guy liked to work out. There's a set of weights and a jump rope. Probably the kid's jump rope—learning the I Work Out and Exercise story. At the far end is an old lamp, a calendar on the wall, from before, and a poster of a mountain lake. On the lake there's a runabout pulling a water skier across the boat's foamy white wake. An old Igloo ice cooler sits in the corner collecting dust. That was the first installment on the dream in the picture—the cooler. I'm guessing they bought it before they bought the house. Then after the cooler they bought the boat, but there was no place to keep it at their cramped little apartment. The neighbor kids played on it when they weren't around to scare them off. When they weren't dreaming of taking the boat up to the lake, they dreamed of parking it in their new driveway when they finally bought a house, so the dream about the boat could be more real. In the dream they always had the little red and white Igloo cooler in the back of the boat where it was filled with ice and cans full of beer and soda pop.

Other things in the basement include a bag of

potting soil for the flower garden they wanted to plant, and a half-empty gallon of redwood stain for the picnic table they had out on the patio. In the dream it had an umbrella stuck in a hole in the center with plastic place mats covered with palm leaves to match the palm leaves on the umbrella. She would bring the hamburger patties out to him on a plate and he would get them sizzling on the grill while the kids fought over some useless toy in the sandbox.

In my backpack I carry a flashlight that I found in one of the houses and every now and then I find batteries. They're essential, because most of the houses have no electricity. The first floor bathroom has soap and toothpaste and an almost clean hand towel. In the family room I see a wallet size school picture on the floor, the smiling face of a little girl who might be eight years old and still in full belief mode, as we all are at that age, her eyes bright and blue with wonder. She's sitting in front of a fake background the photographer unrolled onto the wall behind her—cherry blossoms and blue sky.

In between these houses, out in the crabgrass and vacant fields waiting to be subdivided, it's cold at night and dirty and crawling with insects. Small animals roam and forage. The lawns don't get mowed now and are full of snakes. When the alligators and Burmese Pythons finally arrive it's going to be a real problem. On the other hand, there's nothing here for them to eat except me, which is why I keep moving and like to sleep inside at night. They call this the Sunshine State but don't be fooled. It can be darker than hell here no matter what the time of day when the sun's not out.

I put the picture of the girl in my wallet, which now contains many of the items that I find in each of the houses: airline mileage cards, useless credit cards from closed accounts, pictures of babies and grandchildren, spouses (all female, of course) organ donor cards, receipts, insurance cards. Trying to figure out who I am from my wallet will baffle anyone as I now am all of these people, you could say, a real conglomeration. One family left an entire photo album and genealogy in a closet still pungent with old items of clothing and a pillow missing its pillowcase. That night I laid my head on that pillow and dreamed about the pictures in that album. Wandering through the house earlier that day I imagined them all, each with their little piece of the story they were telling themselves. The father had a job and said, "Love it or leave it," when people complained about the country. "Come and get it," the mother said to the kids watching TV or playing in the pool.

When I wake in the morning I look for the can

of pork and beans I found the day before. It's in my bag where I keep the can opener I found and couldn't believe my good luck when I did. I used to be bothered by eating cold food out of cans, like soup or ravioli, which before I'd never have eaten without heating first. But beans are one of those things that are always just as good eating them cold as they are eating them hot. I still don't eat the bacon fat. Then I pee in the toilet because, hey, why not. Even though there's no running water it doesn't mean jack shit to me anymore, it's not my toilet, and it's not like the people are coming back. That's when I think I see something.

I stop for a second next to the window in the upstairs master bedroom and take in the view. There's one of those greenspace areas with bike trails and trees at the edge of the yard. It's from the Little Piece of Eden story. It runs adjacent to all the houses on this side of the street. The back of the house faces west so the early sun leaves alternating patches of lemony morning light and dark as midnight shadow. Standing behind the slash pine and red mangrove is a girl, could be nine or ten, maybe older, maybe not. She's staring at the house. I'm a little surprised. I haven't seen another person this close in days, maybe a week, much less a child. And she's just standing there. Why? I hide, mostly, from people. I've had enough of that—making my way, pretending. I'd rather read my way through whatever's been left behind and be satisfied that at least I'm not fooling myself anymore.

I take a step back so she won't see me, and wait a second before stepping away from the window, just a few feet, then inch my way around to peek outside again. Not there. I wondered how long it would take to have everything slip a little. A person can get desperate. See things that aren't really there. I dream of people from before it all fell apart, their smiles and the funny things they said. It's only a matter of time before you start seeing things during the day, I told myself. Not to worry. It's better this way—avoiding. My thought, now, though, is to get my bag and find a secure place inside, just in case. Maybe the basement. I'll wait down there; see how it goes. Usually I stay in a house for an hour, or so unless it's getting dark, then make my way to the greenspace where I can move about during the day with less chance of being discovered. I'll look for a likely house—they aren't all empty—and wait, sometimes for hours, just to make sure. Then I'll make a mad dash across the lawn up to the back door. The best houses have a screened back porch where you can mess with the lock—if it isn't already busted —and won't be seen.

Downstairs I poke around, being careful to

stay away from the windows. I open the door to the attached garage and see a basketball sitting on the cement floor and a plastic wading pool leaning against the far wall. I see the mother, then, standing in K-Mart looking at the wading pools on the shelf trying to decide. She is remembering herself as a child and breathing in the memory of those days because she can still smell the grass, almost, and see the diamonds of sunlight jumping from the hose when her mother fills the pool. Now she wants this for her child and imagines it as she looks at each pool on the shelf. Probably for the girl in the school picture I have now in my wallet. In the opposite side by the interior wall to the house is a wooden tool shed built into the corner. I open the door and see only a deflated bicycle tire and a bag of lawn seed with a hole eaten into the bottom of it by mice. I can hide in the shed, I decide, and step in to see if I'll fit. I wait a while, then check to see if the coast is clear. The coast is miles from here, but we say these things in place of reality, which none of us much cares for.

Later, in the kitchen I stand by the window and look into the yard. The half that I can see is empty. I step into the dining room next to see the other half and I am surprised to see the girl again, standing at the back of the yard looking at the house. She is looking up as though trying to see into an upstairs window. Something about her looks familiar. Stepping back into the shadow I take out my wallet. I find the picture I put in there last night. The girl in the picture looks like the girl outside, only younger. If it's her, she's likely to come in. I grab my backpack and head for the garage. Inside the tool shed I scoot down into a sitting position with my knees up in front of me and pull the door shut. In the dark I can see the girl sitting in the wading pool. Her mother and father are there. She fills the little plastic pail with water and pours it over her knee. The pail is yellow, or maybe it's red, and has a strap handle that swivels to either side. She carries the pail across the yard to the sandbox and pours water onto the sand. Her father makes a video of it, and when they watch the video they can hear themselves laughing at their little girl taking water from the pool and pouring it into the sandbox. You'll always have this to remember yourself by, they tell her.

I wait for sounds of someone walking in the house but hear nothing. It is quiet in the garage and the world beyond is disappearing. I doze off and dream about food. In the dream there is lots of it and I can't stop eating. I wake up sometime later, a gnawing feeling in my stomach. An hour passes without anything happening and I am tired of sitting like this in the bottom of the tool shed so I decide to come out and see if the girl is still here. I step inside and wait near the dining room. Nothing. I move quietly across to, look out the window into the yard and see nothing but the yellow grass and the faded bushes baking in the sun. The kitchen is empty and the other half of the backyard is empty, and the living room, too, and so on.

I go upstairs and stand in the hallway. In the first bedroom I come to, I find a page from an old coloring book with red and blue scribbles on it, and see in the closet a doll with no clothes on and a stuffed Curious George slumped together on the floor in the corner. When I pick up the doll and hold her upright the eyes pop open. They are blue and have a kind of starburst ring of gray around the irises. The lashes are long like in the story about beauty we are always telling ourselves. I turn to leave the room but stop because I think I hear something. It sounds like footsteps, someone coming up the stairs, but slowly. I set the doll on the floor and step back into the closet, being careful not to make a sound. I close the door. It is dark in here like the tool shed. After a moment of silence I hear footsteps walk slowly across the hall and into the room. I wait, but there is nothing. Nothing happens. I stand as still as I can, like a child playing hide and seek, wishing I had thought to sit down. My legs are tired from standing. Then I hear footsteps again, someone, whoever it is, maybe the girl, is leaving the room. I hear her walk down the hall and then come back, but not into the room I am in, and then I hear nothing. As quietly as I can I open the closet door. The room is empty. The doll I left on the floor is gone. She must be real, I decide. Both a good sign, and a bad sign.

I stay in the bedroom but after fifteen minutes decide to cross the hallway into the bathroom where I can look out the window. There is nothing in the backyard. I enter the master bedroom and look out that window but figure she must be downstairs still. I may have to stay up here all night. This house has been stripped long ago; even the carpeting is gone. The floors are good hardwood floors, oak or oak veneer. Houses that still have some carpet left are more comfortable for sleeping but have their own stories to tell. If not reeking of pee there can be bloodstains or even semen. If not, then you might imagine there are, and avoid whatever is on that carpet that looks like blood, but may only be rust. I realize I left my backpack in the tool shed. I'll have to go down there and get it but how? What if she comes up here again? I picture the girl finding me in her bedroom holding Curious George. That's mine, she will say. She looks too old to be playing with dolls and is probably why it got left behind, but now it would mean a lot to her to have it. That's why she took the doll just now. Maybe that's why she came back. Outside it's getting dark. I lie down on the mattress and listen for footsteps. Before long I am dozing off and dreaming I'm in a room full of dolls with blue eyes and all the dolls are looking at me. They're just dolls but it's making me anxious. What are you looking at me for, I say.

I wake and the sun is going down and right away I look out the window, checking the slash pine and mangrove for the girl and see only birds and squirrels. The yard is empty, the evening still. I am hungry and decide I will have to make my way downstairs to the garage and get my backpack, which has one more can of food: Chef Boyardee something or other. My water bottle is in there also and I am so thirsty it feels like I swallowed my tongue. It takes a while to get to the garage because I am being so careful. As a kid I was good at playing commando, so I can sneak around this house, now, still, after all these years.

I wait by the tool shed—no sense in taking chances—and look at the picture of the girl again. It could be her. She's come back because her life is in this house. The memory of her life, anyway. Nothing is really here anymore. But now I'm curious about this girl. If she's the story I'm reading in this house it's way better than the poster of the runabout and water skier and the Igloo cooler I found in the basement. It's her story but why is she here all by herself? I have a house somewhere, and a story, too, but I try not to remember what and where it is. Now it is easier to see all these other houses and try not to bother with whatever it was that was my life before. I'm done with all that.

A door closes. It's a very distinct sound, a door closing, so there's no mistaking it. I step in and swing the door to the tool shed closed and wait in darkness. I've been drinking my water so I will have to pee, soon, but expect I have a while before that becomes a problem. I listen, and think I hear her, but it might be my imagination. Maybe I'm dreaming this now like I dreamed finding the doll. Strange what the mind does. I had a life before all this, but I don't remember a doll with eyes that opened and closed. When you wake in the morning and can barely remember a dream, a dream that seemed so real you could swear it really happened, but then your eyes open and it's gone and you can't remember it at all or barely, that's what it's like, what I remember, and don't remember.

I have to decide what to do if she finds me. I could just turn and walk away. Keep walking. By the time she tells someone, if there's anyone to tell, I'll be long gone. Of course, there's no reason to fear her. She's only a child. She'd be more afraid of *me*, I'm sure. She should be. She'd be defenseless. Because now I'm beginning to suspect if she's real she's all alone, herself. Why else is she here? Where are her people if she keeps hanging around this house? I can offer to help her. But that's how it starts, isn't it? Making it up again, like it's anything other than what it really is. I need food and shelter. I need to keep moving. She'd only be in the way. And if they found us together, what would they say? They'd make up their own stories, and I wouldn't like the ending. I know all about that. It's best to sneak away as soon as I can. Avoid her. Don't let her see me, and then whenever she's not looking, I'll get out of the house and make a run for the greenspace out back. Keep going before it's too late.

Two

Dusk and I'm still in the tool shed. Fell asleep once, but now I'm wide awake. How do I know it's dusk? My watch. It glows in the dark. I see it's seven in the evening. I swing open the door. Five steps and I'm across the garage to the door that leads from the garage into the house. The door has been opened and left ajar. I watch through the crack and see nothing but the empty hallway. I push it open further. Nothing. Three more steps and I'm in. Nothing. From the dining room I see into the yard. There's something moving. I step closer to see. It looks like a pack of dogs. They are crouching as though stalking something. They are inching toward the edge of the greenspace. It might be the girl they see. They might be waiting, deciding whether to attack. There's no food now and these stray animals are starving. They've learned to hunt in packs. Nature is always waiting. Everything reverts right back. People are just a blip on the evolutionary scale. I look for the girl but don't see her. If she's there the dogs will overcome their fear and surround her. I move quickly through the kitchen to the back door and, before thinking better of it, I open the door, grab a piece of wood lying on the stoop, and bang it on the side of the house. The dogs flinch and turn in my direction. They see me and begin to growl and bark. It is not what I want to happen. They're making too much noise and will call attention to the house. There is no one around, but I can't risk someone coming, hearing the noise and deciding to investigate. I step back inside and watch the dogs watching the house, now. They come closer and wait. I run through the house to the front door to make sure it is unlocked, and will open, and hurry back to the kitchen. I step outside and run toward the side of the house farthest from the dogs and make it around before they begin chasing me. I hear them barking again as I run to the front of the house and through the front door, slamming it behind me. I keep going straight back through the house. From the kitchen I see the girl emerge from the greenspace and run across the yard to the backdoor. I run to hide but not before opening the back door a little to save her time. The door slamming shut echoes through the house as I enter the garage and step into the tool shed where I slump down and close the door.

I decide I can wait a few hours until it's completely dark and then slip into the house and across to the kitchen and out the back door before she hears me. If I'm lucky she will go upstairs and hide in her old closet where she'll find Curious George, and if she still has the doll they can all stay in there together. It'll be just like before when they had the story they were having, about the house and the boat and the job and the picnic table out back with the umbrella decorated with palm leaves. The umbrella itself is a story about palm leaves. Palm leaves and a sandy white beach. In the store where she bought the wading pool, K-Mart or Wal-Mart, wherever it was, the mother saw the umbrella with the palm leaves and pictured them all eating burgers under it and drinking lemonade. At work, at the job, the father made proposals with PowerPoint, and understood that with his PowerPoint proposals he was really making the umbrella with palm leaves and by extension the sandy beaches, and that with enough key strokes the umbrella would open and bloom, like a flower, right there over the redwood picnic table. And if making the flower simultaneously resulted in a missile delivery system for the military, then whatever! It is not a friendly world. That the system might actually deliver that missile, he tried not to think about. Instead, he thought about the umbrella and the palm leaves and the sandy white beaches.

How long will the dogs wait outside the house for me to appear, I wonder, or will they hang around all night. This could be a problem. I sleep. I dream about dogs. They chase me and I run but my shoes are too big and falling off. Sometime around midnight I wake and wonder if the dogs that just chased me down the street in my dreams are still outside. Carefully, trying hard not to make the slightest sound I push open the door to the tool shed and climb out onto the cement floor. It is dark and I feel the girl's absence in the air. It is palpable like the sound of nothing after the sound of something. Stepping carefully through the house my eyes adjust enough that I see shapes of things and understand the world without their stories to be only geometrical patterns connected by circumstance. I head for the back door. I look; nothing moving. I step out; I move. The episode of the dogs is over apparently, at least for a while. But I know they are out there somewhere and might find me again. I look back at the house and think she is safe, for now, anyway. She is home and can tell herself about the house with all its different parts. The cooler and the wading pool are there and somewhere, if only inside her, are her parents and other people, perhaps, and maybe this will be enough.

I'm not very far into the greenspace when I hear a noise. Something is moving in the bushes, making a rustling sound, and now I hear a low growling like the growling from the dream. A pair of eyes, like lemon drops floating in some endless abyss, appear in the darkness and the growling gets louder and the lemon drops come closer and I begin to step backwards wondering if I should try to run, which I do. Then I hear barking in the distance and I know the other dogs have been alerted and they are heading back here to join in on the hunt. This dog, I assume that's what it is, is right behind me, now, and barking furiously. I have never run so fast in my life—we always say these things and I'm saying it now; it's a little story about fear. My heart is pounding and stuck somewhere in my throat and I expect to feel the dog's teeth sink into my leg at any minute. I want to reach the back door before it happens, but realize like a blow to the head that stopping to open the door will give the dog time to catch up. Then it will have me. Its teeth will rip into my flesh and I will not be able to get that thing off me before the others get here and then it will be all over for me; they will tear me apart. When I am just about there I realize I have no choice. I wheel around and wait the split second necessary, pull my right leg back and with all my strength send it forward into the head of the dog growling and leaping through the air, feel the crack of it connecting, and hear the sharp yelp and dull thud of it hitting the ground and turn, without waiting even a second longer, open the door and tumble inside. I quickly shut the door behind me and know instantly that she must be awake and cowering upstairs, not knowing if it is me, or someone else. I am convulsing with fear, myself, and gulping for air, my heart bursting inside my chest. I lay here thinking that the first lie we tell ourselves is that tomorrow will come in spite of all the evidence to the contrary. And yet, here I am.

An hour passes and I am sitting up now, but still on the floor. There is nothing to eat, which means I will have to go out again, eventually. My rule is not to stay in the same area for more than a day or two. No running from house to house along the same street, either. That's too conspicuous. But the dogs are a new complication. I will have to go to the next house down, in case the dogs are close, sometime soon to look for food. I sleep some more and wake with the morning light. I'm really hungry now. Better check here again, first, I think. I might have missed something. There's a broom closet by the refrigerator. So far I hear nothing from upstairs.

The closet looks empty at first but on further inspection I see a can of tomato paste, a can of soup, and a small can of Vienna sausage. I might be dreaming. I might wake up and still be lying on the floor where I fell in a heap when I burst through the door. But no, I'm not dreaming. I don't think I'm dreaming. I grab the cans of food, thinking: I've just been saved, like it's a miracle, and how can I be so lucky. But, then, I've been finding things to eat all along, ever since this whole thing started. Then, I think: can you hallucinate with your fingers? I can hardly remember what it was like before. I pull the can opener from my backpack and begin to open the tomato paste. The can of Vienna sausage has one of those pull tops. I'm going to dip the sausages into the tomato paste and pretend everything's going to be all right after all. I sit on the floor with my back against the cabinets. Whatever they had to sit on in here is long gone, along with the rest of their life.

I'm biting into my first sausage when I hear footsteps. Someone is coming down the stairs, the girl I guess. I could leave now, but I don't know if the dogs are out there and I don't want to leave this food behind and can't carry it and my backpack at the same time. The cans are already open. I decide to wait and see what happens. Time passes. I want to eat my sausages, but I'm waiting for whoever it is to appear. Then as I'm about to take another bite, the girl, walking slowly, passes the kitchen heading toward the garage. She doesn't see me, but I can tell that it's her. She's wearing an old jacket that looks too big for her. The sleeves are torn. It's dirty. Her jeans are dirty, her hair stringy, her shoes in need of repair. She stops, as if she hears something, as if she can hear me breathing. When she turns around quickly as though catching sight of something in the corner of her eye, I am still sitting on the floor holding the sausage in my hand, looking at her. The cans are sitting beside me on the floor. She looks at them. She looks at me, chewing my food, then back to the can of Vienna sausage. Nothing happens. We wait.

"Okay," I say, "you found me." To which she says nothing. Her face is as blank as an empty page. What's her story, I wonder.

"You have a name?" I ask, finally, after a long moment of silence, tired of waiting.

She looks at me as though trying to figure out what she should do. She's just a kid, maybe ten or eleven. She looks confused. I can see she might be half pretty underneath all the dirt. Cute, like a kid. She is afraid, probably, shrugs her shoulders, thinking more about the food, I suppose, than about what I'm asking her, her face taut and looking tired and hungry.

"What is it?" I say. "Your name," I ask again.

Her face relaxes into a perplexed expression as though thinking what the answer might be. It's not a difficult question, but sometimes answers to the simplest things are the hardest. She stares but does not answer. Her arms are at her side. "Okay," I say, waiting to see what she'll do. Her face goes from perplexed back to somber again. There are dark rings under her eyes. I can't say that I look much better, my hair and my beard wild and overgrown as a mountain forest. I won't smile, and neither will she. What for? I want to eat, but this girl just stands there staring at me. I know she's hungry. So am I.

"This your house?" I ask her. Her eyes shift to take in what there is to see of the kitchen without really moving her head. Without the carpet and the furniture and curtains on the windows it could be anyone's house. How can she tell?

She looks at me through her confusion and blinks her eyes. "That's your doll isn't it?" I try again. She's holding the doll in her left hand. She's got it by the foot and it's dangling there like someone hanging over the edge of a cliff. She's not answering. The doll is from her story. I can tell. When its eyes open she sees into the past. Better to leave it there, but that's her decision. She says nothing. Who's she trying to kid? I know it's hers. She's too old for dolls and still she picks it up and carries it around. Why else would she do it if it weren't hers? She can look at me all she wants but she's not getting any of my food. I tricked the dogs for her; that's all I'm going to do. It's too late, now, for any more stories. I'm done with that.

"I'll be leaving," I say. "Once it's safe outside."

She steps over by the wall where the table used to be, or where you would put one if you lived here. Where the people sat, eating breakfast. Mom they said. Let's have pancakes. But there's no table now and no mom making breakfast. She leans against the wall and slumps to the floor. Underneath the dirt her sneakers have little pink kitten faces all over them. They're cute, but everyone knows there's no such thing as pink kittens. I decide to go ahead and eat. She watches me. I dip the sausage into the tomato paste and put it in my mouth and chew. I wish she'd stop watching me. I swallow and look at the can of food. It makes me wonder what she will do when I leave. She can't stay here. There's no food left after this.

It has been so long since I've been living this way my stomach has shrunk to the size of a golf ball. After I eat three sausages, I feel full. She's still watching me. The doll is lying on her lap. Its eyes are closed, now. The past is gone. There is nothing to see in the doll's face now. If the girl closed her eyes she would have the same face, but her eyes are open. There is a story on her face now I see. It's in her eyes. Blue eyes. In the story I am giving her some of the sausages. If it had a name it would be Sausages and Tomato Paste.

"Here," I say, tired of her looking at me with that sorry face of hers, and lean forward to hand her a sausage. She scrambles across the floor and takes the sausage but doesn't, as I had expected, gobble the thing right down like one of the dogs outside. She sits there looking at the can of tomato paste, instead. I hand her the can of paste and she dips the sausage in and pulls out a big red gob of it with the sausage and stuffs it in her mouth, cheeks bulging while she chews rapidly, her eyes glistening; with what? Gratitude? I doubt it.

I'm thirsty, her eyes are saying. Not thank you; you're so nice and kind. Just, I'm thirsty. I'm not surprised. I wait more long minutes before I give her another sausage. I don't want her to get the wrong idea. Never feed a stray animal, people say. It's the title to a story about what will happen if you do. All you need is the title to know what will happen. So you just say it. People know what you mean. You could make the rest up yourself, depending. That's how we get through life. Make it all up. The house, the job, the flag, the boat, the cooler. It's all the same, really. Sausage and Tomato Paste is just another version. But my ending is going to be different than hers. We're going to have separate endings.

I give her some water just to get her to quit looking at me. I have to take a drink myself and… well…I can let her have one drink, at least. Anything to be rid of her. I put the soup can in my backpack and lean back and close my eyes. I'll sleep just for a minute, so I'm rested and ready to move fast when the time comes.

Three

When I wake it's still mid-morning and she's asleep on the floor, the doll tucked close under her arm. I figure it's as good a time as any to go. I'll have to risk the dogs sooner or later, or it'll mean starving to death, and for some reason I'm just not ready for that right now. As quietly as I can, I stand, knees cracking like twigs in a forest, and step slowly to the front room where I can open the front door without waking her. I pause a moment, then slowly open it and slip into the outside world. A new story begins—me sneaking away, from her and from the dogs. The air feels good; it was stuffy inside. I look around and see an empty street. Somewhere way in the distance a lawnmower is humming. It's the lawn story. You fertilize it, you water it. It turns green and grows. You cut it. It goes with the Picnic Table, if you think about it. The cooler is in there, too. The Lawn, the Picnic Table, the Cooler and the Boat. They're all part of the same story: Life Is Good.

I move to the side of the house and dart around the corner. The back yard is empty and I run fast to get to the greenspace before I am noticed. Once there I duck behind a red mangrove and wait. I listen for the dogs. Except for the humming of the lawnmower, the morning is quiet, the air still. After a moment to make sure everything is okay, I stand up and look back at the house. This is a mistake. She is standing outside the back door on the cement stoop holding her doll, watching me. I look at her long enough to know I don't want her looking at me like that and turn and disappear into the greenspace. I want to put some distance between the house and myself, between her and myself. Too much activity in the same area is not advisable. I will make my way down the street, staying in the greenspace, then pick a promising house and look for food. If there's no food there, I'll go to the next house and keep going until I find some.

I have been walking about ten minutes, taking my time, enjoying the sunshine, and telling myself the Being Out Of Doors story, when I hear something behind me. I duck behind a bush and listen. I hear the sound of someone running, then the sound stops. I wait. A twig snaps. I quickly check out the house across from me in case it is the dogs again and I have to make a run for it, hoping the door is not locked. That would be the end. The other alternative is to find a tree to climb. This is not a good choice because I would be stuck there until I finally lost consciousness and fell to the ground. The dogs would wait. They have beaucoup patience when it comes to waiting, waiting for food, that is; they're all about hunger and food, and a possible meal. They only have one story, the Food story.

I hear footsteps again. Someone is coming and I suspect who it is. Then I see her. She walks right past me, but then turns suddenly, having seen me out of the corner of her eye. I feel foolish crouching here so I stand and continue walking as though I don't see her, as though she isn't even here, and I haven't been crouching and hiding in the bushes like an idiot.

She stays about ten feet behind me, running every now and then to catch up. This is the middle part of Never Feed a Stray Animal. It's not my version of how it ends, now; it's hers. I keep walking. When I see a likely prospect, a house that's empty but looks to be only recently vacated, I stop and assess the situation. At the back door I have to jimmy the lock with a screwdriver, the one I keep in my backpack. I signal for her to be quiet and step through the door. When I determine that the house is safe, I hurry to search for food. There is nothing. I look in every room. I have the can of soup, still, but when that is gone I will have nothing left to eat. Without waiting for the girl, I go back out the way I came in and hurry across to the greenspace. It's not long before she is running and huffing behind me and then we're walking along, single file, looking for another house to search. Three doors down I see a house with a recently cut lawn. I find the sliding doors are open. I go inside and listen. Nothing. The house still has furniture and there are boxes as though whoever lives here is packing. The refrigerator and cupboards are full. This is not a smart move but I feel desperate. I am about to open the cupboard and reach inside for the canned goods when I hear a voice calling from upstairs. "Honey, is that you?" I turn quickly and slip through the sliding door, leaving it open, tripping on my way down the steps. I fall, I get up, then I run across the backyard as fast as I can.

At the edge of the yard I look back to see a man standing at the door with what looks like a rifle in his hands. I fly past the girl, who is waiting patiently like a hungry dog under a tree, but I keep running until I can't run any longer when I collapse behind an Allamanda bush to catch my breath. I'm still lying there when the girl finds me sitting on a boulder. She watches me while I convulse and sweat. The sun is so hot now I am dying of thirst but have second thoughts about getting a drink because you know who will want one too. There is still time left to find a house so I rest a few more minutes and then I'm up and walking again, slower, now, as my spirit has dampened. The sun is taking its toll.

The last house we look in, before darkness arrives, is a mess and smells like a restroom in a gas station somewhere off the main highway where old refrigerators lie rusting in a ravine beside the road. I find exactly nothing anywhere that's edible; there is no water, not a single drop. I look for a room to sleep in that is far enough from the stink that fills the house, and finally decide on the master bedroom where I can at least close the door. There's an old king size mattress with stains on it lying on the floor so we sit on that and I pull out the can of vegetable soup, the kind where you don't need water and just open the can. I find the spoon in my backpack and stir the soup, as though stirring might help in pretending it's hot. I begin eating it, while she watches me until I'm full and can't eat any more and give her the can, which is still half full, and the spoon. When it is dark out I lie down on the mattress, thinking how soft and comfortable it is after sleeping on floors, and try not to imagine what it is I'm lying in. She lies down too and after some turning and fidgeting we both fall asleep.

When I wake in the morning it is cold and she is scrunched up next to me with her arm on my shoulder. This is more of her version of Never Feed a Stray Animal. I remove her arm from my shoulder, get up, and head for the bathroom. The house already smells like a toilet and I can't stay here another day, anyway, so why not. I have to keep moving and searching for food; I have no other choice. I consider leaving without her again, but figure she'll just find me no matter what I do, as in a dream, tracking me down like the stray dog she is. I kick her foot until she opens her eyes and notice again that her eyes are blue like the doll's. I see in there a remnant of who she might have been but only just. Those days I guess are gone for her too.

Today is not as nice; it is overcast, threatening rain. I can smell it in the air. Now I have an extra problem along with the dogs and the risk associated with all the houses—rain. Add starvation to that and you have all the basic worries and burdens, be they stray animals, boats and coolers, or jobs and families. I had a job once in construction, but that was before. Now that job is as untrue as everything else. What I have now is an empty stomach and a stray, whatever she is, following me around and now it's going to rain soon.

I'm quickly coming to the end of the greenspace and the two houses I've tried so far this morning were wrong numbers, both of them. The first raindrops are beginning to fall. "Great!" I say to her but she just hunches her shoulders and looks at me while continuing to press on. I walk a little farther and what I see coming up is one of those mini strip malls with a Cineplex. I feel a little patter of hope because this could turn out to be good. We've run out of houses in this area anyway. There isn't a single car in the entire parking lot. I check again. Nada. Zip. Zero. I keep walking until I get close to the pavement, then I stop at the edge of the property and wait to see what happens. Which is nothing. After ten minutes I cross over to the first building and then after careful consideration I step around the corner to the front. I see that everything is closed up. Going Out Of Business signs had been tacked up but are now half fallen down in all the windows. The place looks as deserted as Chernobyl after the accident, the difference being that this mess was more deliberate if you consider what caused it. We duck under the canopy. Rain is sprinkling more steadily now. Looking through the windows I see that there's not much left for the taking unless you are looking for old Dunkin Donuts cups and fallen plaster. We go down the sidewalk passing each storefront, trying to guess by the remnants inside what kind of stores they were. The signs have been scavenged and the four walls are like book covers with no pages between them. At last we come to the Cineplex. I look around and decide to go closer. It doesn't look half bad.

Peering through the window, I see that it may have been the last one to close, or maybe it's still open. Besides the big sign out front, the building still has carpeting and fixtures inside. A light is on behind the counter. I am surprised to find that the door is not locked. We step inside. The way the place looks, it could be yesterday before all the economy tanked, or last year. It's as if we've stepped into the past. Everything as it was. Then a little miracle. Both of us see it at the same time and gasp in amazement, standing with our mouths open, then look at each other. Besides the full complement of assorted candy in the glass case, there is a popcorn machine with a big pile of golden yellow popcorn sitting in the bottom. Behind the counter against the wall are bags of potato chips and Fritos and Cheezits and Pretzels. There are faucets for dispensing Coke and Pepsi and Lemonade. We are about to take some chips from the rack when we hear a noise. Whistling. We duck into a closet. Through a vent in the door I can see into the lobby, all the way to the front doors and into the parking lot. A man wearing a janitor's uniform is pushing a big trash barrel on wheels across the carpeted lobby floor. He looks Hispanic, maybe Cuban or Dominican. He has a vacuum cleaner that he's pulling with his other hand. The barrel is gray with a broom sticking out of the top of it, and a dustpan hanging on the side. He pushes the barrel to the front door then takes it and the vacuum cleaner and sets them by the curb. Then he locks the door to the Cineplex, shutting them inside. He lights a cigarette and waits under the canopy, leaning against the building, flicking ashes with his thumb. Sometime later a van drives up and the man hurries to put everything in the back, all the while getting wet from the rain. He gets in the front seat and after a moment, the van leaves, tires spinning on the slick pavement as they go.

I wait to make sure there is no one else in the building. First I fill my water bottle. Then I fill my backpack with candy and an assortment of chips and as many boxes of popcorn as will fit. The girl has set the doll down and filled a plastic trash bag full and now fills two Jumbo size cups with ice and Pepsi and puts them in one of those cardboard trays with cup holders in the corners. She fills the center of the tray with a pile of Slim Jims and a few napkins and moves on carrying the tray. The nightlights are all lit so we can see where we are going once our eyes adjust. We enter the theater area just as a hard rain drums on the roof in a noisy din. We take our seats in the middle section about halfway down. The room is empty, except for us. We can see the red glow of the Exit sign in the far corner, like a gentle reminder, and feel confident that if anyone comes, we will hear them in time to get out. We'll escape through the emergency exit before they even see us.

The curtains are open on the stage. The room is dimly lit and a little eerie, but it gives me that hopeful expectant feeling I used to get just before the beginning of a movie, the knowledge that anything might happen, the ultimate stories, exciting, hopeful, even if all untrue. I hand the girl a red and white box with pictures of balloons and smiling faces on it—Life Is Happy it tries to say—and she hands me my Jumbo cup of soda, with more balloons and sprinkling confetti, and a napkin. The rain stops, then, and the noise and its absence echoes through the room. We sit together in the almost dark, eating our popcorn and drinking our Pepsi, her with her feet covered in pink kittens propped up against the seat in front of her, me with my horde of would be food that could last us more than a few days, if we're careful, the two of us just looking up at that great expanse of empty white screen, oddly hopeful, as though something is about to happen.

Then she looks at me, some sort of question on her face. I'm curious so I take out my wallet and show her the picture I took from the house, in the room where the doll was lying on the floor and she looks like she might start to cry. Here we go again, I'm thinking. Now it's the tears and crying. And, of course, after that, it's you know what: The Happy

Ending. But she doesn't cry—just almost. And then we sit back in our seats and wait again and I wonder what the hell I think I'm doing. Now that I've eaten and my stomach's full, I'm eyeing the warm red embers of the exit sign, reminded how we're drawn so to old habits, escaping, running away.

She looks at me, startled, then she puts down her popcorn and jumps up and runs back up the aisle, I don't know why. She's running fast and disappearing through the door when I've turned to look. I only have to think a second. I seize the opportunity and head for the exit, taking whatever I can carry, the drinks and plastic bag, not looking back. No sense getting bogged down now, I say. Who needs it? Here's my opportunity. It's dark and I stumble. I'm almost there when I think I hear a voice that says, "Wait for *me*!" I stop for a second to consider it; was that really her voice? In my desperation, I see myself running out the door, and dashing around behind the building, free of her, and the pitiful stories, and the hassle of feeding her, and looking at that dirty, mopey face all the time, and those ridiculous shoes with the pink kittens all over them, but I can't move, like in a dream where suddenly my legs won't work—the I'm Running In Mud And My Legs Won't Work dream, and I just can't move—so I do it. I wait for her.

THE DREAM

I had a dream
The sky was blue
In the dream I still had you

Four

I'm still here as she hurries down the aisle, not running but walking fast, carrying the doll she had forgotten and looking straight at me. She might cry, looks like—either because I tried to sneak out, or because I didn't leave her, after all, I'm not sure which. Then I see she's also carrying two Dixie Cups of ice cream. The ice cream might already be melting and she stands there looking at me until I reach out and take one, a little Dixie Cup with a wooden spoon on top still in its wrapper. I hold it up where I can see it. Chocolate, it says on the side. Whatever tears she's worked up are holding tight as she sticks her Dixie Cup under her arm so she can peel the wrapper off the wooden spoon. I feel like shit, now, and full of regret, but I'm not sure why and which regret it is I'm feeling. We take a seat beside the Exit doors and I'm thinking, we have the whole theater to ourselves and can sit anywhere we want. That's always the way, blessed with everything when it's of no use to you, like dying of thirst in the middle of the ocean. Since there's no movie, for us, or ever going to be, apparently, close to the door is best in my opinion. Someone might come.

The ice cream's that cheap crap, with the fake flavor, but feels good on my tongue. I can't remember the last time I had ice cream. She's finished already and staring into the bottom of her empty cup. Then she looks at me with that quizzical funny face she gets. Mopey but curious. She's staring at me.

"What?" I say, annoyed with her for always looking at me like she expects something. As always, she says nothing. "What?" I say again as though she's going to speak.

And then, surprisingly, she does, after a bit, just like that.

"Are you Jesus?" she asks in a soft, whispery, reluctant voice, looking serious, now, and sincere in spite of the dumb question. I don't know what surprises me more: her speaking, or the stupidity of what she's asking.

"Am I Jesus?" I want to laugh. Then, "You spoke!"

She blinks and stares.

"No," I say. "I'm not Jesus. Why would you ask me that?"

She continues to stare at me for a long moment, staring and blinking.

"C'mon. Why?" I persist, surprised still by the sound of her voice.

"Because," she says, timidly.

"Yeah…"

She's clamming up again like whatever it is

that's there is stuck in her throat. Then, "He's supposed to come back," she says, matter-of-factly. Her eyes are dark now and penetrating. She's not joking.

"Listen kid," I say to her. "Don't waste your time waiting for him. He's not coming. I'm all you've got. That's gonna have to be good enough for now. Let's go." I get up to leave and she's right on my heels with the plastic bag and the doll in tow. "Gotta find a place to sleep tonight before it gets dark." And I hurry out the door.

Outside, the sky is gray with self-doubt. It's how it feels, anyway. Seeing it takes whatever's left of my joy from eating something, even that junk, and files it away with the rest of my life in the *YEAH, WHATEVER!* bin. Unhappy should be a weather forecast like rain or snow. Looking around, there seems no place to go but back into the Greenbelt. I hesitate, but then we go. Between the stray dogs, Burmese Pythons, and occasional meth-heads a person might be afraid to venture out where it's so secluded. I wish I had a choice. But it's been like this a while now. And I used to think hanging sheetrock was the worst thing that could ever happen to me. Then it was prison, even if only for a year. Then it was losing whatever I thought was waiting for me when I got out.

I take a quick tour of all the crap that went before—the wife, the house, the kids, the job—and find it's harder and harder to revisit. I've been over it and over it so many times, I just slide right through it all, now, like hurrying past an old drunk passed out on the sidewalk. Don't look, just keep moving, you might see yourself lying there. And who wants to see that? Okay, I miss them, but that's not going to bring them back. Just move on and maybe it will get better. Nobody's counting on it. I'm no fool. Have been, okay? But not no more.

It's muggy as all get out and I could use a cool drink. I figure it's my turn to carry the garbage bag full of junk food we took from the movie theater. Looking around like there might actually be some place we could sleep, I see bushes and tall grass and trees, no more greenspace, just woods and tall weeds and the neighborhood's going downhill fast. The farther we go, the worse it gets. I have a queasy feeling that what's coming up next is a trailer park, or a motel for truckers and whores or something worse, and sure enough we come through a thicket and out into a goddamn transfer station full of all the stories ever told put into one big blender and pureed into a giant spew of reeking garbage. An End of Days like material mixed in, splintered and rearranged into formations that could be an installation in a museum of modern art, or cleanup from a tornado, take your pick. I can tell by the rats and seagulls it's not the former and see then that there's a huge sign just beyond the dump that says in faded letters:

Day's Bible Camp
Church of the Nazarene
Jesus Welcomes You

The girl wrinkles her nose and pulls a face like she might get sick. We keep wide of the garbage and the rats and make our way through some skunk vine and torpedo grass to where there's an opening in the chain link fence and a narrow dirt path that eventually winds its way around to the edge of the abandoned Bible Camp. The buildings are mostly small cabins set on cinder blocks, exfoliating paint, or what's left of it, leaving weathered boards to silver in the Florida sun, and little else. In the middle is a large barn-like congregation hall with a wooden cross over its front door. The door itself is off its hinges and tilts halfway open. Pigeons fly in and out of the broken windows. No one at all, much less Jesus, has been here for decades, probably, and if God ever blessed these tinder boxes, it must have been during the Eisenhower administration. This is not The Greatest Story Ever Told; it's more like Lord of the Flies. Speaking of flies, there are more than a few of them, and where they aren't whirling in some kind of weird vortex of their own making, they're sitting it out in the sun as though waiting for the Rapture, or recovering from the big dizzy anyone would feel if they flew around in circles like that. I'm walking toward the cabins, deciding if it's worth the trouble to stick around, even one more minute, but the girl is just standing back as if the Rapture's come and she's too afraid to move. This place certainly isn't Heaven.

Carved into the door of the first cabin are crooked, barely legible letters. JESUS LOVES YOU. There's a rusted metal cot with a long cardboard box flattened and spread out to make a mattress on it, scavenged from the dump, no doubt, so a bum could sleep it off or some high school kid could get-it-on with his girlfriend. The Yes, Of Course I Love You Story. I turn and look outside and see her standing there waiting for me. She squats, resting her elbows on her knees, chin resting on the heels of her curled, upturned hands, her eyes downcast. Then I see beyond where she's sitting, behind her, way back in the bushes near a dirt path, leading to God knows where, a man, holding what looks like a black garbage bag filled with something, his clothes, or cans and bottles, most likely. He's staring at the girl, not likely able to see me standing inside the cabin where it's dark, the sun behind me and the building. She's looking at me now and frowning until she realizes I'm not looking at her but at something behind her and feeling concerned. She stands, slowly, then turns to look and sees the man. He doesn't move but continues to stare at her. No expression whatsoever. She turns back towards me and walks toward the cabin, then stops and faces the man again. He's older than me, could be anywhere between fifty or sixty. His hair is long and stringy. He's unshaven and wears a T-shirt that's filthy and worn, and might have once been blue, with some sort of design on the front, a fish or something. He's thin and wears a baseball cap, the Daytona Cubs, maybe. The I'm A Regular Guy costume, in spite of the way I look. See, it says, I'm okay. I have a baseball cap. But clearly, he's not okay. He's about as regular as Siamese twins. Then again, that's what anyone would probably say about me.

He's still staring. I wait to see what he'll do, then he takes a step forward. I come out of the cabin and stand on its little porch. This gets his attention, but still, nothing shows on his face. I don't know if he's attracted because she too has a garbage bag full of stuff, or he thinks he might have a little friend here at long last.

"Praise the Lord," he says, thinking maybe we're with the Church of the Nazarene, I suppose, the ghost of it still here in these buildings.

"Jesus has come and gone," I say. "Now beat it."

At first he doesn't move, then he turns and heads for the dump. Probably harmless, but one can never tell. What would he do to the girl if I wasn't here? The girl watches him as he disappears into the skunk vine then turns and looks at me with a flush of relief on her face.

Taking another quick look around, I realize we can't stay here, now; Quasimodo might be back for another peek at the girl. That's a story I hate to think about. We leave through one of the many paths that intersect at the Bible Camp and find one that borders the highway. Cars whiz by in a vroom and woosh, the familiar whine, then drop in pitch, as they come and go. Rush hour at full tilt. Those people who still have jobs to go to, now getting an early start on their way home. Of course, plenty of them are doing okay, still, because that's how it works. Losers naturally beget winners. That's the point of it.

We walk for half an hour keeping to the scrub pine, saw palmetto, and devilwood growing unchecked behind all the Laundromats, car washes, and liquor stores we pass. She's slowing down, and I have to stop and wait for her, which pisses me off until I remember the creep at the Bible Camp. We sit on a rock and snack on popcorn. It's buttery and still crunchy but quickly makes us thirsty and wondering what to do about it. It's hot today and we're losing water through our pores so fast I'm getting worried. We have less than a nickel between us so I consider breaking a rule I have about no shop lifting, and then get a better idea.

"Break's over," I say.

We walk again looking for a gas station, one with a soda machine outside. It's an old trick. Pretend you lost money in the machine; get a refund. There's a Citgo up the road a ways, so off we go. We're there in no time and I'm beginning to taste the syrupy effervescence already. I tell her to wait behind the station and stay out of sight while I head for the machine with my head up like I'm a regular person. I pretend to put money in and push the button a bunch of times, stopping to look for my can of Pepsi as if I really expect to see it then push the button some more, banging the side of the machine a few times for effect. I walk into the station where a man who looks like he might raise Pit Bulls is putting packs of cigarettes into the slots of the display on the wall behind the register. He knows I'm here, but won't turn around. Another smug bastard hoarding his little piece of the power.

"I put money in the machine but nothing came out," I say, trying to sound indignant. He stops what he's doing, but still doesn't turn around, as though pissed off by my very existence, deciding, maybe, if he should let one of his dogs loose. When he does turn around he's not looking too happy, or too clean either. I should talk.

"How much?" he says.

I'm stumped. "How much?" I'm losing my nerve but trying not to show it.

"Yeah. How much? How much you put in the machine?"

Of course I don't have the faintest fucking idea and scramble to think how much a Pepsi would cost these days. I take a wild guess and say, "Dollar."

With a face already smoldering he snorts, "Hmnnn! That's why," and turns back around and stuffs three packs of Newports into a Newport slot. "It's a buck fifty," he says still facing the shelf.

Feeling stupid, but glad to be done with my little con gone haywire, I head back around by the machine and give the button one more quick push for good measure, and for luck I push the coin return. I hear money fall and out comes a quarter and a dime. Feeling lucky and a little better about myself after failing so miserably at my scheme I pocket the money, and as I round the corner of the building I notice the restroom on the side and try the door so I can at least get a drink of water at the sink. But the door's locked, of course, and just as I give the door a kick to register my anger a police cruiser pulls into the station and sits with the engine running. The cop spots me and gives me a thorough going over with his If Looks Could Kill stare-down only a man acquainted with correctional facilities can appreciate. It's bad enough having a record, but to walk around with a wallet full of other people's photos, ID's, and credit cards—even if they are just souvenirs and probably no longer open accounts, just dead, useless plastic—is not a good idea, the full import of it only now becoming clear to me. I try to look relaxed while I walk back around behind the station, but know he'll wonder why I'm going back there. I hope I can get to the girl and lost in the brush and scrub before he decides to pull the cruiser around back to see what I'm up to, which eventually he does. I hear the engine rev and I begin to relax just as we disappear into the weeds. If I was thirsty before, my mouth is parched and sprouting fields of cotton now, and by the time we stop running I'm swallowing my tongue. We're out of breath, too, and she's wondering where our Pepsi is.

"Plan B," I say.

Which is what?

I have no idea.

Five

The sun is down. It's halfway dark by the time we come to what looks like a deserted motel. Bull Thistle and Goose Grass is shooting up out of the cracked pavement. Windows are broken, doors are hanging loose. The neon lights have seen a little target practice, looks like; looters and squatters have come and gone. I don't like the place one bit. The rooms could be a trap. There's no back door; no way out. The office is a wreck, but I notice the back room was once made into some kind of living quarters. The bathroom has a rusty shower stall and a window a person could exit through. There's also a back door leading right out into the weeds and skunk vine. I go out back to investigate and find a dumpster full of rainwater, old ripped up motel carpet marinating in the stew of water and garbage, and home now probably to giant gestating mosquitoes harboring little doses of Breakbone Fever. There's a whole story in that single name right there, just so you can know what's in store for you when you get bit. It's really Dengue Fever, but where's the story in that name? Lost in a foreign language and merely exotic sounding.

The girl is not looking too thrilled with our new digs, but I don't want to get caught out after dark. They all come alive, then, at night: feral dogs; alligators; Burmese pythons; druggies; gangbangers; pimps; whores; degenerates; and your ordinary garden variety crazies. We'll take our chances with the mosquitoes and Palmetto bugs and whatever else resides inside. I do a quick reconnaissance for spiders, ticks, bedbugs, and used hypodermic needles. The fact that there's no evidence of drug use here makes me think we might be far enough off the beaten path to sleep safely and unbothered. No drug dens for me, thank you. Still, it's good I'm not a sound sleeper.

When I trip and almost fall on my face I catch her hiding a grin. It's nothing monumental, but better than the dead fish she's been wearing on her face since we met. It's a pleasant surprise. Up until now she's looked pretty glum. Shell shocked, really. Whatever brought her to this place in her life, wandering around out here all by herself, must have been pretty bad. And now all she has in the world as far as I know are the clothes she's wearing, the doll, and me. A pretty sad state of affairs right there. I don't know how long I can keep this up. One guy creeping around under the radar by himself is a lot easier than having this kid tag along. Don't know why I'm doing it. Life is a mystery from beginning to end. That part I've known for quite some time. A mystery, and a tragedy. No news there. Any high hopes I ever had you could put inside a thimble, and you'd still have room left over for all of my dreams. Instead, I have her.

I find an old 2x4 to prop up against the front door. Won't hold forever, but might last long enough for us to get out the back door if it comes to that. Amazingly, the back door still has a working lock. I clear out a space in the middle for us to sleep, but all I can find for a mattress, something to cushion the linoleum floor, are some heavy damp drapes from one of the other rooms. We can hear traffic occasionally from out on the road, but everyone is in a hurry. There's nothing nearby, apparently, to make them want to stop. We have some more popcorn, a beef jerky, and a couple of Snickers bars for dessert, only too aware of how desperately we need to find some water, and soon. Our thirst is getting dangerous. I already feel dehydrated, less able to function. Job one tomorrow will be getting to another gas station or a burger joint and, if we can find an empty quart bottle somewhere, wash it out real good and get a couple day's supply of water before moving on, we'll be okay.

I have trouble sleeping and turn fitfully, worrying about giant mosquitoes and heat seeking reptiles. She, on the other hand, is out as soon as she puts her head down, curled up to me like I was someone she could actually count on. I guess I'm sleeping eventually, because I'm dreaming about stuff —people and places that seem familiar in the dream but are really, like in all dreams, just nonsense—when I'm wakened by her pulling on my shirt. I roll over but can't really see her. That's when I hear the car. It's right outside and the engine's still running. No voices, no radio playing, just a car idling in the parking lot. I keep quiet, trying to listen, but eventually have to crawl over to the window to find out what's going on. The car's parked with its lights out facing the entrance from the street. I see a glow from the dashboard, but that's it, except for the occasional slow winking of a cigarette. I wait and watch for the longest time, hours the way it feels, but really only five or ten minutes, I suppose, when suddenly a pair of headlights swings around the entrance and the whole window lights up like we're live in concert and I'm supposed sing a song. Then just as suddenly the driver switches to his parking lights and pulls up beside the first car. I hear voices and the low rumble of the speakers, which I now feel in my chest. Then the parking lights wink off and only the periodic embers of cigarettes glow randomly like red fireflies, letting me know there are several people in the second car.

Hesitating at a time like this can be a big

mistake so I run through my options, quickly in my head, which are two, really: run out the back, now, or stay and risk getting caught. I crawl back over to the girl, grab the bag, handing her the doll, and taking her by the hand we make our way as quietly as we can to the back door. Sitting there we wait a moment and listen. Then I unlock the door and out we go, slowly, trying not to make a sound. In no time we're in the weeds, then find a little spot behind a bush and listen again, and wait. We're already getting bitten. We can't see a thing. Eons of nothing but crickets and bug bites go by before we finally hear a car leave, or both of them, we don't know which. I wait some more, then decide to have a look. We can't sit out here all night being eaten by bugs.

I head for the back of the building and decide to slip around the side so I can get a peek and have the best chance of running if I think I've been seen. I stick my head out and hope no one is looking. To my relief there's no one there. I heave a big sigh and find the girl waiting for me by the door. Together we go back to our musty pile of drapery where we now lie in darkness, afraid to close our eyes and already scratching at umpteen million bug bites. Still thirsty I tell myself we need to upgrade our operation and wonder if it would be possible to find some place where we can stay for a while, Stop wandering like a couple of hunter gatherers and stay put. Make it halfway livable and accumulate some provisions, and not have to walk all day. But then what? I stop myself, realizing what I'm doing: being foolish. It's all bullshit and make believe. It makes sense until you're in it and all the crap starts. You lose your job and it all falls apart because it's all a dream, and then I am dreaming, a real dream I realize as I doze off and I'm in a place where it seems real enough but can't possibly be. I'm walking down some street, trying to get somewhere and can't quite ever seem to get there, but something keeps me walking.

I wake to the sound of crows cawing and the girl looking at me in distress. "I'm thirsty." She looks a little pukey, too, but who wouldn't after a night like the one we just had and almost a day without anything to drink. We sit for a moment to wake up while I pretend I'm drinking my coffee, something I used to enjoy with uncommon delight before it all went to shit and I lost my job. One minute you're in the Honey I'm Home Story drinking coffee and the next minute you're in the I'm Leaving You Forever And Taking The Kids With Me Story. Hello Safe House, goodbye split-level-two car garage-with a garbage disposal. I'm glad, at least, I didn't buy her that goddamned refrigerator with the ice maker. Truth is I would have given two hundred ice makers to get her and the kids back, but that wasn't going to happen. End of story.

"Are we going soon," she says.

"Yeah, kid. Just let me finish feeling sorry for myself and we'll be out of here in no time."

The gas station we find has a water cooler with those little cups in a chrome tube so I pretend to look for a map while she gets a drink. She has been walking kind of slow this morning and I'm wondering if she needs some better food in her and just needs some hydration or if she's actually feeling sick. "I'm okay," she says. I get my drink and then it's around to the restroom to see if we can fill an empty bottle I find sitting at the top of a trash can. I read somewhere once that germs are good for people and try to console myself with that fact while washing out the bottle. I can tell right away it won't fit under the tap in the sink so I won't be able to fill it. Out back there's a spigot on the wall, so I fill the bottle there, giving us a fresh supply of Cholera, Polio, and Hepatitis, along with the H2o. Then it's back to the overgrown Right-of-Way that runs between the highway and the back of the muffler shops and strip malls that run for the next half mile or so. After that it's open terrain with nothing but giant power lines straddling a scrubby looking field. We walk a long way toward what I think might be another development but I'm not sure exactly where we are, but there's a little foot path worn in the grass and we follow it. On the other side of the field we see a water tower, which seems promising, and to my surprise the unmistakable arc of a Ferris wheel pitched high against a blue sky but no longer turning, then a moment later I see the mountainous scaffolding of a roller coaster and other buildings that seem eerily silent even from this distance.

We keep walking. She's been falling farther and farther behind, and stops to pick up the doll, which she has dropped, so I'm glad for a place to stop when we finally get where we can rest ourselves and quench our thirst with the by now warm water. "You don't look too hot," I say to her. She doesn't answer, just finds a spot in the shade and takes a long drink from the bottle. We look at the Ferris wheel. The place appears to be a derelict amusement park more than just a few seasons out of commission. A big sign says: FUN-O-RAMA. On the wall behind her is the faded mural of a big clown with orange hair, a tiny hat on his head and a big red nose at the center of his white face. "I think the candy bars are melting," I say as I hand her one and get more popcorn that neither of us really wants and some pretzels. "We're going to have to find one of those food pantry places where they give away free food," I say. "I don't know what else to do. It's either that or steal some."

The buildings are pretty well boarded up so there's no place to go to get out of the sun. We walk around behind one of buildings that line what must have been the midway and find a building that has an open doorway. Looks like it must have been some kind of gallery where you throw the balls and try to knock over the milk cans and win something, a Kewpie doll, or stuffed animal. She right away sits on the floor and leans against the wall. In my head I'm going over the logistics of shoplifting something healthy she can eat that doesn't need to be cooked, but without a coat to hide it in, I can't quite work out the details. My scheme becomes more and more elaborate—I'm kind of the Cecil B. DeMille of daydreamers when I get myself going—*the two of us causing one failed ruse after another to distract the employees while I wheel a shopping cart full of milk and eggs and cold cuts and green vegetables and orange juice, Flintstones chewable vitamins, peaches, pears, apples, and bananas right out the front door. All this while the cop outside gets called away suddenly by a code red alert on his VHF radio.* How I get all that food the hundred miles back to where we are sitting right now before it goes bad in the heat will take a whole new production in my mind, which is now apparently on a sit-down strike. I'm too tired to think. This heat is melting my brain along with the candy.

Which is fine, I guess, because at that moment I hear a truck pull up outside somewhere near the roller coaster. A peek through a slit in the boards nailed over the front of the little building with the rigged milk bottles and I see a man climbing up the scaffolding to a track on top of the coaster where he appears to be working on some part of it. I watch a while and see him tossing sections of track off onto the ground below and decide he must be trying to dismantle it. Seems like a lot of work for one man. And hot out there in the sun like that.

"You be okay here by yourself for a while?" I say to the girl.

"Where are you going?" she says.

"Not far. Just right over there by the roller coaster. There's a man there working on it. Gonna talk to him."

She thinks it over a second and says, "Okay."

She looks pitiful, but resolute, so I go out the back and head over to where the man is working and already stopping now and then to wipe his forehead.

He sees me and pauses to see what I want, glad probably for the distraction. "Lot of work for one man," I say.

"Whata'ya want?" he says right away looking

down at me.

"I'm kind of hard up. Got a sick kid. I need some money."

"Ain't got no money." He lifts a big crow bar so I can see what it is he does have.

"I'll help you work on that for five bucks an hour," I say. "Just for the afternoon. A few hours. That's all. Whata'ya say?"

"Why should I do that?"

"Like I said. I got a sick kid. She needs to eat, something to drink. That's the truth, Mr."

He's got kids of his own, no doubt, and grandkids, and I can tell he's the type of guy who would wonder the rest of the week if there really was a sick kid out there that he refused to help. "Just for the day," he says. "My regular man's out sick. I've got fifteen dollars in my wallet, give or take. Stay busy and earn your money. Stay outa my way and don't piss me off."

I'm at least fifteen to twenty years younger than this guy and have more muscle left on my bones than he does, in spite of the shape I'm in from wandering around doing nothing, so I make a big dent in the work he's doing. And I almost halfway enjoy it, since I know it's only temporary and tomorrow I can go back to being a useless bum living off what's left of the American Dream as it falls flat on its face all around us. I'm also somehow uplifted slightly by the thought of being able to help the kid, even though it's not my job to save the fucking world. The world could give a shit less about me. My boss doesn't talk much, which is okay by me, the less he knows the better. And I don't really want to hear about his model train hobby or whatever the fuck it is he does to keep his mind off how badly his life sucks when he turns the lights on and takes a good look at it. Which must be sometime. I don't know; I could be wrong. Maybe he does like his life. I'm being unfair. I used to like mine. Emphasis on the past tense. But still, maybe it's just me. I do miss my kids, which having the girl around has brought back from where I'd hidden them.

We knock out a few hours of work and he gives me my fifteen bucks and says, "My name's Ray." He shakes my hand. "You done pretty good. A hard worker and you don't run your mouth like a lot'a people do. I'd use you again if you want. Hope your kid's all right." I thank him and head back to the rigged milk can game and find the girl asleep on the floor. When I wake her I show her the money and ask if she feels like she can walk and we head out looking for a Wendy's, Burger King, or McDonalds, some place uplifting in that pretend plastic air-conditioned way. Lots of comfort food. After we get some carbohydrates in her we can think about some kind of healthy stuff like peaches, oranges, and fruit drinks or V-8 Juice. It's not too long before we find a strip of shops and fast food places. There's a Whataburger next to a Sonic, but she opts for the Burger King farther down. By the time we get there she's fading again but happy we're about to eat something real for a change. What's better than a hamburger to a little kid?

After we order and sit down she says, "Did you steal it?"

"Steal what?" I ask.

"The money."

I'm insulted and tell her I earned it so we could put some food in her stomach and you're welcome, too, thank you very much. She seems surprised and lowers her head a little as though there's more scolding to come. "I'm sorry," she says. And then, as a kind of afterthought, she remembers to say, "Thanks." Our first thought at the sight of all the food up on the wall is to get two Cheeseburgers each, French fries, and onion rings, all that heart attack stuff that tastes so good and fills you up to your eyeballs. Chocolate shakes and large Root Beers to wash it all down. Then I realize we could never eat all that stuff and would just be making another down payment on a heart attack and so I get a grease and cheese sandwich with lettuce and pickles and order a small hamburger for her and one large order of fries for the two of us to share, and two small Root Beers. Even that takes us a while, our stomachs are so small and we're in no hurry to go anywhere. We take some napkins and plastic forks and spoons and a few straws. Once again we have no place to go and I'm worried we'll be doing last night all over again. We head back to the rigged milk can shack since we have already been there and checked it out and have full stomachs and have no idea what else to do. We can stop at a convenience store on the way for more liquids and as many cans of food as we can carry. Beans and meatball spaghetti, one can of Ravioli and one can of peas. Gotta have some green vegetables. She's still a kid for Christ sake. We start out and find it's cooler now that the sun's so low in the sky. It's not long before we're back to FUN-O-RAMA and staring up at the big roller coaster looking stark and ominous against the evening sky. "Ever been on one of those," I ask her.

"No," she says.

"Well, trust me; you wouldn't like it. Supposed to be fun, but they'll make you crap your pants they're so scary." This amuses her. She smiles and gasps. A little giggle escapes her lips like she needs permission to laugh or something. I wink at her and walk around like I've got a full diaper and she laughs a little more. We scan the vacant buildings covered with once colorful but now faded stripes and polka dots, a carousel horse sitting on the ground mid gallop—*look Mommy, I'm a cowboy*—and it says Life Is Only Make Believe. A giant clown's head from some missing paper mache statue lies sideways on the ground looking at the world with its wide-eyed perpetually smiling face. No calliope music here, now, only crickets and the faraway whir of traffic somewhere in a different world than this one: *the world that used to be.*

Back to the milk can shed, then, and looking for a bit of padding for the floor so we can sleep without dislocating our spines. She seems happy and looking a little better so I'm happy and pretty soon we're sitting in the dark again and hoping we can sleep through the night without any excitement. I for one am tired from working my puny three hours on the roller coaster and walking all day. Once upon a time I worked all day every day for years and slept like a dead man. Now this is all I have to show for it. Nothing. Like maybe I *am* a dead man.

Six

We wake up hungry and tired in the morning and not too thrilled knowing it's about to begin all over again. She stares at the wall like she's in a trance and I think maybe I'll just stay where I am for another hour but finally drag myself off the floor and go outside to see the sky and have a look around. It's early yet and no sign of that guy Ray. At least we have some Orange Gatorade to drink, and we haven't been up all night listening for drug dealers, or sitting outside in the weeds swatting at mosquitoes. We've got the canned stuff for later so that's something. "Time to head out," I say, sticking my head back in the already sweltering wood building. I wrack my brain for a place to go and decide only that we need to get back into a more residential type area where all the empty upside down houses are just sitting there waiting for us, to be plundered and otherwise made use of, pick them clean like the vultures we are. It was so much easier when it was just me because I got used to moving around and starving and just dealing with it all, but with her it's different. She's a constant reminder of how fucked up this actually is. I'm taking care of her, sort of, and I don't like seeing her looking so hungry all the time, and now she's looking pukey again in spite of the big meal we had yesterday. I have no idea where to go. I'm not sure exactly where we are and don't exactly have a plan. That was supposed to be the idea: no plan, no people, no anything. Just keep moving and don't let them find you. Why I don't just tell the kid to wait here, that I'll be back in a few minutes, and then disappear again back into nowhere is beyond me. Then again it's not. She's looking at me, waiting and chewing on the inside of her cheek, like she does, that worried look on her face that I can't bear to see. Both of us are starting to scratch our mosquito bites. "Let's go," I say.

We walk and walk and drink our Gatorade while she practices her whistling, which she's not very good at. Eventually I've had enough and tell her to give it a rest. We walk some more and then we come to a big field with a clearing where we see at the far end there's a little wooden shack with a small front porch that might once have been someone's would-be weekend getaway. A sign that's fallen on the ground says **Keep Out No Trespassing** but fuck that, nobody's been here for years; I can tell. If someone comes we'll just say we're with the Environmental Protection Agency looking for signs of illegal dumping or some kind of crap like that. My partner here is a pituitary dwarf if you have to know, but don't say anything to her, she's very sensitive about it. We pass through the rickety gate and cross the field, a short hike through tall grass where the remnants of a road (tire tracks) are still visible. Inside the shack there are remnants of a lost weekend or two, a table, rusty beer cans, an old wooden chair, twin beds with dirty moth eaten mattresses lying askew, a little refrigerator in the corner with its door open that's been defrosting now for about eight years at least and probably done now, a lamp with mallards landing in the marsh on its shade, a 1993 calendar on the wall with pictures of the Everglades, and a few plastic cups on a shelf by a kitchen sink around which are some cabinets. The windows are broken but the screens are intact, a big plus, and even better, I see through the window that there's a well pump out back like my granddad used to have. Man's capacity for self-delusion is infinite, so I immediately run outside and give the handle a healthy pump. Nothing comes out at first, but then there it is, water, wouldn't you know, clear as a baby's tears and gushing out, so while my luck is running high I chance a drink and find it tastes okay. Like regular water, and really cold, too. I figure I'll know in an hour or so if I've just poisoned myself so I tell the girl not to drink any until I live through the night. If I'm still alive tomorrow she can have some.

Not far away in the trees there's a one-hole

shitter complete with webs and spiders and a hornets nest or two, and if I can believe my eyes a half roll of toilet paper frayed and discolored and sitting on a nail. Turning around I see the girl pushing an old wooden wheel barrow and whistling The Entertainer, sounding like the goddamn ice cream truck, the same eight bar loop and buzzing in my ear. "Hey," I yell at her and, when she looks, give her a thumb slash across my throat. "Can it!"

After a rest we have our meal. My backpack still has that can opener I picked up months ago so I get that and grab one of the cans. We have Ravioli and Cheesits and Gatorade. A regular banquet. "Would you care to see the wine list?" I ask her but she doesn't know what I'm talking about. Then right away she breaks her plastic fork. I give her another one and tell her if she breaks this one she'll have to eat with her fingers from now on. She frowns and I know what this routine is. "Okay, whatever," I say. "But plastic forks don't grow on trees." It's annoying having to say shit like *forks don't grow on trees*. Especially with someone else's kid. But there you have it. Goddamn forks *don't* grow on trees and now hers is broken.

Later, she's rummaging around in the cabinets on the wall by the sink, and finds a fly swatter and a pencil, and then she pulls out a candle stuck onto an upside down Skippy Peanut Butter lid. She's trying out the swatter on a few flies while I go outside and have a look around. There might be some useful junk out here, who knows, so I kick at the weeds and walk in circles. What I find is a shovel with a broken handle behind the shitter and a pile of rusted out cans. Not far away is a galvanized metal bucket. Amazingly there's no hole in the bottom of it. Then I find the top half of an old fishing rod. Where's the rest of it? I want to know, but it's a mystery. It's like an archaeological record of the boom times around here. Then I get the bright idea that if I climb up the tree behind the shack I might be able to see what's in the distance, like where some stores might be that are closer than where we ate yesterday. Sure enough, when I'm all the way up near the top of the tree, I see a tall sign like outside a strip mall or at a gas station. One of those signs that cars can see from the highway. When it's time to get more food I will take a long walk and check out what's over there. With any luck I can find a Denny's or something with a dumpster out back. Wouldn't be the first time I lucked out and found old bread they'd thrown out just because it had a little mold on it, or it had gotten too hard to put on a table.

Back inside she's got the paper grocery bag that we saved from getting the canned goods, and spreads it out flat. She's sitting at the table drawing on the back of the bag with the pencil. Her brow is creased from concentrating really hard, and every so often she pushes a strand of her hair back over an ear so she can see better, all the while drawing away, then sitting back and studying what she's working on. Her feet are wrapped around either side of the front legs of the chair and resting on the horizontal rungs that brace the legs on the side. Pretty soon I take a look and she sits back so I can see. I can make out what looks like a pretty good rendition of a roller coaster and Ferris wheel. There's something like a circus tent with flags on it in the background and people standing right in the middle. A man, a woman, and two children—a boy and a girl.

"Pretty good," I say. She begins drawing again, a classic sun with rays coming away from it in the upper right hand corner. "Who're the people?" I ask. She shrugs her shoulders but keeps her eyes on the drawing. I'm curious now about the picture, like it must be one of those ink blotch tests the psychiatrist gives you to find out why you are a compulsive shoplifter, or if maybe you're some kind of serial killer. "So where's your family?" I ask, just for the hell of it, wondering about it and realizing she should be in school or something, not here camping out in the middle of nowhere with me. "C'mon," I nudge, "you must have some idea." She continues to stare at the picture then adds what looks like it might be a car. Then, looking right at me with her deadpan mopey face meant to shut me up she says, "They're in heaven." The matter-of-factness of it is a little unsettling. I say nothing. She goes back to drawing and I get the feeling I should drop it. I pick up the fly swatter and pretend to look for flies, not wanting to pry, but I can't let it go and say, "You must have been staying with someone before you ran away. Where are they?" She stops drawing, closes her eyes and purses her lips to let me know I'm annoying her, then tilts her head to one side. Without looking at me, but at the picture, instead, she says, "So where's your family, then?" I don't want to get into that and she knows it, and that's why she asked. I've spent the last two years trying to forget it all, so I give it up. "Okay, you win," I say. Conversation over!

The next day I decide to walk over to where I saw the big sign, which could be a mile or more. I take my back pack and tell her to stay here.

"Why can't I go?" she asks.

I say, "Because I can walk much faster without you." I'm also afraid, which I don't tell her, that people, meaning police, might be looking for her, which had crossed my mind when we were at the hamburger joint. I don't need that kind of attention.

She looks away and stares at the sink like she thinks there's something there to see but I know she's just pouting.

"Are you coming back?" she says.

"Of course I'm coming back. Why wouldn't I?"

She shrugs her shoulders and picks up the fly swatter, watches it while she waves it back and forth like it's a flag. Maybe to her it's a magic wand. Kids want to believe that stuff. Suddenly she looks a mess to me. Her clothes are dirty and wrinkled, her sneakers are so covered with dirt you can barely see the kittens. Her hair's getting stringy and tangled. I don't know when the last time was that she had a bath, but I haven't had one in ages myself. We both look like shit and probably smell like a couple of old hound dogs. It's one thing for me to be living like this, but somehow I can't recommend it for her. I'm having second thoughts, so I start to leave and tell her to keep a watch on the entrance and hide out back in the trees if someone comes. "Okay," she says, refusing to look at me because she's mad she can't go too.

I feel bad and tell her, "Hey listen. I'll be back before you know it."

Once I get away from the would-be cottage I feel guilty but liberated. I walk fast through the tall grass and pretty soon I feel like my old self again, on my own, nobody to slow me down or worry about. I realize I've made a big mistake getting tied up with her and tell myself I've got to figure out how to put an end to it. I could just not come back, just keep going. But then what would happen to her out here all by herself. I'll have to come back, I decide, and then take her somewhere else and leave her. I'm such a fool I think in disgust. You'd think I'd have learned my lesson. *Goddamn that kid*, I mumble to the weeds and the birds flying overhead and take long determined strides through the grass and think to myself now I'm the one pouting.

The sun was out earlier but now it's clouding over and looking like it might rain. I pick up my pace and in a while I can make out the sign just over the tree line. It's a Texaco station. I continue walking and before long I come to a road. I follow it to an intersection and turn right and I see where I can reach a main thoroughfare where there are shops and a Cracker Barrel restaurant. There's another gas station right beside it. I keep going until I'm there. Out back I'm not finding much that looks edible but I am finding that I need to pee so I go next door to the Chevron station and get the key to the restroom. What I notice is that the soap dispenser is empty so they've left a bar of soap on the sink. When I'm done I pocket the soap thinking the girl can wash her face and hands at least and maybe I'll give my armpits a good scrubbing. When I come out of the restroom someone yells "Hey!" and I think, Great! I'm busted for stealing a lousy fucking bar of soap, but when I turn around I see it's Ray over at the pumps filling his truck with gas. I stand there a minute then go over to say hi and he tells me his other worker is still out sick. If I want to work some more, he says, I should just show up at the roller coaster tomorrow and the next day. I tell him yeah, I'll do that, thinking I could use the money for the girl, but not liking the trap I'm getting myself into. Next it'll be a steady job and renting a little place somewhere with a shower and electricity and then you need a TV and a microwave and that's how it all begins. "Okay," I say and wonder what I'm doing while I take a walk farther up the street looking for another restaurant that might have something out back for me, and find a Pizza Hut.

I happen to arrive just as a guy is dumping a couple of garbage bags full of trash and what looks like it might be food into the dumpster. It's garbage when you're the busboy, but it's food when you haven't eaten much in the last two days. When he's gone I take a look and find boxes of untouched slices of pizzas inside, along with all the other crap they're throwing out. I go through the boxes and find the best looking pieces and dump them all into one smaller box, which I stuff into a trash bag that was full of paper trash, which he'd dumped. Just then the back door opens and a man wearing a white apron stands there, hands on his hips, watching me just as I'm walking away. The sky's getting darker and the wind's picking up, so I figure I'd better start back and make a quick look around to see if there's a grocery store nearby for future reference. I don't see one but ask a guy walking by if there's one around here anywhere and he points up the street. "About half a mile," he says. "Food King."

Halfway back it starts raining and thunder rolls in like a war going on two towns over. Now I'm worrying about the girl, again, and wondering if she's going to be scared of the thunder, and if she's been all right there by herself, and hoping nothing's happened to her while I was away. I'm beating myself up about it, imagining some moron showing up at the little cabin and snatching her up, or maybe a big snake hiding in the shitter bites her and she's been turning blue while I've been scavenging pizzas, or else she's fallen down outside somewhere and hurt herself, a spider bite, maybe, or a bee sting, a splinter. It's ludicrous. I know this and tell myself to calm down. She's perfectly all right, you'll see. I'm getting worked up over nothing, but I can't help myself.

I'm pretty well soaked when I get back and find her curled up on one of the beds falling asleep. She flinches and sits up quick when I make some noise. She's giving me a hard look as though she really thought I was never coming back. "You okay?" I say. She nods her head but still scolds me with her eyes and I all of a sudden feel guilty. I hold up the bag and say, "Pizza!" She's still glaring at me, but fearfully, like I put her through some bad shit leaving her alone like that and she doesn't appreciate it. I feel bad about it but I had to get some food. And I'm also a little disappointed because I thought she'd be just a little bit excited about what I've brought back. Pizza for Christ sake! But she doesn't care. That's gratitude! So much for that. When I pull out the box it's a little wet on the outside, but inside the pizzas are fine—I hope. They smell good even though they're cold, and I'm counting on them being from an early lunch crowd and shouldn't go bad for another day or two, at least, or maybe not. I don't really know, so I decide I should eat some first and wait a while before letting her have any, just to be safe. I take a bite and it tastes pretty good. I decide to eat a whole piece, so I do and then sit down and wait to die. The rain's really coming down now and sounds like those people in that show, Riverdance, are performing on the roof, the whole troop all at once, legs flying, heels and toes banging it out; I can almost hear a little piper and hand drums. I make a mental note to get some matches so we can light the candle and think a flashlight and some batteries would be good, too. I figure I'll work at least one more day for Ray and get some additional cash. I'm not dead yet, so I pull out the bar of soap and toss it over to her. "What's that?" she says.

"It's called soap. People use it for washing. Tomorrow you can wash your face, and maybe have a sponge bath out by the water pump if it's hot out, which it should be, if it ever stops raining."

"Need a wash cloth," she says.

"Well…don't have one. Use your undies. Kill two birds. Wash yourself, clean some clothes."

"Undies?" she says, mocking me.

"Don't get cute," I say.

She picks up the soap and smells it, remembering how it was, probably. Somebody must have made her take a bath every night before putting her to bed. The You're Safe With Us Honey story. Now you go to bed and say your prayers so nothing bad will happen. Lights out on that I guess. 'Cause here we are, out on the edge of the world, poisoning ourselves with food from a dumpster, sleeping in this dump of a weekend getaway, drops of rain falling on our heads from a leak in the roof.

"Want some pizza?" I say.

She's still smelling the soap. "I guess."

"Well, sorry. We're all out of prime rib today, Miss, and I guess the cappuccino maker must be broken, too, because there isn't any of that either."

"I said yeah."

"Yeah…well." I'm looking around for some place to set it. "Okay, okay. I'm just…never mind. It's good, actually, this pizza. Sausage or pepperoni?"

She shrugs. "Sausage."

"I'm just kidding. It's all hamburger and cheese. What'll it be?"

"Well…hamburger and cheese then."

"Excellent choice."

She eats one piece but doesn't want another so I suspect she's not feeling well again. It keeps raining all afternoon and I'm thinking if it rains tomorrow I won't have to work. I never used to be lazy. On the other hand, who's fond of work? Not that hanging sheet rock wasn't a total blast, but I wasn't too broken up when they bumped me up to the office to do some estimating and bidding on future jobs. I got pretty good at it. Made good money and it lasted for several years. Then the bottom fell out and that was the end of that. Instead of working I was in the unemployment line waiting for my check. There's a story for you. From Here To Eternity. That's how long the line was.

Fact: Riverdance is much louder in the dark. It's enough to drive you batty. There's nothing to do, so we play the spelling game where you write a word on each other's back with your index finger. She's a pretty good speller, so I never stumped her, which got me to thinking. I decide to test her on her multiplication tables after the spelling game gets old and worn out. She misses a few, but knows them pretty good for the most part. We'll do division next. If we had our own place to stay, like a little apartment or something, I'd need to enroll her in school. I'm not sure why I'm thinking about this, it just sort of pops into my head. Then I ask myself, *why*? She's not *my* goddamn kid. Before long she's asleep on the bed so I take a pee out the front door into the rain. Then I lie down on the other bed and listen to the distant cannon fire, and the remnants of Irish step dancing tapping away somewhere above me until I fall asleep.

Seven

Morning and the sun's out. I wake to the sound of a crow, a loud sonofabitch, announcing something to the entire goddamn world. I wonder what the hell they could have to say that is so damned important. Couldn't it wait until after lunch? I stir and look over at the girl. She's not moving and looking pukey again, so I figure I'll make some more money and take her somewhere for more Calories and Cholesterol. Or a big salad, if she'll eat it, and some fruit. That's my plan; it's what she needs. I fill an empty Gatorade bottle with water from the pump and tell her I'll be back after I go over to FUN-O-RAMA and work some more so we'll have some money for food. "Then we'll go out for some more burgers, or pizza, hot this time, or fish and chips, or whatever you want." Her eyes fail to light up when I say this, so I play my trump card. "Ice Cream!" I say, as in, "Ta Da!" She forces a smile, so I say, "Get some more sleep, if you want, and I'll be back soon. And don't worry. If I say I'm coming back, then I'm coming back. Trust me." She nods and rolls on her side and I go out the door and on my way.

Everyone's happy about the rain, apparently. Besides the goddamn crows there are frogs and crickets and jays and magpies and ravens and swallows and egrets and who knows what. They're all flying around singing Zip-A-Dee-Doo-Dah. You'd think they'd never seen rain before. I'm not that happy, myself, because I know I have to work for a few hours today, and I'm a little worried about the girl not feeling well. She gets sick too easily. What if she can't walk to the restaurant later? Do I have to get take out and bring it back to her? Will she even eat what we order if she manages to get all the way there?

Ray's glad to see me. He couldn't work yesterday on account of all the rain and his guy's being out sick, still, so he's getting behind. I climb up where he is and start unbolting things and prying girders and braces apart and whacking on the metal track with a fifteen pound sledge hammer. The metal was cold when we started, but is fast heating up as the sun hits it. By midafternoon it'll be hot to the touch, burn your skin almost. It takes all night to cool off again, unless it rains, when steam rises from it in veils of thin, wispy smoke. Otherwise at night the heat leaks off the track and its inch and a half bolts into the night air, sucked by colder places to where heat is missing, toward all those crevices of darkness and shadow. Here's what you can count on: nothing lasts, and things don't stay in one place. In high school we heard about this thing in Science class—Entropy—and thought like most people that it was supposed to be evidence of disorder and the world's preference for chaos. The teacher, trying to be upbeat about it, said it was more about equilibrium. Either way nothing stays the same, especially these things we build. It all goes to shit eventually. Ray is beginning to suspect it; we both are. Whatever stays the same? Not a damn thing.

An hour later we take a break and drink some water. I'm looking at the Ferris wheel. On its side, in faded yellow paint, it says: **THE GREAT MANDALA** . I'm imagining it full of people. It's night time and the colored lights are all on, the wheel turning slowly, three different kinds of music going all at once, wild screams coming from the roller coaster, as if life isn't exciting enough the way it is, you have to do that to yourself, scare yourself silly, just to get your blood moving, feel something besides a dull hum in your ears.

"Four years ago," Ray says out of the blue, staring down at the giant clown's head lying on its side on the ground, like he might be telling the clown head instead of me, "we were building so many houses we couldn't keep up with 'em. New developments everywhere. Boomburgs we called 'em. Everywhere you looked. Everybody and his brother was buying up houses, or building new ones, then flipping them six months later for a whopping big profit. It was a fuckin' goddamn free for all. Then it all came to a screeching halt. Just like that. Kapow! It was over. Damn shame, is all I got to say. A goddamn shame. Now it's all demolition work. Tearing it all down, taking it all apart. I got a nephew that trashes-out houses that've turned upside down. They had put up next to no down payment. There's no way to refinance so the people just take off and leave everything behind. Most of the furniture was all on credit. Appliances too. So they just disappear and start all over somewhere else out of state. What's it all coming to? That's what I want to know." Then he spits and gets up and goes back to work without another word. I don't know what to say. I know all about it, of course. Been in most of those empty houses, every one of them, feels like, although, truth is, there's gotta be thousands more.

We keep working and the sun gets hotter and I'm at that old place again where you feel good about working but can't wait for it to stop. I tell myself the Work Builds Character story and keep going. Later, we take another break. Okay by me. How much character does one guy need? After the break Ray wants to load the truck with the scrap metal, so we climb down and drink some water, then start loading. He has to take a leak after a while, so I decide to look around for something to use for a cushion on the beds. I find something that looks like the quilted, padded blankets movers use that's actually in pretty good shape. "What's that for?" Ray asks me when I bring it back to the truck. "Gotta help move a chest of drawers for a friend," I say. No use telling him the truth. What's he going to think? *I'm doing what?*

We're back up on top of the coaster for a while when Ray nudges me with his hand. When I look up he points to the ground over by the giant clown's head. An old man is standing there sideways to us looking straight ahead at something, we're not sure what.

"Who's that?" I say.

"Don't know," he says and draws the back of his hand across his forehead to wipe the sweat from his brow. We watch as the man stands there, statue like, his gray hair hanging below his ears in a thin, wispy tangle, his old T-shirt damp and dirty with sweat sagging over baggy, soiled khaki trousers. He shifts position slightly to take in another part of the grounds looking, apparently, at what's left of the place. He appears to be lost in thought. Or maybe the old man is just lost. My guess right away is he's remembering how the place used to be. He stands that way for a good five minutes then turns toward us looking up. He squints and takes us in, a long protracted judgment that hints somehow of loss and sadness, then he turns and looks toward the Ferris wheel. We watch some more as he stares, deep in thought, as though studying the place for some significant detail, an omen, maybe, or some sign of where it all went. We go back to working and look up every now and then to see what might well be an apparition appearing and disappearing around the place, standing statue like and looking at all the buildings and the big rides, then drifting away to appear moments later in another spot when we look up again. Half real but no less there since we both see him.

"What the hell," Ray grumbles and drops his wrench and crow bar with a clang and descends from the coaster to see what the man wants. I follow behind. We head for the water jug first as a way to justify taking a break and wait for the man to come over but he doesn't. He could be eighty years old, if a day, by my estimation, or ninety. Stoop shouldered and shoddy, needing a shave, looking underfed and forlorn: He seems in a daze. I'm thinking we should offer him some water at least.

Ray finishes a long drink and calls out to him. "Help you with something, Mister?" To which the old man says nothing. He keeps his back to us like maybe he can't hear, so Ray walks over and stands beside him and waits.

"No," the man says without turning toward

Ray, still half lost in something that might be the past, or the past might be where he still lives and it has come now to visit us.

"We got water if you're thirsty," Ray says. "Kind'a hot out."

The man doesn't answer or acknowledge us, but continues to stare. Then after a few minutes he says, "Haven't been here in fifty years." He says this softly, to himself maybe, so you'd think he didn't care whether we heard him or not. I walk over by them and Ray gives me a look like this guy might not be right in the head. It's hard to tell. Could be suffering from sunstroke. Alzheimer's maybe. His feeble manner indicates advanced decline. He has trouble breathing, his speech slow and halting. He's listless and slow moving. Majestic in a strange way.

"That's a long time," Ray says.

No response for a long moment then, "Yup." Then he lowers himself down on an old ticket booth that's lying on its side in the sun bleached grass, deep in the weeds, and runs his hands through his hair pushing it back. He sighs in a long and breathless exhale that might be his last then says, "It was a lot different then." He's looking at the ground around his feet. His shoes are worn and cracked and might last another month if he's lucky. He doesn't wear a watch. His arms are leathery and dark from the sun, sag at the elbows and freckle heavily with age spots where the sun has baked him dry. A fine net of wrinkles has him wrapped from head to toe from the looks of him, if his face and neck and arms are any indication. A sadder pair of eyes you'd never want to see. Could be *me* some day if I don't start smiling more often, I think, and make a mental note to store a picture of his face for future reference. This is what the end looks like, I say. Or maybe just right before it.

"Well, take a good look," Ray says, "because in a few weeks won't none of this be here anymore. Takin it down and hauling it away. It's all goin for scrap except the wheel."

A long silence, and then he says, "Too bad. It was a beautiful place back then. A lot of pretty girls came here in them days. My wife was one of them. Sixteen years old and hell bent to have a good time." Pause, then, to take a breath. Another long exhale. "So I gave her one." He's got his sense of humor still, I tell myself.

"What happened?" I ask.

"Her old man put a shotgun to my forehead."

"And then?" I wanted to know.

"I married her. What d'ya think? Had no other choice. That or get shot. She died five years ago."

"Did you work here?" Ray asks him. "Or what?"

"You could say that."

"I *am* saying it. Are *you*?"

"I am."

"Must have been a popular place once upon a time."

He looks at the buildings and the Ferris wheel. "Was. Nothin else to do. They came here every night to escape the heat inside their houses."

I notice then he doesn't have any teeth. His eyebrows curl down over his eyes in a white, feathery tuft like two miniature waterfalls, the lobes of his ears heavy and drooping with age, wiry hairs gone astray sprouting from them. His brow and cheekbones heavy and chiseled with the stoic pride of a stone precipice.

"You miss it then, I guess," Ray says.

"I do," he says, and lets a few beats pass. "And it misses me. Wants me back. That's why I'm here." Another pause. His long white hair lifts momentarily in a little breeze and falls. "We were so young then. Had the whole world before us. I had a strong back, good for working. I could do anything." He comes to life now, as though the memory of it stirs his blood. "Work all day and half the night. Drank and made love to the ladies until morning. And then…that's when I met my future." His eyes seem to sparkle at the thought of it. "The light was striking back then. The evening sky was so clear and bright it would hurt your eyes. People had money. They were happy. Plenty of work if you weren't too lazy to get up off your ass and go out the door in the morning. All kinds of jobs, too, for a good worker. Steel mills, auto plants, machine shops, all kinds of factories everywhere. I joined the Teamsters Union soon as I got back from Korea. I worked here at this place for extra money, that and because there were so damn many pretty girls. At twilight they'd come out in droves like night blooming flowers, butterflies catching the light, and goddamned pretty, too. All of them. Then I met Louise and her father's shotgun. She was wild as hell and I saw her standing by the carousel with a friend, her face all afire with some kind of mischief and that was all she wrote. But I kept working here. Had to. She got pregnant faster than apples fall from trees. We got married. I kept working. It was a good time to be an American. You didn't need much money and what you bought lasted a good long while. Different then. Never did lock our front door. It was a good time to be alive. Not like now."

He stops talking as suddenly as he had started and kind of freezes mid-thought. We watch as he searches the air for a glimpse of some memory that seems to plague him. Like he can see it all again if he looks hard enough.

"Then it all changed," he says after a bit. "One day we woke up and the world was gone—the one we knew, the one we'd lived in. There was a new world here in its place, seemed like. They shot the president. That was the beginning of it. Now it's all I can think about, that time. I'd go back if I could. If I could just see it again one more time the way it was. Sit here on a summer evening and see all the lights again and hear the noise of all the people and the music playing and hear the ball game on the radio the way you did back then. The smoke and food venders filling the air with smells that would make you drunk with hunger. The old cars and the sweet smell of the night air, the cigarette smoke drifting invisibly through the dark. Look across at the carousel and see Louise in her summer dress laughing at something her girlfriend said and then seeing me for the first time and turning away pretending shyness before looking back to see if I was still watching her. I was. And she wasn't shy at all. But it's all gone now. I know that. I'm not crazy, just old and tired out. I'll take that drink of water, now, if you don't mind. I'm feeling a little dizzy. Must be this awful heat. Bothers me now. Didn't used to."

Ray gets the man some water and waits while he drinks it to see if he wants some more. "You need something to eat?" Rays asks. "We've got some."

"No thank you," he says. "I'm okay now."

We have to get back and finish the section we've been working on before we're done for the day. We turn and head toward the coaster and Ray stops and turns back again to ask the old man if he needs a ride somewhere when we're done, but the old man is no longer there. It was such a short few seconds of time we had turned away that it feels like he's vanished into thin air. It gives us a start. For a second I wonder if we had maybe only just imagined seeing him, but for two of us to have the same hallucination at exactly the same time seems unlikely. Maybe he was a ghost. Two people can see that at the same time, can't they? Whatever he was, he had to have been here. A story like that one, like the one he'd just told us, was way too elaborate to be a mere figment. But in an instant it all feels as though it was, like it was only a dream, or a ghost of a dream, and now we're waking up.

Eight

It's a long walk back to the house, but I'm feeling pretty good, so I just keep going and try not to think about having to carry this padded blanket. I think about the old man instead. Then I get tired of carrying the blanket so I pretend I'm somebody in a movie. It's supposed to give me motivation, but it doesn't help. The exotic setting I'm imagining and the inspiring soundtrack to accompany it is fake, the weight of the blanket and heat on the other hand are real. I'll be glad once I get there. Ray asked me if I would be back tomorrow and I said yes, though I'm not sure why. Not that I have anything better to do. Then I see the little cabin. It warms my heart so I pick up the pace. Why is that? Not sure I know. The girl's still lying down when I get there so I hold up the blanket, and she slowly gets herself up so I can put the blanket on the bed. She lies down again, right away, and says she's chilled, so I fold half the blanket over her and feel her forehead. She feels kind of clammy. "You been drinking plenty of water?" I ask, then wonder if that's what's making her sick. I realize it would have to make me sick, too, so I rule that out. "Guess you don't feel like walking anywhere do you?" She shakes her head "no" and I ask her what she did all day. She shrugs and says, "Nothing." She's not my responsibility, I remind myself, but know instinctively that this is no life for a child. "Listen," I say because I'm not in my right mind, apparently, and delirious from working outside in the hot sun then carrying that heavy blanket all the way home. "I'll keep working so we can get you in a school somewhere, okay?" This is a lie I realize after saying it but I'm trying to cheer her up. "You can't just lie around all day doing nothing." And then trying to lift her spirits when she looks at me like I'm nuts, I say, "Or you can work for Ray and I'll go to school."

She doesn't laugh and just stares at me with a blank look on her mopey face until she says, softly, now with a quizzical look on her face, "Who's Ray?"

I open the beans and eat half the can and hand it to her with her Ravioli fork from the other night. I had washed it and saved it, like it was: You Wash And I'll Dry Then We'll Watch Wheel Of Fortune. She's sick and I don't know what's wrong with her and I'm no doctor, anyway and, of course, there's no TV. I'm just a guy taking FUN-O-RAMA apart piece by piece because it's been the Rise and Fall of the Roman Empire around here, lately, and all over the rest of the country, for all I know, and now I have a little bird here with a broken wing and no way to fix her. She takes only a few bites of her beans and says she can't eat anymore. I get some more water from the pump for her and try to get her to drink, but she doesn't want much water either. I know enough to insist that she keeps drinking it because she's starting to perspire and that means fever. I think. How would I know? I'm not a nurse, either. It's hot out and this little wooden crate we're hiding out in is just a sweat box when there's no breeze, which there isn't. "Gatorade?" I ask and she nods, but when I look I see there isn't any left. In the Before I was always working and you-know-who took care of the kids. It was always "Daddy's home" and then "Lights out." Like I hardly saw them. Now I've got both jobs, it seems.

Tonight there's no noise, no dancing on the roof, but I can't sleep wondering what's wrong with the girl and trying to decide what I should be doing to help her. Plenty of water seems obvious, but is that enough? Maybe after work I could get some more Gatorade. It's a long walk and she'll be waiting for me. It's the best thing, though, for dehydration. I know; I saw it in a movie. And the Jaguars drink it at all the games, don't they? Now I'm trying to think what else I should do. I'm lying here getting pissed off because I can't sleep, and all I do is worry about the girl, and having to get up and go to work, and thinking how hot it is, then the weird dreams start. An old man in a dirty T-shirt is standing in a field and chanting something like he's a medicine man and raising his hands up to the sky, gazing upward to look at it, and it starts to rain. He closes his eyes and the raindrops splash on his face.

Suddenly the sun's out and the crows are back making all their usual racket.

It's morning.

I look at the girl and see she's sweating profusely. I try but can't wake her up. She's making little groaning noises and moving around a bit, but she won't open her eyes. I take my shirt off and go out to the pump and soak the shirt with water, wring it out, and come back inside and wipe down her forehead. I feel her forehead again. She's burning up. I run outside and find the bucket and fill it with water from the pump and bring it back inside. I pull her legs over and off the side of the bed and put her feet in the bucket. Startled, she opens her eyes with a little jolt but is still too listless to do anything but make a face. The pink kittens on her shoes stare at me from on the floor beside the bucket where she'd left them when she pulled them off still tied. It fills me with dread.

I'm supposed to be leaving for work, and don't want to let Ray down, or piss him off, but I can't leave her alone here like this, so I sit beside her on the bed and push her tangled, dirty hair, most of which is soaked in sweat, off her forehead and wonder what I should do next. She needs to go to a hospital, I know this much, but how will I get her there? The cold water on her feet seems to help, so I take my shirt out to the pump again and run water on it and wring it out, a little less this time, and bring it back. I leave it lying across her forehead. I'm saying, "Open your eyes," to her and stroking her hair, but she only moves her head back and forth, so I know this is really serious. I'm scared, now. She could die. I'm getting really nervous and want to do whatever I can to help her, just make her well again, please. That might be a prayer. Whatever, I don't care. I need all the help I can get. If she died I would never forgive myself. How could I? I'm supposed to be taking care of her, whether I want to or not. She's just a little girl. It will be my fault if that happens. Somehow I didn't do what I should have done, whatever it is, like in the Before when I didn't do what I should have done there. Lesson learned.

Then I think, maybe I could put her in that old wooden wheel barrow. I could push her to the gas station in that, or maybe over to FUN-O-RAMA and get Ray to take us to the hospital in his truck. Then I think no, she'll fucking cook to death out there in that hot sun. It would be for an hour or more, which is how far Ray is. If I have to push that wheel barrow with ninety pounds of sweaty kid in it, it'll take forever. The gas station is closer. I decide that's the better way to go, but then wonder if I should just go alone and get Ray and come back. I could run the whole way. But then I think how I'd have to leave her here alone with no way to keep herself cooled off, and what if she didn't make it? Plus, what if Ray isn't there?

"Fuck this!" I say, after sitting here a while feeling helpless and like a dumb jerk for not doing anything, so I pick her up and take her outside and put her in the wheel barrow. I get my shirt and dump it in the bucket to soak it and put it on her head and start pushing. It's harder than I thought it would be, and I start to wonder what the fuck I think I'm doing, but I've got to do this, and I get the thing moving and we're on our way. It's a little bumpy, but I can't help that. I can't sit in that cabin with her all day going back and forth about it, doing nothing while she's getting worse and worse. Just do it, I tell myself. Get her there. Do something right for a change. My fucking father went to Vietnam, my grandfather fought somewhere in the Pacific and got himself shot in the leg, so I can goddamn well do this.

We're about two thirds of the way there when the axle on the wheel barrow starts to squeak and squeal and I'm wondering what the hell is that? Will it hold up? And then it finally breaks, or rather the bracing for the axle splits and falls apart so we have to stop. I'm about to drop and about out of breath, but realize it could take an hour or more farting around out here trying to fix this thing. Even if it's possible, there's nothing but weeds and dirt and twigs and grasshoppers to work with. I scream a string of obscenities at the sky for being so blue and peaceful today and allowing this to happen, which doesn't accomplish a goddamn thing, of course, except I'm so pissed off it revs my juices and I pick her up out of the wheel barrow and hold her in my arms and start walking. I try to distract myself by deciding which movie I'm in: Cowboy In The Desert; Soldier In The War; or Lost In The Jungle, but I'm too worried to do that shit now and I just concentrate on not stumbling on a rock, and put one foot in front of the other so I can make it another ten feet. Then I work on the next ten feet. All the while she's getting heavier or at least it feels that way. I'll never make it, I'm thinking, but have to keep going, so I do, I keep going. Then I have to stop and rest; my legs are buckling. I look at her face and can't believe how bad she looks. This puts the fear back in me. I can't quit now, I think. So I make myself get up; I keep going.

By the time we get to the road I'm soaked and getting a second wind, but when cars whiz by and no one stops I wonder what the fuck is wrong with these people, and start to lose hope, or in my case, the memory of it. I'm pissed off all over again until I see the gas station and as I get closer I notice what looks like a cab driver putting gas in his car and can't believe my good luck. When I'm finally there he's just gotten in and started the engine.

"Hey, man," I yell, "I need to get this girl to a hospital, quick. It's an emergency. I don't have any money, but…." The bastard only has to hear "no money" and drives off so fast I don't have time to yell anything he can hear. I yell anyway. By now I'm totally unhinged. "ASSHOLE! ASSSSS HOOOOOOLE!" The attendant comes running out of the station to see what all the commotion is and sees the girl. "Fuckin cab driver!" I say. "Wouldn't take us to the goddamn hospital!" The man's Hispanic and apparently doesn't speak English too well. He looks concerned, like I might be crazy or might have murdered the girl. "Hospital!" I say. He looks at the girl again, who's looking dead or close to it, and says, "Descuide usted! Me conducir! Descuide usted!" Which means nothing to me, but it sounds like he wants to help us. He motions for me to follow him and hollers something in Spanish at the other guy inside. There's an old Chevy parked beside the building. He opens the back door, and I get in with the girl holding her in my lap, her head falling against my arm and shoulder. He gets in and backs the car out and away we go. I'm saying, "Hospital! Hospital!" Like he speaks English, not knowing that it's the same word in Spanish, which I find out later. And he says back to me, "Si! Si! Hospital!"

We're going pretty fast, and naturally a cop pulls us over. When the driver points to the girl and says, "Hospital!" the cop takes one look at her and says, "Okay," and gets back in his car and on go the lights and the siren makes a quick "WOOP! WOOP! at the intersection and we now have our own private police escort. I'm not thinking anything but, please God just let us get her there in time, which definitely is a prayer this time. It must be working, because the cop takes us right up to the Emergency entrance, and I get out with the girl in my arms and then immediately we're surrounded by nurses and orderlies in white coats with a gurney who have been waiting for us because, of course, the cop has radioed ahead. I try to give the driver what little money I have but he won't take it and drives off after telling me, "Buena suerte!" They wheel her in and start with the fluids and questions and I tell them what I know, which is next to nothing, really, just that she's been feeling bad and has a fever. And then just like that they take her away and I'm left behind to fill out the forms and give them all my information, which is what exactly? Homeless, no insurance? I know nothing, actually, not even her name. I don't exist anymore for all practical purposes and don't know who that girl is. Now they're looking at me funny and telling me I need to put a shirt on. I tell them the girl has it, so they send someone to get it. The cop, I notice, is deciding to stick around and get to know me better, and someone in the office is pointing at something, and then they all look up and over at me. I realize right away what movie I'm in now: YOU'RE FUCKED! The Sequel! How I know is that I've already been in the first one. That one didn't end well and neither will this.

Nine

"Is she going to be all right?" I ask.

"Yes, I think so," the nurse says, still giving me that look like I have two heads and it's annoying her. I try to act casual, but how can I when I'm freaking out about the girl and I feel now like maybe I do have two heads?

The cop takes me down a hallway to a little waiting area and sits me down and says he wants to see my I.D. That's when the other officers arrive—what they call "Backup" on TV—and also in real life. Now it starts. They run my name and find out I have a record. "You're going to have to go with us," they say, and hand me my shirt and tell me to put it on. I know enough not ask what I've done. To start with, I'm me; that's always been enough right there. "We'll have to cuff you just as a standard precaution, so we'd appreciate it if you'd cooperate." I know the drill, of course; only idiots resist arrest, so I put my hands behind me. There's four of them and one of me and I'm not that big, anyway. Plus they have police issue weapons: service revolvers, Tasers, batons, pepper spray and no mercy when things get to that point. They take me out like I'm fucking Jeffrey Dahmer, and put me in the back of a patrol car pushing my head down as I get in just like in the movies. They don't say a word all the way to the station, which I expect, so I sit listening to the calls coming in on the radio, which squawks too much—like they're too damn lazy to adjust the squelch on the set.

Once inside the station they put me in a holding cell and I wait and sweat it out like reliving an old nightmare, the kind insomniacs have. The one where they're afraid to fall asleep because of the dream that haunts them, so they try to stay awake all night, but can't until they do finally, only I haven't fallen asleep I'm living it. Here I am again staring at four walls, with no window, and bars across the door. I'm left to stew and simmer while they dig up everything there is on me. I sit staring at nothing so I don't have to look at the metal bed with the prison gray paint chipping off to show its dank metallic railing underneath, tiny patches of *nobody cares* staring me in the face. Looks like the inside of a black hole, the one I've just been sucked into. Sitting here in my jail cell, it becomes a magnetic vortex, the kind that will sap all your energy and give you that faraway look in your eyes, that blank stare that convicts have that I've seen way too much of. I catch myself and look at the walls instead and picture the girl lying in a hospital bed surrounded by nurses and doctors all knowing what to do, fully invested in saving her. I just want to know how she is, and when they finally come to get me, that's the first thing I ask.

"We'll ask the questions," is what they say like, really? We'll ask the questions! How much TV have *you* guys been watching? Too many cop shows, clearly! This is not good. All the old insolence from my previous prison experience has come roaring back. It's how you stay alive in there and the one thread of comradery that all inmates share, mistrust of and hatred for the guards.

They take me to a room with some chairs and a table like on Dateline NBC where the wife's been found murdered, the husband's bloody hunting knife beside her on the floor. Now I'm sitting at the table and look around the room. A short man with thinning hair and creases in his brow, looking full to the gills with what must have been a lot of beer and too many Krispy Kremes comes in and takes a seat without looking at me. He slaps a manila folder on the table and starts thumbing through it, like he hardly knows where to begin, my crimes are so numerous and I'm so deplorable. If he shakes his head and tells me I have a rap sheet as long as his arm I'm going to laugh in his face.

Then he speaks. "So you were dealing and got caught? That it?"

Well, no small talk for him, thank you, just get

right to it—my prison record rearing its ugly head. "No," I say. "That's not it." I know it's a waste of time to talk to this guy, but I do anyway. I'm going to die a fool. Been one all my life, why change now. "I was only buying." He's not even listening, but I continue, anyway. "Wrong place; wrong time."

"Yeah," the cop says with a smirk. "They all say that." Now he's looking at me affecting his best I've Seen It All And Don't Believe A Fuckin Thing You Say look. "Try again," he says.

"Well I'm saying it because it's true. Look in your file. You guys never heard of me before that. Nothing more than a traffic ticket."

"We all gotta start somewhere," he says. "So what were you doing with that girl?"

"I've been homeless."

"Okay. You're homeless. And the girl? Do you know her name? We were just wondering."

"Actually, I don't know her name. She wouldn't tell me."

"She's pretty sick, ya know. You got her there just in time. You must have been real worried about her."

He's acting now like we're waiting for a bus and he's just making conversation. Why doesn't he ask me why I'm homeless? Because then I'll say I can't get a job. And when he asks me why not I'll say it's because of my prison record that's why. But he doesn't want to go there; they never do. "She just showed up one day," I tell him, "and I gave her something to eat."

"Why's that?"

"Because she was hungry. Why d'ya think?"

"That the only reason?"

"What other reason is there?"

He's nonplussed by my response, and to show me how much, he takes a deep breath and lets a bunch of air out through his nose while turning pages in the file. Maybe he took acting lessons. I think so. My guess is half those pages are scrap paper he took from the copier before coming in here to make me nervous. Does he think I don't know my own record?

"Says here you're a pedophile."

"That's bullshit and you know it."

"On the contrary," he says. "I don't know anything. I was kind of hoping you could fill me in on a few things. Like that girl and what you were doing with her."

"I told you. I just gave her something to eat and she just kept hanging around."

"Why would she hang around a guy like you?"

"I don't know. You tell me. She was hungry and I fed her."

"Maybe you were enticing her with food so you could take advantage of her. Take her clothes off and…"

"FUCK you!"

"Your ex-wife seemed to think so. She said you were a pedophile."

"Yeah, like I said at the time that was just something she came up with because she wanted custody of the kids. She wanted to be able to leave the state with them, go back to Alabama. So she pulled that rabbit out of her ass."

"That where she's from?"

"Yeah."

"Said you molested your daughter."

"None of that crap stuck and you know it. I was never charged with anything. Nobody believed her because they knew it was all bullshit. It all got thrown out."

"You lost custody."

"I was in prison. What'a you expect?"

"You know that girl you were with is a runaway?"

"I guess I knew it had to be something like that."

"But you just couldn't pass up the opportunity to hide out with her every night somewhere. You must have enjoyed that some."

"Like I said, Fuck you!"

"Nice!"

"I just felt bad for her because she was alone and hungry and had nowhere to go. Is that a crime?"

"She could have gone home if you'd let someone know where she was."

"Well there had to be a reason why she left in the first place, didn't there? Why send her back to that? It was none of my fucking business."

"Back to what? Did she tell you something?"

"No. We never talked about it. I asked her once and she wouldn't say anything so I let it go."

"What do you suppose it was?"

"I have no idea. Maybe *they* were abusing her."

"Who's they?"

"Whoever she was with."

"Did they abuse her?"

"I wouldn't be surprised."

"I guess you know all about that, don't you?"

"Did she say I abused her?"

"Did you?"

"Ask the girl."

"We're going to. So if there's anything to tell us it'll be better for you if you tell us right now."

"Look, is there a point to all this, or do you just like jerking people around?"

"No one's jerking you around. We're just trying to find out what's been going on." He's put on a new face. The *I'm just trying to do my job and we all want what's best for the little girl* face, *and you could help us maybe if you'd only calm yourself down a little.*

"Well I told you. Nothing. Just that I've been homeless and all the fun stuff that goes with it: hunger, boredom, and fear. That, and recently I've been working."

"Yeah, well, we're talking to Ray right now."

"To Ray? Terrific! That should win me a bunch of points with him. Well so much for that job."

"You always have this big a chip on your shoulder?"

"Not until I met you, I didn't. You and that asshole judge who sent me to prison in the first place."

"He had no choice, given what you did. We have these zero tolerance laws, now, put in place by decent law abiding people like me to clean up that sewer of a neighborhood you were hanging out and selling your drugs in."

"Buying, asshole. I told you. I was only buying."

"Whatever you say."

"Well I *am* saying. You just know all about

everything, don't you? Have everyone on the street all figured out."

"That's my job, to know. I have to know what's happening and who all it's happening to and who all is doing it."

"Yeah? Well while you're at it why don't you see about a hair transplant and leave me the fuck alone?"

"Christ. You guys are all alike. Comedians, two bit criminals, and perverts."

"Yeah, well up yours!"

Back in my cell I'm left to cool my jets while they come up with something to hang me with. There's old vagrancy laws, but working for Ray kind of screws that up for them. Although that's gotta be over now. The kid thing is perfect for them. I probably wouldn't believe me either. And all they have to do is accuse me. They don't really have to prove it. How do I prove I *didn't* abuse her? A lie detector test? No fuckin way! Not with my luck! I know better than that!

MY STORY

I'm starting to wonder if my story is ever going to be uplifting!
- BEK from a cartoon in the New Yorker.

Ten

The next morning a woman shows up. She tells me her name is Mariela Perez and she's from Child Protective Services. Wants to talk to me about the girl. Only half awake, I look at her thinking this might be a dream. I had slept okay until about 2:00 AM but then woke suddenly with the sensation of being buried alive. The thought of being locked up again is only slightly more tolerable, but feels kind of like it. Including the part where you're in Hell, not that other place. We read about Dante's Inferno in college. A few years later I took the graduate course: A YEAR IN PRISON. Now I'm in here.

They take me to a room with a table and chairs. She takes a seat and motions for me to sit across from her. I'm cuffed again and sit with my hands behind me. Ms. Perez seems nice enough. Doesn't come in with that nasty look on her face. Nice looking, actually. My age. Might be younger. Has a yellow pad for taking notes, which she gets out and sets on the table. Holds on to her pen like she's all business. Nice hair. A little plump. Sexy plump. On the healthy side. Nice smile. Seems genuine enough so sure I'll talk to her about whatever she likes.

"Can't we take the cuffs off," she asks the

guard. “That looks awfully uncomfortable.”

The cop tells her it’s for her own safety but she shakes her head and insists. They remove the cuffs and he leans forward with his arms on the table.

“Thanks,” I say.

She writes something on her yellow pad then underlines it with her pen. “Can you tell me how you came to meet her?” is how she starts off. “Where it was.”

How many times are they going to ask me this? Instead of answering I ask, “How is she?”

She gives me that humoring Yes Of Course smile with pursed lips and raised cheeks and relaxed shoulders, puts her pen down, hands folded in her lap. “She’s better.” She tilts her head a tiny bit to one side. It supposed to convey that she’s touched by my concern. “They think she might have a virus. West Nile or something. They were waiting on her blood work, last I heard. She’s able to talk. She asked where you were.”

“Yeah? She did, hunh.”

“Does that surprise you?”

“In a way. She never said much at all. Not a big talker.”

“Where’d you meet her?”

I tell her about the house with the doll on the floor. The pack of dogs. How I tried to run out on her twice, once at the house and once at the movie theater, but couldn't do it. "Big mistake, wasn't it?"

"What would have happened to her if you had? She might already have been sick. She could have died. Or somebody else could have found her and been less…caring."

This gets my attention. Unless it's a trick. Did I hear that right? "So you believe me then? That I didn't molest her."

"I want to."

"Well, I didn't."

"We have reason to believe someone did. There's evidence of abuse. Are you aware of that?"

"No. How could I be aware of that? Besides… what evidence?"

"I can't tell you that."

"What're you here for then?"

"To find out if she said anything. She had been in foster care before she ran away."

"Oh yeah? I wondered. Said her family was in Heaven. Is that right? They're all dead?"

"Yes, that's right. Car accident. Both parents and her little brother. A year ago. Truck crossed the median. Head on collision. Whole family killed instantly, except for her, of course. She was at a friend's house. I can't imagine how she must feel."

"Poor kid. No wonder."

"How's that?"

"Nothing. Just how she was."

"How was she?"

"You know, withdrawn. Inside herself somewhere. Didn't say much. Kind of sad like. Really sad, to be honest."

"How long were you with her?"

"I don't know. Not long; more than a few days. Not quite a week. I lose track of time. There's no real reason to know what day it is in my line of work."

"Which is?"

"Nothing. I'm kidding."

"Did she say anything else?"

"Anything else?"

"About why she ran away. Her family."

"Not really. That was it. Don't even know her name."

"She didn't tell you?"

"Didn't talk. I tried."

"I'm not surprised.

"Yeah?"

"People do that. It's a way of coping. It's easier that way. Leave it all behind. Her name's Jessie, by the way."

"Jessie." I picture her face, when I carried her in my arms, wet hair sticking to her forehead. "Hunh.

Looks like a Jessie. Wouldn't talk but was feisty. I could tell that much, if it weren't for being messed up. Maybe that's why we got along." I say this mostly to myself, not really to Ms. Perez.

"What do you mean?"

"Well…we were both disappearing, in a way, or trying to. We almost had, really. But it's hard. You have to eat. If you don't keep moving you get caught."

"Is that what happened?"

"That's it. I quit moving. Didn't want to. But, you know. Had to."

"Why's that? Why quit moving?"

"Because of her. She got sick. Got to be too hard dragging her around from place to place. I could sleep anywhere. Jump out a window and run if I had to. With her it was more complicated. Then she got sick."

"What did you think you were going to do? I mean the two of you."

"We didn't. That was the whole point. Not to think. Just survive and stay low. But you can't. Not with a kid. After a while I started thinking about how it was for her, moving around scavenging for food. She was too sick to keep going. She blonged with other kids in school, anyway. I could see that. So I took the job with this guy Ray so we could get some decent food."

"Why would you do that, if you were trying to disappear?"

"For her, I guess. It was a mistake, of course. She needed to eat. Real food I mean. I let myself believe for a second. Just a little, but it was a mistake. Now I'm here."

"Believe?"

"In the movie. You know…"

"What movie?"

"All of them. Pick one. Once Upon A Time. Honey I'm Home."

She is shaking her head now and frowning at him. "I don't understand."

"That's because you're still in the world. You have to believe that shit to be in the real world. So it seems normal. I don't. I've left. I'm somewhere else."

"Believe what?"

"In the movie like I said. You know. Believe. Blue skies. Pink kittens."

"Pink kittens?"

"Yeah. That's right."

She's knitting her brow and seems upset, making notes furiously with her pen, her face telling me that it's gone off the tracks again. "Sorry," she says. "You've really kind of lost me here."

"Well…Exactly," I say. "That's what I'm

saying. That's exactly what I'm saying."

The look on her face is one of disappointment. Or dismay. She shakes her head while getting up to leave, putting her pen away. The look on her face has taken on an icy edge. She was feeling good about me, initially. Now she's not. "Well I'm glad we got to talk," she says. "I feel better about her having been with you. At least I was. Now I'm not sure again. You have a lot of problems, I can see. And yet…when she asked about you it wasn't out of fear. I could tell that. You seem to have made a good impression on her in spite of yourself, and…the impression you made on me. I probably do believe in blue skies, by the way. You have to."

"If you see her, tell her I said Hey. Can you do that for me?"

"Okay. I'll do that. Anything else?"

I think about her walking around that little cabin with that fly swatter, and sitting in the chair drawing with her pencil. The candle we never got to light. "No. No that's all. Just that. Tell her I said hello."

I'm sitting here wondering when I'm going to get fed. I have no idea what time it is. Late afternoon, maybe? I've lost track. Getting a little claustrophobic in here. The room seems smaller. I have to get out of here, like I might lose it if this goes on much longer. They can't keep me in here forever, can they? Not without charging me with something. They said I could make a phone call but who the fuck would I call? The Mayor? And when I *do* get out. Then what? Find a new bunch of empty houses? There's plenty more out there. Back to the old routine, then. Nonexistence. Weight Loss The Easy Way. Join the Homeless ; disappear. Shed pounds fast. Weigh less in just a few weeks without exhausting, complicated exercises. Fuck pilates. Snack at the dumpster. Have microbes for dessert. All the flavor with zero fat. I'm an idiot.

Hours pass. Nothing happens. I stare at the wall. The wall stays the same. The wall stares back; the wall stays the same. Even a fly landing and taking off would be a welcome distraction. But no flies here, only myself.

Someone's coming and I'm thinking food, but it's only Bubba with a toothpick in his mouth. I'm thinking he could do a circus routine with his tongue and that toothpick. Like a fucking baton twirler he is, if you could stand to look at it. Smug and content, he's unlocking my cell. "Let's go," he says. "Looks like you're outa here."

"Careful," I say. "Don't choke on that

toothpick." He gives me that look like, *Give me a break!*

In the station office I'm surprised to see Ray waiting by the counter. He's not smiling. Doesn't even look at me or acknowledge me in any way. Then he does.

"Let's go Cisco," he says. "They're done with you for the time being."

I can't believe he's here, and can't believe I'm getting out, either. I would have thought he'd be all done with me after this. They sign me out and tell me not to go anywhere. They might want to talk to me again. A clock on the wall says it's five o'clock. I wait until we're outside and ask Ray where we're going.

"I don't know where you're going," he says, "but I'm going home." He puts the truck in gear. "You ready to go back to work in the morning? I've gotten way behind. My other guy quit. He wasn't really sick, it turns out. He was looking for other work. The sonofabitch."

"All right," I tell him, not knowing what else to say. "I'll be there."

We drive a while. The world is still turning apparently. The sky is still blue. "You eaten?" Ray asks.

"No. Not since this morning."

"Well, come on, then, I'll take you to a Burger

King out near the roller coaster. I don't care where you're staying and don't want to know. Here's ten bucks to buy your dinner. I can take it out of your pay. You didn't kidnap that kid did ya?"

The question takes me by surprise. "Would you be here right now if you thought I had?" I ask.

"Hell no," he says.

"Well okay then. There's your answer."

We drive out towards FUN-O-RAMA and find a Burger King not far from the hospital. While waiting in the drive-thru after ordering my burger and fries I say I wonder how the girl is doing. It seems odd to call her by her name. Jessie. I don't know a Jessie. I just know her as the girl that showed up one day with a mopey face and kittens on her shoes and followed me around.

"Don't even think about it," Ray says. "You show up at that hospital and they'll put you back in jail. Go ahead and eat," he says when we get my food. "I've got dinner waiting on me at home." He drives me out to where what's left of the dirt drive to the cabin is and I tell him I can walk from here.

"This is where you live?" he asks, seeing only the empty field.

"That's the place. Can't see it from here, but there's an old shack back there. Not much, but the rent's cheap."

Ray frowns and mumbles something I can't hear and suppose I don't really want to hear and then puts his truck in reverse. "Tomorrow, then."

Ray nods his head, makes a three pointer and drives off into the evening light. Now I'm alone, again, with the crickets, looking across the wiregrass at the trees in the distance. Clouds hang low on the horizon, white and puffy against a violet, blue sky. Getting past evening, now. Late. Long, long shadows spill across the field. There's a warm breeze on my arms and face. Being in jail again has reset my brain a little and I suck in the night air like it's my last breath and it's all the better for it. I finish off my fries while walking through the grass to the cabin. It looks the same as when we left it. The metal bucket sits half full of water by the door. I stand there a moment and wonder why I'm here. I could be anywhere. I could keep walking and never stop. I could walk forever. Inside I see the blanket I had wrapped her in. It's all in a mess on the bed. The table sits in a swath of graying light from the window over the sink. The candle, unlit, is still there, waiting. The chair, pulled out, is sitting on its four legs beside the table near the wall. The fly swatter sits on top of the table, beside the paper bag, the bag with her drawing on it. I don't want to look at it, but I do, I look anyway. There are two trees in the distance. The obligatory sun is still shining down on them, the little family, all neatly resurrected from their graves for a fun day at FUN-O-RAMA. They'll eat cotton candy and ride the Ferris wheel after. The car's all back together, again, like the family, without a scratch, right there behind them, a testimony to their spirit. Like it never happened. All new and shiny. Just like before. Heartbreaking. The poor kid.

I take the chair and sit outside to watch the birds flit along the tops of the wiregrass bending downward as if burdened by some hidden oppression. The sun, most likely, and the wind. A white trail from a plane makes a long arc across the sky. I follow it to its logical conclusion: lost in once blue sky now paling to a violet and lavender gray tinged with pink soon to devolve into nothingness. When I turn and look back up in the direction of the road that can't be seen from here, I think I see someone coming. Just the top of the head, at first, bobbing up and down, a steady wobble on the horizon. I watch and wait. Coming closer. It's her. Same ragged clothes and dirty face, messy brown hair. She walks at an easy pace and I sit in my chair waiting for her. I'm anxious to know how she is. I will ask her, when she gets here. How are you? I'll say. I still have the drawing. It's right inside on the table where you left it. Do you want something to eat? Aren't you hungry yet? Your hair's a mess. You better comb it.

The sun is down and the light dies its usual slow death. A breeze, still warm, blows past me, feeling good on my skin like soft hands massaging my aching muscles. I wait here while the crickets sing louder and louder. The night air cools and stars appear above me ever so slowly like something wished for and now here. I wait. And I wait. When the darkness is complete I go inside and lie down on the blanket and wait some more. When sleep finally comes I am, for a few hours, like the dead, without any care, oblivious. I dream, but the dreams are lost as they spin out into hopeless nonsensical reverie, lost to me forever in the morning. When I wake it's to an empty room filling with light. Outside, the crows are calling, again. I feel the urge to answer them, if only I knew what they were saying. It's important from the sound of it. I listen closely. I worry that I'm missing something vital that I need to know. There's a lot I don't know. But somewhere I lost my appetite for it. What I do know leaves a bad taste and often scares me.

I leave to make the trek back to FUN-O-RAMA, telling myself to get some matches somewhere if I can. It's not as hot today, more clouds, now, and I'm hopeful it won't be another long day of baking in the sun. I see a turkey buzzard riding a thermal, circling way up pretty high, and wonder if he's checking me out. I pick up the pace a little just in case. With my luck I have to be ready for anything.

When I get there Ray's up top already and waiting. I make the climb and find I'm not really motivated to work, anymore, but I owe him ten bucks worth and feel obligated to be here. So I am. I can walk off the edge of the earth some other day. Tomorrow, maybe. It's always an option. Something that gives me strength, a little peace of mind, knowing that I can at any time I want make myself disappear, or seem to. It's my personal ace in the hole. Like magic, only I'm both the magician and the trick.

Eleven

A week later I'm still here. I'm not sure why except Ray needs my help and working keeps my mind off the girl. I've been unbolting a half mile of steel track that the cars ran on, people in all the seats, up and over the hills and down again with such great speed their stomachs were in their throats pushing out cries of terror. Sometimes, standing up top, I can almost hear the screams of all those people, as though frozen mid-air, held in place by the weight of all that fear. It floats there, suspended, rarefied by the altitude and so much light, which has carried it aloft, the sun so hot it's a hammer blow to my senses. I hear sounds from the past. Barkers hawking their wares are luring people in, selling tickets, the noise of business in its most elemental form. Spend your money here, they say, and be transformed. See the bearded lady. Ring the bell; win a prize. Ride the ride of a lifetime. We manufacture fun, they say by way of implication. Fun! The most desirable of all the American gizmos. And with it comes excitement! The ghosts of more people are walking below, laughing and smiling, entranced by all the noise and wonders. A night at FUN-O-RAMA. A summer night, it once more descends, full of June bugs buzzing against the neon lights, long, long ago. Darkness just beyond, and all around. Like the sea around an island. Ray doesn't see them. But I do. Sometimes I think I see the old man, again, standing beside the Ferris wheel waiting for Louise. Sometimes I see the car from the drawing (I look at it every night, now, while waiting for all the nothing that's coming my way) parked just beyond the giant clown's head. It sits quietly. A reminder. Be transported; but to where?

"Ferris Wheel's next," Ray says. "Need to hire more people."

He's still working, not really looking at me, sort of thinking out loud. I tell him, "If I stay I'm going to need more money, Ray." Now he *is* looking at me.

"Wondered when you'd get around to that."

"Well, you can stop your wondering now."

"How much you figure you want, then?"

"Same as you'll be payin the others. Whatever that is. I doubt they'll be working for five dollars."

"You're right there. I'll give you ten. How's that?"

"If that's what the others get. I'll know sooner or later, though. So better stay honest."

"Trusting sort, aren't you."

"Not really, no," I say, and drag my arm across my forehead to wipe the sweat away.

He turns back to his work. "Okay, I'll give

you twelve."

He pays me in cash, which I hide in a tin can buried in the ground with a big rock on top, to mark it. I stock up on canned food and Fig Newtons, and buy a big thermos to fill with water and take with me to work. I don't know what to spend the rest of the money on, that's too much to think about. I stand outside the hospital sometimes, but a nurse finally recognizes me and says not to bother waiting around here anymore because the girl is gone.

"Where to," I ask her, and she says probably to her new foster home.

"Not the old one?"

"A different one," she says. "Nice people. I met them."

"That's good. You're not going to tell me their names, or anything, *are* you?"

"No sir," she says. "I'm not."

"Well…," I say.

"She was a pretty girl once we got her cleaned up," the nurse says. "Didn't say much. Not a talker."

"Nothin' to say," I tell her.

"Well…I doubt that."

She's looking at me now like she's not sure what to think. With a job like she has she's probably seen enough people to know you can't always tell the good ones from the bad ones just by looking. She's sparing me that and I'm grateful.

On my day off I decide to buy an old bike out of the Want Advertiser at the Quick Trip. I'm tired of walking back and forth to work and to the store. It's one of those road bikes. There's a scratch on the fender. It has twenty one speeds and a flat tire. They're asking fifty dollars. I buy a new tire and ride the bike home in a snap. On the way I have an idea. At the library I ask the woman behind the desk if she can help me find an article in the paper. She takes me to a computer and tells me how she can access a database for the local news rag and put in search words to find the article. I tell her to search *Runaway Taken To Hospital*. After a few false tries she gets the right wording and we get a hit. What she finds tells us there are two articles and which paper they're in. The first article tells all about the girl—they don't say Jessie's name—running away from foster care and being brought to the hospital two weeks later by a homeless man, and a pending investigation to see whether or not she had been abused by this man. The second article tells how she is recovering well and has gone to live in a new foster home where there are three other children. Without saying so, exactly, it has Happy Ending written all over it. I sit and stare at the article for a few long minutes. I should be happy for her. The librarian comes back and asks me if I need help with anything else. She's had a chance to get a better look at me, since I've been here, and has come to the conclusion that I am not from the neighborhood, and that perhaps I'm not from any neighborhood at all. She is right, of course, and I am sure, as Ray has pointed out to me more than once, I'm in need of a bath. On my way home, I buy a bar of soap, a small box of detergent for my clothes, and deodorant.

My new life is starting to overwhelm me. It's amazing how quickly you can go from a whole lot of nothing to a little bit of something, and how unbelievably taxing even a small amount of something can be. I'm working hard on finding a reason to keep this up. It has no plus to it that I can see—it's all minus. I like my new bike. But not that much.

I ride my bike to Glendale, the neighborhood where she is. Another story there in that name. Like all the names they give places, but especially housing developments. GLENDALE. A leafy glade type of place. Hill and Dale sounding. To grandmother's house we go. I'm there in Glendale checking it out. I don't find her, and I knew I probably wouldn't. What could I say, anyway? I just wanted to return her doll. Stay at home moms pull their kids in off the street when they see me ride by on my road bike with 21 speeds and a scratch on the fender. The gears could use some oil. I ride up and down every street, but it's no use. It feels good in a way knowing she's in a proper home. And bad. I go home feeling there is probably something wrong with me. This isn't healthy, I tell myself. Time to let go. It's just that for a brief moment I had …what? A reason to go on with this endless repetition of days. Now it's back to nothing, again, but why the difficulty going back?

When I get to FUN-O-RAMA on Monday there are two new guys. They arrive together in a pickup truck and both wear camo pants and John Deer hats. They're good friends, apparently. While working they talk Nascar and guns, outdo each other with their knowledge of different types of ammo. Buzz and Earl. I keep clear of them. Ray sees this but doesn't say anything. He lets me keep my space. Doesn't matter to him what the hell's wrong with me. I do my work and don't flap my gums all day talking Indy 500 and how to kill a wild boar with a bow and arrow. I just put my head down and go to work.

"You're an awfully quiet sonofabitch," Buzz and Earl say to me on the break.

I think not answering would be the perfect answer to that comment, but catch Ray looking so I say, “Pretty much, yeah.”

They’ve known Ray a while so are comfortable being themselves around him. They each chew a pinch of Red Man and now and then have to spit, one after the other. “What’s the matter?” they say. “You don’t think you’re too good for us, do ya?”

“I don’t know,” I say back. “Do I look like someone who’d think he’s too good for you, or anyone else for that matter?”

They laugh and Earl says with a grin, “Not really, no. You look like kind of a grubby little shit to be honest about it.”

“Well, there you go,” I say back to them. “I’m a grubby little shit. No offense though. I just don’t go in for all that chit chat. That’s all.”

This brings more laughter. They are a happy couple, it seems, plus some. Better happy than mad I say. “Chit chat, hunh?” Buzz says through a wheezy laugh that has him coughing up this morning’s dose of cigarettes. He lights another one now. There are more creases in his forehead than a roll and pleated vinyl seat. When he laughs or coughs his eyes disappear completely in the meat packed in under his eyebrows. They both each weigh more than me and Ray put together.

“Well, you little shit. You’ll just have to go with us out to CHICKLETS sometime. That’ll get yer chit chat a goin."

"What's that?" I say.

"It's a titty bar over in the next county. Pool tables, lap dances, and beer. We do Tequila shots until everyone falls down. It's a ton of fun. It'll be the best night of your life, if you can remember any of it the next day." Wheezy goes into another coughing fit after laughing at this and spits across Earl's knee, which gets him a nasty look from Earl. He's the meaner looking of the two. He's also a tad bigger and playing with a few more cards in his deck. If he made a fist, it would be about the size of my head.

I want no part of these two, but say nothing so as to keep the peace. They seem okay enough as long as they're laughing, but I wouldn't want them getting pissed off at me. Then I just can't help myself. I say, "Sorry, can't go to no bars. It'd break my parole."

"Yeah?" Buzz says. "Now what'd you go and do to get yourself on parole?"

I hear Ray chuckle at this.

"You tell 'em Ray," I call out. "I don't like to think about it."

Ray looks at me as I walk away and then says to them without a blink, "Murder one, I believe it was. Slit a guy's throat for him. He was only sixteen at the time. That's how he got out so soon. He was a juvenile. I wouldn't mess with him if I was you. He's got kind of a short fuse and he's a little fucked up in the head. Something wrong with him. Good worker, though."

"He's ugly too," Buzz says. "But I don't believe a word of this shit you're feeding us. You're just a lying old bastard, Ray. You know that?"

"It's the truth," I say looking right at him with my best hard ass look.

"You know," Earl says, "For someone who's no chit chatter, you're an awfully funny guy."

"Okay, boys," Ray says, thinking probably that this could go on a while. "That's enough of the bull shit festival for now. Get your asses back to work. This here coaster won't take itself down."

Another week goes by. Buzz and Earl like to give me a hard time, but so far it has stayed friendly. I can put up with their dumb ass humor and don't show fear. That's the trick. In prison it's the first thing you learn. The weak get eaten alive. Convicts can smell fear, drawn to it like flies to a rotten piece of meat. So even if you're scared you put on a good show. Give'em your best performance. Tell a good story. And they're all telling stories in there; you have to. The main story is: I'm A Bad Assed Motherfucker So Stay The Fuck Away. Whether you really are one or not, you have to act like you are, or unafraid anyway and maybe a little crazy too. Of course, a lot of them really are bad-assed and crazy; that's the problem But there's bad, and then there's really goddamn bad. Their stories came with plenty of pictures too. Like they say—worth a thousand words. The tats tell the tale. Swastikas. Bleeding hearts. Skulls with snakes coming out the eye sockets.That kind of shit. What gang you're in. Your ethnic background. And of course there's another way to tell a story. The old way. Letting blood. Wasting someone. Me? I just stayed the fuck out of everyone's way. That's the easiest. Won't say any more about it. So I can deal with these two jokers. They aren't shit compared to what I've seen.

Then I hear Ray call my name. I stop what I'm doing and look over at him. He's pointing down by the truck. There's a car there and a woman standing beside it looking up at us. It's that woman, Mariela Perez, from Child Protective Services. Buzz and Earl are looking her over like we're at the titty bar and they're getting ready to put a ten dollar bill in her thong. I climb down and grab my thermos.

"You're hard to track down," she says.

"No I'm not," I answer. "I'm right here. Just got to know where to look, that's all."

"Must be hot up there," she says getting an eyeful of the crew.

She's looking good outside in the daylight. I take too long a look and feel bad but can't help myself. "You come all the way out here to tell me that?" I say.

"I'm glad to see you, too."

"Sorry. My conversation has degenerated some since I've been working here."

"I'm here about Jessie," she says.

"Why? She all right?"

"She's having some problems. Having a little trouble adapting. I finally realized that she was…"

"Hey," Ray calls down to us. "This going to take long?"

I look at her for an answer so she says she needs to talk to me. We agree to meet at a pizza place on Highland Avenue after I get off work. We decide on 6:30. I'll have to go home and clean up, then I'll ride my bike over there to meet her.

"See you later," she says with what might pass for a smile.

After she leaves, Buzz and Earl are full of every kind of horseshit remark they can think of, which with both of them working hard as they can at it, doesn't amount to anything better than, "Hey! You boning that are ya?"

"Christ!" I say. "Does she look like someone who would waste her time with a guy like me?"

"Well, no," they say, "now that you mention it. Not in the least."

"I never win the lottery either."

Buzz squints hard and says, "You don't even play the lottery, do ya?"

I look but don't smile. "You are just one fast actor, aren't ya Buzz?"

"I believe I am, queer bait."

"Well you're half right, anyway."

Now he's perplexed and trying to figure out which half I'm talking about and looks at Earl for assistance. "Don't ask *me,"* Earl says. "You're the one doin the talkin, dipshit!"

At Papa John's Pizza she is waiting for me at a booth when I get there. I've bought a new shirt and jeans so I'll have something to wear on my day off. You get tired of people treating you like a rabid dog or a panhandler. Besides, my other clothes are starting to fall apart and too dirty to clean.

"Well that's a change," she says, relieved I didn't show up looking like I did earlier. "You don't look half bad when you get cleaned up. All you need now is a haircut and a shave."

"I actually was a person once," I say.

"You still are, I think. Aren't you?"

"I'm not sure, anymore. It's getting harder to

tell." I take a quick glance around the room, feeling awkward, then down at the table and finally look up at her. "So tell me," I say to get her from talking anymore about me." I hear an accent. Latino?"

"Cuban. Grandparents came over after Castro came to power. Born and raised in Miami. Second generation Salsa baby."

"Salsa baby, huh."

"Yeah. But Miami might as well be Havana most of the time. You know? Little Havana."

"Okay," I say before she has time to ask me where I'm from. "What's up with Jessie?"

She nods and gives me that Being Patient look. Then it comes. "I need your help."

"*My* help."

"Yes." Her voice is very deliberate. Calm but serious. She's thinking what to say. "What I think is that, as you would expect, losing her parents and little brother was so traumatic for her that, naturally, she just kind of closed herself off. I'm sure you already know this. Blocking is what they call it. People, but kids especially, will just go numb. They stop talking. Can't relate, go deep inside themselves. It's quite typical. Like I said when we met, she just cut herself off from her past. So then she meets you and must have formed a bond with you somehow; I'm not sure I get why. You let her be, I suppose, that's the best I can make of it. No pressure. Basically, then, you replaced her family in a way, not completely, of course, but you became some kind of source of attachment. Gave her a center. Something to hang onto. This is the simplified layman's version. Then boom, all of a sudden you're gone, and now she's lost you, too. It's a double whammy, if you will. So she's acting out, now. Pulling away again. A way to get rid of the anger that's stuffed inside somewhere. One of the five stages of loss and grief. Same old, same old. So she takes it out on the new family, fights with the other kids, withdraws."

She looks at me now to see if I'm following this, like maybe I won't understand. "Okay, I get it. And so where do I fit in? Why come to me?"

"She needs help."

"You've made that clear. So help her."

"I'm trying to. She needs *your* help."

"How can I help her? What is it you want me to do?"

"She needs closure."

"Meaning what, exactly? What kind of closure?"

"To see you again, for starters. Just so she doesn't feel so cut off."

"See me again. That's easy enough. And then what? What's the catch?"

"Don't know, exactly. We…"

"Never mind. I think I know what it is; I know what's coming. You want me to see her, get her back on track, and then say goodbye," I say. "Is that it?"

"See her and be around a while, until she transitions is more like it."

"And then I'm history, right?"

"That's not how I'd put it, but…yes. She needs that if she's going to heal. You understand? It's what she needs. You should do that for her, if you care about her. I'm sorry, but it has to be that way. The administrators at CPS will never agree to your having a permanent relationship with her. Just not going to happen. Not given your background and your… current circumstances."

"I'm not asking to have a relationship with her. Am I? Who said I wanted that? I just don't like be seen as some kind of creep who's unfit for contact with…"

"Whatever," she snaps, exasperated. Fuck me and my self-respect, is what I'm thinking.

"I saved her life," I say.

"I know that. Try to be reasonable. Think about her. Think about…"

A waitress appears at our table to take our orders. Iced tea for her, and I order a beer for myself. We need more time to look at the menu, she tells the waitress. I was hungry after work, but now my appetite is disappearing fast. I don't like the sound of this. First they accuse me of molesting her; now they want my help and then it's get lost again.

"Look," she says. "We can't do anything about your screwed up life, but we can help her, and right now she really needs it." I'm looking at her and can't quite hide my anger. I understand what she's saying but I see this for what it is. She can see you, then you have to disappear like the scum that you are. You're good enough when they need your help, but then you have to get lost. Something about it just isn't right.

"Listen," she says. "I know that deep down inside somewhere you're not a bad guy…"

"Great. That's nice of you." She gives me a peevish look but goes on.

"…Things go wrong for some people, they get lost in all of it, nothing ever seems to work out. But, no offense please, stop thinking about yourself, here, and think about her."

"I'm glad you have me all figured out," I say.

"I'm only trying to help Jessie."

I know she's right about the girl, but somehow I can't help being pissed off for the way their portraying me; I'm homeless, not degenerate. She's looking at the menu, now, and I'm wanting to just get up and walk out of here. I didn't sign up for any of this shit, anyway. I see the girl's face when she sat there in that house the first day and waited for me to give her some of my food. Didn't say a fucking word, just stood there looking at my can of Vienna sausages holding that goddamn doll. "I wanna help her," I say, getting up, and dropping five dollars on the table for the beer and turning to leave. "But not this way."

"So you agree, then? You'll help us?" she says.

I keep walking. "I didn't say that," I yell back to her.

"Your beer!" she says as the waitress arrives at the table.

"You drink it," I say, halfway to the door. In the parking lot I'm already feeling like a dope, but I keep on walking. Old habits die hard, apparently. But fuck this! I'm done. I'm still walking but I don't know how to explain why I'm so mad. I'm just sick of the attitude of all these self-righteous people. And yet I know she's only trying to help the girl, so I just might be as pissed off at myself as I am at those fucking people.

I'm a half mile down the road when along comes Mariela Perez in her car. She pulls ahead of me and stops at the curb in front of me. She has her window down trying to hand me something, a card, looks like. "You're acting like a child," she says, scolding me, like somebody's mother. I know she's right, and it stings, but fuck her.

"If that's supposed to be persuasive," I fire back, "you're way off your mark."

"Here's my number. Call me when you calm down."

"I don't have a phone, remember. I'm homeless."

"No, you wouldn't have a phone," she says, "but Ray does. And I'll bet those co-workers of yours both have cell phones."

"And here I thought you were pretty nice, when we first met," I say. "Can you believe that shit?"

"Listen, I'm just trying to do my job. This isn't my only case you know. In fact thanks to budget cuts and wishful thinking my case load has almost doubled in the last month. So for what it's worth, you don't have to like me. Just help the girl. That's all I'm asking." She gives me a hard look, then speeds off leaving me there holding the card with her number on it in one hand and batting away the road dust she churned up with her car that I am now eating. I'm feeling worse than ever and don't like this fucking movie I'm in now. She's trying to make me the bad guy. But fuck that! I'm a bum, maybe, but I'm not a bad guy. Now all I want is to ride this damn bike into a new movie somewhere. Take off and never come back. Like the movie where I mind my own business and make my way through abandoned, foreclosed houses, again, finding what I can find and staying the fuck away from other people. I'm about to toss the card but put it in my back pocket instead. Don't ask me why. I guess because I'm not a bad guy, and I'm not a goddamned litter bug either. Of course, she isn't a bad person either and I know that. She's only trying to help the girl, who Christ knows really needs it.

At work the next day Ray says, "Ya know, Hopalong, feeling sorry for yourself doesn't look too good on you."

"Who says I'm feeling sorry for myself?" I say, wondering what the fuck business it is of his.

"*You* do, hangin your bottom lip out there like that. I got a granddaughter that's not as bad with her pouting as you are."

I resist the temptation to walk away. It's his way of trying to get me out of my funk, I suppose. "What I am, is pissed off, if you have to know. Not that it's any of your business."

"When you slow down at work and trip over you bottom lip it sure as hell *is* my business," he says.

"Well then say that. Save the therapy session for someone else."

"Fine, if that's the way you want it. Get'cher ass back to work then and quit your mope'n around."

At lunch I sit by myself and wonder how this movie is going to end. None of it looks too good, but me running out on the kid looks the worst. Then the twins come over for a little fun at my expense. They just can't resist. I should have expected it.

"Hey sweetie," Buzz says, "You're acting like such a little girl lately I thought you might need someone to come over and hold your hand for you."

"Yeah," Earl joins in. "You're awfully cute when you pout like this. You know that? Gives me a regular hard on."

"How'd you two like a steel railroad track up your ass?"

"Whoah," they say in unison. "Listen to the man talk. Hey, why don't you settle down there, shit lips. We're just dickin with you," Earl says. "What we really want to know is if you wanna go to CHICKLETS with us tonight. You need something to get you out of this pity party you're havin and what's better for that than titties and beer? Lemme answer for you…Nothin!"

"Well, shots are better, for one," Buzz says like Earl expected an answer.

"Well, that'll work, too, Buzzy. Now what say? Go with us after work and have at least one beer.

We're not taking no for an answer."

"And a lap dance," Buzz adds. "Best therapy in the world."

Calming down a little and seeing no way out I say, "You think I believe for one second that you two care about what's bothering me?"

"You're right," they say. "We don't. We're just tired of looking at that sorry assed face of yours all day, and you mooning around like a puppy dog who needs a home. Plus you're slowing us down. Time to grow a pair and act like a man."

"Yeah," Buzz says. "It's makin us all kinda sad."

"Fuck you guys." I spit on the ground to emphasize it but I'm softening a bit and showing a little bit of a grin. Have half a mind to go with them if only so I can get a little drunk.

"So you'll go?"

"One beer!" I say.

"Beauty!"

"And you assholes are paying for it."

"We knew you were a cheapskate," Earl says. "As well as a candy ass. Now it's official."

Ray hollers over, then, "If you girls are through with that little tea party you're havin over there we have to get ourselves back to work."

Twelve

I don't call the number on the card. Maybe tomorrow. Instead I go to the bar with Buzz and Earl. I'm getting used to them, and they're friendly enough, if not a little too deep in the weeds for me. The conversation is like talking to some of those guys back in the joint. It veers from bravado about going to Iraq or somewhere similar and "wasting some sandniggers!" to "the best way to field dress a deer." Not a skill I've ever felt like acquiring. Too much information I'm never going to use. Then it goes off the rails completely after a few drinks when they start talking about all the shit they've pulled over the years, which is mostly the fights they've gotten themselves into and heads they've busted, including their own. It doesn't bode well for a night out with them. I'm half expecting a fight to break out at any moment, something I did my best to stay clear of in the pen. The noise is almost overwhelming, but I find the naked girls are worth the trip. Haven't been with a woman since my wife left unless you count the crack whore I wound up with before I got sent away, when I was at rock bottom and didn't know where I was half the time. We were usually too loaded for much carnal excitement and even in my delirium I was too leery of her past acquaintances to sustain much interest.

Probably saved myself a world of trouble there. Then I got busted. When I got out I tried to get my life back but no one would hire me. Soon as they find out you're a convicted felon they say *thanks we'll let you know, don't slam the door on the way out*. You have to tell them; they'll find out sooner or later anyway. Now I'm here, and between the music and everybody yelling into each other's ears about towelheads, camel-jockeys, and semi-automatic weapons, weather proof boots, and football, I'm getting jumpy. I stand at the bar with my beer in hand looking at all the T & A when Buzz hands me a shot of tequila. I know I'm making a mistake, but can't refuse a full shot glass in CHICKLETS with all these alligator wrestling dudes standing around me shoulder to shoulder pouring them down like they're leaving for the Bagdad first thing in the morning. Down she goes, and in goes the beer chaser right after. It's been a long time, but drinking's like riding a bike. You never forget how. Now Earl's putting twenties in a girl's thong so she'll take them off and give him a close up grind. You wonder about these girls, sometimes, but they seem happy enough to take everyone's money. Not exactly shy, either. Mostly they're fighting off boredom. Like everyone else at the job, they just want to know how long before their shift is over. My guess is half of them are paying for college on the Sell Your Body

For Cash Plan. One of them has her eye on me, now, but I know this movie. Manipulate me out of all my money then disappear in a puff of smoke. Go home and give all my hard earned money (now her hard earned money) to her man, some jackass with a coke habit, a nose ring, and propensity for violence and then he'll send her right back out again. It's amazing how many of these bozos fall for it, though, but then again I'm not quite drunk yet. "Cowgirls Don't Cry" and "Everybody Wants To Go To Heaven" comes blasting out of speakers all over the walls and ceiling so you feel the bass guitar in your stomach. If it was any louder my eardrums would burst. They hand me another beer and I tell them, "No more shots!" So they answer by handing me another shot. Now I am drunk and thinking, fine, if I fall down I'll just sleep here tonight.

I watch the girls some more and pick out the one I like best. She looks bored and puts too many convoluted moves into her performance, like she has that What I Really Wanted To Be Was A Famous Ballerina way about her, like she studied tap, and jazz, and ballet when she was a kid, and thinks this is only temporary while she gets her shit together even though she's been at it for ten years now. The I'm Better Than This, Really I Am story. Well, really she's not, but has a perfect body and a pretty face so might as well cash in on it, right?

We drink and stand around yacking for another hour to where the girls have an amazing appeal and yet are becoming tiresome at the same time, if only because my eyes are going in and out of focus. Buzz is trying to tell someone how he caught a giant catfish barehanded once. "You reach in where they're hiding underwater and grab'em by the mouth. What we call Noodling."

Eventually a very hot looking babe comes over and says, "Haven't seen you in here before." Good looking doesn't quite cover it, and even though she's got more makeup on than a drag queen she still has a sorority girl face and perfect teeth. She could be in a whiskey add or on the cover of Sports Illustrated wearing a bikini. She is wearing street clothes to make her seem more available. You know not to get too friendly with the half-naked lap dancers. But this one seems off the clock. I know better than to think this is anything other than a hustle, but I remember her now from her turn on the pole and can still see her fake tits but otherwise perfect body. Little wisps of hair fall in loose curls around her ears. I'm driving over a cliff at sixty miles per hour but can't seem to get my foot off the pedal. "First time here," I say in answer to her question as though she gives a shit.

"First time for everything," she says back. Oh,

I'm thinking. This girl wouldn't tell me if my hair was on fire anywhere else but what the fuck, I'll play along. She finishes off what's left of her drink, looks at it and shakes it then looks back at me like I'm supposed to do something. Even a dead man can see what's coming. Meanwhile over her shoulder I spot another dancer in her street clothes looking to fleece some other poor bastard out of his hard earned money buying seventy five dollar bottles of champagne for her, or twenty five dollar daiquiris made of ginger ale and pink food coloring. I remember this one too from her moment of glory because she was the one girl of the bunch who wasn't particularly awesome in the looks department or her body either. Flat chested by comparison, she had breasts that would make most men happy back at the homestead but just seem insufficient on a stripper. On the other hand some of these women are just too big and most of the fake ones look freakish and their tits look about as erotic as two halves of a coconut. It's part of the What Were They Thinking story. Plastic surgeons should be required to take a figure drawing class with live models before they get their scalpels awarded them.

"Am I boring you?"

She seems a little pissed that I'm not as infatuated as I should be but I can't see parting with my money for something that's going absolutely nowhere unless maybe she's a hooker. In my drunken haze I'm thinking *well, maybe,* but still have enough mathematical ability to guess how much of my bankroll a blow job from her is going to cost me. The skinny stripper in the corner probably has a discount rate and maybe if she doesn't have a boyfriend she might be one of those types that goes for ex-cons. In here we're all glass half full types because we're drunk and revved up from looking at all this naked pussy.

"Sorry," I say. "I promise to do better." It's all I can think of at the spur of the moment. Even I don't like the way it sounds coming out.

"You're sorry all right," she says. Then she turns to the bartender and yells, "Pedro! Jo Jo here wants to buy me a drink!" I don't like this but push my way through to the bar to collect the drink. Pedro wants the money up front. "Okay," I tell him. "Here's for the drink," and I hand him a twenty to which he says it's thirty five, "and when I hand him another twenty I say, "but the drink is for that girl at the corner of the bar there." I point to the skinny one with the zits covered in makeup and head towards where she's sitting and looking a bit forlorn.

I get about as far as "Hi," when the drink arrives and a very pissed off stripper comes up behind me and says, "Are you fucking kidding me!" She's now waving a bouncer over, which brings a couple of gorillas whom I think I've seen before in the weight room back in the slammer, or maybe it was their first cousins. They look anxious to see me.

"This fucking asshole called me a stupid cunt," she tells them. The skinny stripper looks on in astonishment. Her life has just gone from abject boredom to interesting to What The Fuck Is This in all of seven seconds. Her mouth is hanging open in the form of a big question mark. I like the way it's puckered and in my boozy haze imagine kissing it.

"That right?" the clod closest to me says.

"I never said that," I scream stupidly. I'm not so drunk as to not realize they don't give a rat's ass whether I said it or not. They only care that she wants me to have my ass kicked the way it should be if I *had* said it. In return for the thirty five dollar drink I had to buy, and the ass kicking I'm about to get for something I never actually did, I decide what the hell. "You *are* a stupid cunt," I tell her. They have me by the arms now as I'm saying, "Bye," to the skinny stripper still suspended in the grip of shock when the cunt with the coconuts for breasts snatches the drink out of her hands and dumps it on my head. They drag me to the door and shove me through it where I land on my face in the parking lot. When attacked by a grizzly bear you're supposed to play dead, but my brain is telling me that in another minute and a half I won't have to *play* dead because I'm going to *be* dead. And I'm being attacked by a pair of Grizzlies, which has to make a huge difference. Waiting for the first blow and before I can get up and attempt to run I feel someone pulling on my arms. "C'mon," Earl says to me. "We're goin."

"Going!" I hear Buzz say. "We ain't had no lap dance yet,"

On my feet in a sudden reversal of gravity like a movie played backwards I see the two grizzly's lying on the ground, where I used to be, shaking and holding onto their heads and making authentic bearlike sounds, but no longer in too much of a hurry to finish what they started.

"Forget that," Earl tells him. "Next time."

They drag me towards the truck. "You are one real pussy," Earl says to me. "You know that?"

"Just one fuckin lap dance," Buzz says. "That's all I wanted."

"Gotta work tomorrow," Earl says. "Besides. You know how nasty your wife can be when you're late." And then to me, "She's hell on wheels, jailbird! Nice lady, but a real don't mess with momma type."

"What did you say to that bitch, anyway?"

I'm feeling my jaw to see if it still works and pleased to find it does. "She says I called her a cunt."

Earl nods his head. "That'll do it all right. Did you?"

"Did I what?"

"Call her a cunt?"

"Well, not right away."

On the way back he takes a slight detour and we arrive at Buzz's house. A dog barks when we stop the truck, and Buzz says to me, "Come on inside a minute. I have to show you something." We climb out and walk past the barking dog, which Buzz kicks away and barks back at. "I'll bite *you*, ya little fucker," he snarls, "now outa the way." The dog seems used to it and takes it in stride, bounding back with a tongue hanging grin and sniffs at every pair of legs he can find.

"Don't *tell* me," his wife says by way of a greeting, pushing her way through the screen door. "They threw'ya all out of the titty bar for impersonating men."

"Meet the little wife, Viola. Like Earl said, Hell on wheels."

"Earl said that?" she asks, looking at Earl who pretends he's not hearing any of this and quickly reaches down to pat the dog.

Buzz goes to the fridge and grabs three beers and hands me one and gives the other to Earl. "Just one," Buzz says.

"A quickie," Viola says, and chuckles. "Listen," she says to me, "anyone ever tell you you need a haircut and a trim for your beard?"

"Not until recently," I say.

"Well next time you're here I'll give you one. When I'm not cleaning up after the Buzzsaw here I work at a beauty salon. Thelma's, out on the highway next to the video store. I can do your nails too if you want. They're not lookin' too good, either."

Buzz grabs my arm and takes us into the TV room full of oversized furniture covered in pictures of pheasants and bird dogs, so big and plump you could fall into one of them and never come of out again. Against one wall there's a small table and chair with trophies and ribbons and medals spread out on top, and a couple of those fat candles on short fat pedestals. On the wall above the table is a picture of a young soldier in his blue Marine dress uniform. Beside that is a picture of the same soldier in his regular desert camo sitting on one of those armored personnel carriers. He's holding an M16 across his chest, sort of cradling it. Buzz lights the candles. Over the pictures it says Lance Corporal Robert H. Hanson, United States Marine Corps 1984 – 2005. There are a few newspaper clippings in a picture frame behind the candles. Beside that is a photo album. What looks like some kind of a shrine to the dead soldier.

Buzz sits in the chair and stares at the pictures. "That there's my little brother," he says. "He was a fuckin goddamn hero, ya know?" He says it like he's mad, but when I look over at him the tears are rolling off his face like he was a baby in a wet diaper. "Best sonofabitch God ever made. Died near Fallujah so we can live in freedom back here at home."

I don't know what to make of it and can't think of what to say. I go from one movie to another so fast, anymore, I don't have time to switch. "Played football?" I ask looking at the trophies and ribbons.

"Varsity," he says. "Could have gone to any college he wanted on a scholarship. They all wanted him. But he had to go and join up, and go to that fuckin shithole Iraq, instead."

I dig down real deep for something to say and all I can come up with is how sorry I am. He looks pathetic sitting there in front of his brother's pictures and trophies. I can chalk it up to all the booze if I want but I can imagine how he feels losing his brother like that. Life is a bad deal most of the time and in between it's not much better.

"You boys better go," he says. "We gotta work in the morning."

"Don't mind him," Viola says in a quieter voice coming up beside me. "He's like this every time he has a few, and looks at those pictures. 'Bout broke his heart when he heard what happened to Bobby. We all just couldn't understand it. Losing someone like that so early in life. It's a damn shame."

We head off into the night with nothing more to say. No radio this time, just the sound of the engine winding in and out of gear, the in and out of the universe packed into Earl's red F-150 360 V-8. All of life in one little moment. Life and death over and over again. We're halfway to my place when Earl says, "He's really just a big pussy cat. Unless you piss him off, of course. Then it's time to get the hell outa there. Otherwise he's not a bad guy. We been friends a long time. You just have to get to know him."

Which I have, a little bit, I guess, after tonight. You never can tell about people. We all have our shit to deal with. We all need a little help sometimes. So I'm thinking, maybe I ought to call Mariela and help the girl. It's the least I can do. Why punish her because I'm pissed off at Mariela? What did this runaway girl named Jessie ever do to me besides show up in my life out of nowhere and…what? That's what I can't figure out. Not sure why I give a damn but it sure seems like I do.

Thirteen

Still, I don't call. In the morning things look different. In the morning things *always* look different. I don't have a hangover, but I am dragging my ass around like an old man. I make it to work and the boys are there, tired too and dragging their asses around like they'll never make it until lunchtime. Ray's brought in a big flatbed truck he's rented to haul away the long pieces of track. They're heavy bastards and hard to maneuver. Have to lower them from the top with a block and tackle we've rigged up. When we get all the metal off we'll take down the scaffolding. You just make some strategic cuts halfway through some of the vertical posts, then push on it somewhere with a power shovel and get her out of column. Then we'll get the hell out of the way and wait a few seconds and watch the show. That'll bring the whole thing down. Once a few key supports go, the whole shebang will buckle faster than a loser in a prizefight. Boom! It'll all be over, just like that, except for the dust. It'll be something to see, but it's kind of sad, too. That roller coaster represents a lot of good things to a lot of different people. It's an escape from their troubles, and brings in money for the people that worked here. Paying money to have the crap scared out of you is not my idea of fun, but some people think it's a stimulating alternative to everyday life. Exciting, they would say. You've got to hand it to the guy who invented the roller coaster. He must have been one hell of a guy. I can't fix the world, he must have said, but I sure can scare the worry right out of all the people.

The next day around lunch time Ray gets a call on his cell phone and says it's for me. I know who it might be, but worry it could be the boys down at the police station with some new thing they've cooked up to hassle me with.

"I was hoping you'd have called by now," Mariela says.

I think of her call as a mixed blessing. There's two ways to look at everything. I'm not sure which this is. "Well…I didn't," I say. Sounds a bit harsh, but I don't know what else to say. This phone call is a bit unexpected. "Sorry I didn't mean to be…"

"This is kind of spur of the moment for me, actually. I got to thinking about things and decided that maybe I owe you an apology."

This is also unexpected. "What for?" I ask, thinking, *I thought so, too, but now I'm more or less over it*. "Don't worry about it," I say, but try not to sound like I really mean it, even though I do.

"You were pretty mad when you left," she says. "Can I buy you a beer so we can talk and try again?"

"What's there to talk about?"

"Say yes and find out. I still owe you one. You didn't get your beer the other night."

"Okay," I say, tired of jerking her around and getting the look from Ray. "When?"

"I can pick you up after work."

"Sorry. I don't have my tux with me today."

"Don't sweat it," she says. For an educated woman she can sound a lot like regular people. I should knock off the crap and be more agreeable.

"All right."

The day drags and we all regret going to Chicklets. Ray's annoyed with us but can't fire us so we go slow and make minimal progress. It's hot as usual and what they're doing today requires some teamwork. This translates into being harder to coast on the job. We are all glad when the day's over. Except for Ray who had planned on getting more accomplished by now. But he has noticed that the tension in the crew has eased.

Buzz and Earl are not as smart assed this time but can't help gawking when she shows up. "Tomorrow then," Earl says to me and tips his hat to Mariela on his way past her car. Ray cranks up the diesel engine on the flatbed and sends a cloud of black smoke up and out the stack. The boys sit and watch as I load my bike into the trunk of her car and we head out for our big talk.

We find a quiet lounge that's a little closer, and take a table in the corner out of the way. The place is half empty. You can hear yourself think in here, which might come in handy and I wait for what she has to say. I get my beer and she has a gin and tonic. I like the way the ice tinkles in her glass when she stirs it. It cools me off just to look at it sitting there on the napkin in front of her, relaxes me, the green wedge of lime floating among the ice cubes, visible but only just.

"At first I was as mad as you were," she says by way of kicking things off. I'm thinking, oh no, here it comes. Like my mother and all her received wisdom pouring over me like hot cooking oil. "But then when I thought about it some more I realized that I wasn't looking at things properly. I was just thinking of Jessie. Which is my job, of course, but then as a professional, you know, you're supposed to see the whole picture. In this case that picture includes you. There's always other people involved."

I take a big swig of my beer thinking this could be a long night, but she's no match for my mother who could drag out a lecture so long you'd rather have taken the whipping. "I wouldn't want to be left out," I said, but she lets this pass.

"So when I was thinking about it, I realized that all that stuff I said about Jessie the other night could just as easily have been said about you. Correct me if I'm wrong, but it seems to me that, for whatever reason, you've apparently blocked out your past, or at least you're trying to as much as you can, living by yourself like a hermit, avoiding any kind of normal life the way you are. And from what I understand you had a life somewhere once. A family. A wife and kids. Now I don't know what happened but…"

I hold up my hand like a traffic cop. "Okay," I say, trying not to sound too nasty. "Maybe we should just stick to talking about Jessie, if that's okay."

"Well, see. You're making my case for me. I haven't even finished saying what I wanted to say, and you're shutting me down. It proves my point. Doesn't it?"

"I don't know if it does or it doesn't. Except it's my business, nobody else's. Besides…" I stop in the middle of my sentence and look at the silverware on the table in front of me. It's all rolled up in a napkin with a paper ring around it, buttoned up to keep the world out, all neat, and tidy, and most of all clean. Tables are dirty. You have to protect yourself. "Look, whatever," I say and realize what I must sound like. I'm still proving her point. I know this.

"Whatever," I say again like a moron.

"Well fine," she says, "I'm not asking to hear about your past. I'm just saying you have one and you're trying to wipe it out, just like Jessie. You two are the same, in a lot of ways."

Annoyed and fidgety, I reach out and grab the silverware in its bundled up napkin and pick at the paper ring where its edges are loose and sticking up. I want to explain myself but there's just too much to say. I wasn't expecting this to be about me. And now she keeps going whether I want to listen or not.

"In a way, I think Jessie was beginning to replace something of your past. You were easing your guilt and pain vicariously by taking care of Jessie, and of course you were replacing something for her. If that makes any sense to you."

I keep picking at the paper until it comes apart and part of the knife peeks through catching light from a lamp in the ceiling. For a split second I have to close my eyes. I thought I had forgotten what my wife's face looked like but then I see it as clearly as when I first met her. Then it's gone again just like that. Like a little lightning bug going off in my brain —brief but illuminating.

She ignores my attempt at inattention and goes on with her theories about my life. "What I'm saying is that this is traumatic for both of you; you're just better at pretending it isn't than she is."

I almost don't hear her because I'm trying hard to decide why it is I'm making such a mess of the napkin and paper holder. "Considering how badly it ended," I say, completely out of the blue but still not looking at her, "it was amazingly good at the start, you know." That little pin prick of light has me remembering.

"What was?"

"Us. You know, my wife and I. We were just kids, really. I worked and came home every night. We were happy."

She folds her hands and leans in towards me. "I see. And your kids? What about them?"

"What can I say? Life gets complicated. They were good kids. We loved them. It gets tough. We were still happy. Just…not so much. Like most people. We were busy. Went in opposite directions, seems like. I can see it now. When you're there, in the middle of it, you don't always notice what's going on. It kind of happens all in slow motion. A little bit here, a little bit there. Then the bottom falls out and it's over." I put the silverware and napkin down but still continue to look at it and the mess I've made of it.

"What happened?"

"I told you before. Economy failed. I lost my job. End of story."

"Lots of people lose their jobs."

"Yeah. That's right. Listen. My family meant everything to me. But I couldn't pay the bills. So…I lost my way. I couldn't get work. It went on like that for a long time, me looking and getting some crap work that we couldn't live on, so eventually I started getting high, thinking I'll feel better at least, it's just for today or one more night. Then I'll quit. When I get back to work I'll be all right. But there was no work to get back to. Then it just gets worse and worse. Then no one's going to hire you because you've been out of work so long and you're fucked up on drugs and your attitude sucks. Then you're not careful and all of a sudden you find yourself in jail. Then you're really fucked. It's a whole new ball game. When you're locked up like an animal you have to change in a hurry. If you don't then you don't survive. You can't let yourself think about things or you'll go crazy. The ones that do let themselves think, and remember all the shit they've lost, don't survive. The guards find them in the morning, a torn sheet around their neck, eyes bulging, or they've bled out on the floor from cuts they've delivered to themselves. There's ways when you're desperate, believe me. Doesn't matter what anybody else thinks. You just get to where there's no reason to live. And remember, there's nothing to do in there but sit in your cell and think about how fucked up your life is."

This seems to take her down a peg but she's no light-weight so she comes right back with, "Well, you're not locked up now. And you can change things. You can remember your life before and you should. You need to talk about it. And I'm a good listener. You need to do this, you know. You really need to."

I look her in the eyes but want to change the subject. "Well…I suppose. You know Buzz lost his younger brother over in Iraq. Did I tell you that? Makes you think. There's a lot going on in the world. A lot of shit out there to think about."

"That's too bad. I'm sorry to hear it."

"What do you suppose happened to her, anyway? Jessie?"

"We don't know. She won't talk about it. We need to get her to trust us so she will. Maybe if you help us, we can find out what we need to know."

"You think?"

"It's possible. Kids do open up, eventually. They have to."

"Yeah?"

"Sometimes. When they find someone they can trust."

"You think she trusts me?"

"Yes I do. I think she trusts you."

"Yeah? Well,…she should."

We are almost done removing the steel track. One more week and we'll be able to start on the wood scaffolding and frame. Ray brings the flatbed back and we spend most of the day getting the long pieces of track up and onto the truck bed. Once they're all in place they have to be secured with ratcheting tie down straps. A car dealership in Orlando is buying the giant clown. They arrive on a Wednesday with another flatbed and a boom truck type crane. We lay the body on its back on top of the flatbed like a headless corpse. Strap it down. Then set the head upright at the end by the clown's feet and tie it in place. The clown seems happier to be sitting upright, at least the head, anyway, its permanent smile frozen in perfect glee, never mind that it's fake. This is good for the car dealer. They'll be able to sell a lot more cars with the clown story to attract new customers. The giant clown standing there says to them *you'll have more fun at Dixie AutoMart where the big clown is*. If you don't know where it is, your kids will know. They'll tell you where it is. Takes the worry out of buying a car. Makes it better. Clowns are fun and happy and don't live in the real world. They throw buckets of colored confetti at you, instead of cold water. And it's like throwing buckets of fun, in a way. *Life isn't real*, it says. So don't worry about buying the car. We'll help you. Just remember: *You're having fun!* You're not buying a car; *you're having fun!*

The day she brings Jessie I'm sitting outside on the chair throwing pebbles at a scrub lizard sunning itself in the grass. It tolerates me for a while, pulsing its throat but otherwise keeping very still. I look away for a second and then when I look back it's gone. Was it really there? It could have been real, or maybe I imagined it. I amuse myself thinking about it. There's no way to know, now that it's gone. Things are like that; they are there, and then they are not. What's real is a question of how much you believe what you see. One of the buildings at FUN-O-RAMA says MAGIC SHOW in faded red paint all over the front. I've seen magic. Seems real when you watch it happen. Seeing is believing, people say. I'm not so sure. We all know magic's not real. Or is it?

They're walking. Coming towards me through the grass. I see them, but I'm not sure about this either. Maybe I'm just being hopeful. I look away and then back again to confirm it. They are still there and getting closer. Mariela has a proud walk. Attractive. Assertive. The girl looks different. Is she taller? In the heat and sunlight they begin to wobble. They see me and Mariela waves. I look in the grass where I had been throwing pebbles and the scrub lizard is there again. I look back at Mariela and Jessie and then back at the grass, again, and the lizard is gone.

They're standing in front of me, now. Mariela is saying something but I'm not listening; I'm looking at the girl. She's not the same. Then I realize that her hair is washed and combed and has a barrette in it, a mermaid. She also has new clothes. That's what's so different. They are clean and I notice also how kind of pretty she is. She still has a mopey face, and it's getting mopier. Her eyes are wet, and her face is crumpling. I stand up and the girl runs over to me and throws her arms around me, buries her face in my chest, sobbing. If I had any tears left in my head I would cry, too, but tears, if I ever had any, are all just history now. They're back there in the past somewhere with my socket wrenches and my wedding ring. It's all lost now. The whole thing. The goal was to have season tickets to something, football games or baseball games. Something like that. That's how you know your life is full and can say it's all real. It's like the FUN-O-RAMA sign, only it says Season Tickets. But it wasn't real. It was a story I told myself, like dumping buckets of confetti on my own head. This, now, I'm thinking, is better than season tickets. I can feel this. The memory of tears are filling my head, along with the smell of her hair. Mariela is tearing up now too. I'm just standing there with my arms around the girl and thinking how glad I am to see her. I don't know what to do.

"Hey," I say.

"Hey," she says back.

"Well," Mariela says. "Someone sure is happy to see you."

Jessie pulls back and looks at something on the ground. I look over just in time to see the scrub lizard dart away into the taller grass. "Have any trouble finding the place?" I ask Mariela.

"No," she says. "She remembered how to get here."

She takes a step toward the front door then goes inside for a look around. Mariela sees this and grabs me by the elbow. In a lowered voice she says, "I have something to tell you while she's not around." She looks to see if Jessie is still inside. I check and see that she is standing at the table looking at her drawing. I step further away from the door and around to the side. Mariela follows.

"What?" I ask, thinking from the way she's acting that this is no bucket of confetti she's about to throw.

"Remember the aunt in Alabama I told you about? The one that couldn't, or wouldn't, for some reason, take Jessie after the accident? Well the Police notified her when Jessie was found, you know, to let her know they'd found her and that she's all right. So now the aunt says she wants to take the girl after all. And, of course, because she's a blood relative she kind of gets top priority by the people who make the final decision. So she might be going to Alabama to live with them."

"Does she know?" I ask.

"She only knows that her aunt is talking to us about her. Nothing else. She didn't seem anxious to see her, I can tell you that."

"Yeah. Well I'm not surprised. Just when you think the lizard's there, it's not."

"Whatever that was supposed to mean," she says, frowning.

"Sorry. I was just...thinking out loud."

"Well, if that's what you were thinking then you're in worse shape than I thought."

"Okay," I say. "Whatever."

"On top of everything else the psychologist that's been talking to her is convinced she's been abused in some way. Problem is she can't get her to open up about anything. She only talks a little bit and what she says is not much."

"So."

"*So* is right," she says. "So I want to know what happened."

We both turn and see Jessie standing at the corner of the house watching us. She's holding the fly swatter. A souvenir from her time staying here, I guess.

"You're not going to leave me without a fly swatter are you?" I say to her.

She shakes her head, No.

"Well good. Those flies get to be a nuisance."

She swats at the side of the cabin with the fly swatter absentmindedly while watching us. "I like your new clothes," I say. She tilts her head to one side a little and looks at me. The sun's in her eyes and she squints at the light. I don't want her to go to Alabama but don't say that. I tell her I'm glad she's all better. "I was worried about you. Ya know that?" She turns around and faces the other direction, swings halfheartedly at the air with the fly swatter. She could be any child at that age. They need everything, and they have so little. Especially her. What the hell has she got?

When it's time for them to go I make her promise to come and see me again. She nods her head and says, "Okay." She hugs me again and I watch as they walk back out to the road where Mariela's car is parked. The farther they get from the cabin the louder the crickets sound. It's a pulsing sound, like the pulsing in the lizard's neck. Maybe it's the lizard's heartbeat. Must be; I can feel it. Or can I? Might be my own heartbeat I'm feeling. It's a hard worker, my heart. Always pumping away whether I tell it to or not. Like it's got a mind of its own.

She has set the doll in the chair by the table and I wonder why she didn't take it with her. I put the fly swatter back on the table and look at the drawing. When I go to hang it on the wall it falls to the floor, turning over. I see she has made another drawing on the other side. It's a picture of a tree. A girl is standing on a limb halfway up in the tree. A man is standing beside the tree and a short distance away, but doesn't see the girl. There's a dog beside the tree looking up at the girl. No sun in the corner. She drew this in a hurry while we were outside talking. It's not as good a drawing as the other one. She didn't finish. If she's the girl, then who's the man? The dog sees her; why can't he?

Fourteen

When all the steel track is down and hauled off, we set about preparing the wood frame for take down. Ray has a chain saw for making the cuts. Buzz has another one. A can of orange spray paint will be used to mark the verticals that Ray has chosen to cut. The last cut will be to a cross-brace Ray has picked for its structural location. I'm not sure what engineering principles he's based this on. Most likely it's a hunch and a guess and a lot of common sense, so now I'm nervous. Nevertheless, Ray seems confident enough about what he's doing and walks around shaking his paint can, looking at the structure like there's some kind of complex mathematical calculation unraveling in his brain. It's a plan just waiting to be revealed in orange blotches carefully placed near the base of the coaster. This takes time, as Ray wants to get it right. It's a small coaster compared to other ones. FUN-O-RAMA is no Coney Island. But this isn't Tinker Toys, either. The maximum height is seventy five feet at the beginning, which is the tallest hill. You need this much height to keep the cars going up and down and over all the way to the end. We stand aside and watch him work. He takes a few steps back and scans the structure, tilts his head a bit to sift a calculation loose inside, then steps forward quickly, before he changes his mind, and sprays a big blob of orange paint onto a vertical post with quiet deliberation. Michelangelo was hardly more careful with his masterpieces, nor did he take more time than Ray does in his cautious and careful application of color to the posts. He even takes time to check the direction of the wind, which is light today as he has hoped and planned for. Once done with the masterpiece of orange dots, he stations Buzz on one side, and himself on the other, and they crank up their saws and take turns making precise surgical cuts halfway through the painted members. Ready at any moment to kick ass and get out of the way if the structure starts to creak and waver, they cut and hurry to the next spot, chainsaw horror filling the morning air with its hysterical whining tirade. When the cuts are made and Ray assures himself that everyone is at least eighty feet from the coaster, he makes the final cut to the cross brace, then quickly runs to the nearest exit.

Nothing happens.

We wait, hearing only birds and morning crickets and the sound of our own hearts beating. This particular coaster, built in 1946—after the war in Europe and the Pacific was over, after we have dropped Little Boy and Fat Man on Hiroshima and Nagasaki, and America takes off like a rocket as The

Dream Machine, a capitalism of the free world, goes into full gear—this particular roller coaster has been sitting here for so long, it has settled in for good, apparently, and, like the Dream Machine itself, doesn't know enough to fall down. We wait some more. Now Ray is wishing there was at least a little wind. "Crank up the shovel," he says, finally, and Earl climbs into the cab of the power shovel Ray has rented to pick up the pile of match sticks the coaster will be once it all falls over. The diesel engine roars to life and slowly makes its way towards the reluctant object of demolition. Earl extends the shovel to its full length and stops just shy of the wooden frame. Then he slowly gives the thing a tiny shove until it begins to lean. He quickly backs up, watching in front of him to make sure he isn't about to be in a disaster movie called Roller Coaster Falls On Man Operating Power Shovel. If Ray's calculations are accurate it will tend to fall in on itself and come straight down. It doesn't.

Earl is lucky this morning and, though he won't be a movie star just yet, he will be spared having the skeleton of a Roller Coaster tumble quickly into his lap. At lunch time he should buy a lottery ticket I tell him. You never know how extensive and long lasting a run on good luck can be. The coaster frame comes down slightly to one side in a brief but splintering wall of sound, slightly concussive, and we're all present and accounted for when it's over. A small cloud of dust rises and hovers over the fallen ride, its life of terror and excitement now over, ceased forever and permanently transfigured. We give a little holler and whoop of relief, knowing how unpredictable life can be, and take our morning break. Ray sits wondering where he went wrong in his calculations, but we all think he must have done something right as the demise of such a big and ungainly structure could have been a whole lot worse. Then, again, taking things apart is always quicker and easier than building them in the first place. Once you get started, it all goes pretty fast.

Fifteen

Against my better judgment I am accumulating things. Buzz gave me an old five gallon joint compound bucket he'd cleaned out and used around the house the last few years. He had an extra one and gave it to me for washing up, which he's recommended on good authority—Viola's. I bought a Coleman lantern and some propane. I still have the candle that the girl found. I brought home some matches, but haven't used the candle yet. I'm saving it, but for what I don't really know, just feel like I should. Might come in handy. I have soap and a washcloth, now. Viola gave me an old towel. A hint, I think, but she couldn't resist making her point clear as a bell. "Take a bath now and then," is what she said when she handed it to me. Earl said he has an old Coleman stove he'd be willing to sell me cheap. I'm still deciding about that but will no doubt buy it sooner or later. I bought a tooth brush and tooth paste. Work boots. A new sweatshirt and jeans. A pillow. Sleeping bag. It starts to add up after a while. Like I'm somewhere again and have a life and an address. What the address *is* for this place, I have no idea. I also bought a drawing pad and crayons and colored pencils—not for me.

Saturday morning I wake to total quiet. It's so

quiet it bothers me. I go outside and look up toward the road and see only an overcast sky and a quarter mile of wiregrass and Jimson weed. The air is as still as a body in a casket. I turn and walk around behind the cabin and have to stop at the sight of something in the trees, all over them, in fact, hanging like black fruit on the branches, a giant cloud of what looks like crows, so many there must be hundreds. The odd thing is they aren't making a sound. It's like a bad Omen so I wait for something bad to happen, which does not. Nothing falls from the sky. No massive crevice opens up in the ground. My strategy on how to deal with this is to go back inside. Here I drink some water to distract myself, and I peel an orange. I've taken to keeping fruit around. It's healthy and you don't need a refrigerator for it, or a stove. After eating the orange, I sit around inside staring at the picture of the girl in the tree, and try not to make any dumb comparisons between her wellbeing and the presence of the birds outside. Later today I'm invited to spend the afternoon at a cookout Buzz and Viola are having. I'll focus on that instead. It's just them and their two boys and Earl and his wife and kids, so I said I would come by for a little bit. I'll just eat and leave. No harm in that. Maybe I'll take a shower while I'm there to please Viola.

Later, walking my bike out to the road, I turn

to see if the birds are still there. They are. Maybe I'll tell Buzz that he can give my bike to the boys if something bad happens to me. I feel privileged in a way. My legacy. Most people don't get a warning. Especially one this cinematic, unnerving, and prescient looking; Stephen King would give it a thumbs up, I'm sure. I tell myself they're only birds, but apparently I'm not listening; I'm walking a lot faster—in case!

Buzz has fired up the grill and has burgers and hot dogs sizzling away when I get there. Here we are again. Another movie. I look around for a picnic table with an umbrella that has palm leaves on it. None there. Only the table appears, but it does have a red checked chuck wagon type plastic cloth on it just like at all the western roundups where they brand cattle and cook beans on an open fire, roast weenies, and sing cowboy songs. All that's missing is the baked beans and then out comes Viola in her "*I'm Still Sexy*" apron carrying a big bowl of beans, and wearing an oven mitt on each hand. I'm about to turn around and leave when Earl comes out carrying a plate full of blackened short ribs that are glistening and hot and have my immediate attention. Some appear to have been dry rubbed and set in a smoker for the last sixteen hours. "My specialty," Earl tells me as he struts proudly by. "I got my own smoker back at the house. Secret dry rub recipe and know to cook it slow." He has a quiet grin on his face that you'd never see at work. He's in his element with a cold beer and a plate full of ribs.

Inside Buzz and Viola's house, two boys that look like miniature Buzzes and another boy I take to be Earl's kid completely ignore me while I watch them play some sort of Virtual Reality game, the latest thing, where they wear headsets that cover their eyes and they shoot, stab, blowup, and otherwise murder people that appear to be in the same room with them but are not. There's blood all over the place, or should be from the sound of it. This is like the umbrella with palm leaves on steroids. The umbrella and table cloth are just a reminder that there's another way to live. The power boat in your driveway is real, but the experience you think you're going to have in it, is not. Somehow you always know that. You just like the reminder that life could be fun if it was. It just isn't. But this thing these boys are into is on a whole different level of make believe. The reality they're playing with may be fake, but it's a real fake. They don't care if the guy they just splattered all over the fake wall is not really real. It feels like it's real, and it looks like it's real, which according to some people, namely my guy Plato, is what real things actually are: real fakes that only feel real but are not. What's real is the idea of them. The ideas are the only actual reality. I can't believe I remember this shit after so many years, and having these thoughts is making me start to hyperventilate. They remind me too much of when I was back in school and had a life. I was kind of into it all back then. It was a surprise and a shock, everything I was learning. I began to think I could actually be something besides a guy in a trade. Thinking about all this has made me want a beer. I go to the kitchen and look hard and long at the refrigerator. "Beer's outside in the cooler," A woman says. "Hi, I'm Earl's wife, Ellen," she's extending her tiny hand towards me like a weapon. "Hi," I say taking a step back and then carefully taking her hand and shaking it. It's surprisingly warm and soft and I wonder if women in Virtual Reality will ever feel this good. "Nice to meet you," I say. Then I'm stymied. Now what?

Mother's little helper is at the kitchen table, but she's not helping. I don't think they do that anymore. What she's doing is playing, talking with much animation, an embarrassing amount of animation, in my opinion, to something called a My Little Pony Rainbow Power Pinkie Pie, according to the box sitting beside it on the table. It's some kind of little horse that's pink and has more hair than Rapunzel. I don't know whose kid she is, but she could be close to Jessie's age, maybe younger. The difference is striking. Jessie knows too much about life; this kid knows nothing. I can tell. She's in a world all her own called Me Myself and I. I've had enough and head for the beer cooler outside, wondering how things could have gotten this bad. Pink kittens are one thing. They're just cute. That Pinkie Pie horse whatever is obnoxious and has me spooked and worried and kind of sad for these kids. Whatever happened to Hopscotch and riding your bike?

Outside, Buzz points me to the cooler. I grab a Bud and join Buzz and Earl by the barbecued ribs. It seems easy enough, and I try to act normal, but I can't quite remember how to make unnecessary talk with people about football and the weather, so I stand here and listen. After making jokes about the look on Ray's face when they made the cuts to the coaster frame and nothing happened, and then the look on his face when it fell but not the way it was supposed to, Buzz nods his head for me to follow him to the garage. Earl and I go with him and watch as Buzz finds a mason jar in the paint cabinet on the wall and holds it up for me to see. It's about half full of what looks like water. "This here shit is the real deal," he says.

I look and say, "Real water, huh?"

"Water my ass," he says. "This here is real White Lightnin.' It's gen-u-wine moonshine. Made the way the old timers used to make it, in a still way back in the woods so far the bears can't even find it. Came all the way from Mississippi where my family's all from. Guaranteed to make you acquainted where you're not well known!"

He unscrews the lid and hands it to me. I take a whiff and hand it right back. "You first," I say. "Smells like Acetone or something. Bet you could strip furniture with this stuff."

He takes the jar from me and sniffs a little, then drinks a baby sip. With his nose curled up and tears forming in his eyes he makes a face and says, "Wheweeeee that's strong. You probably could strip furniture with this. I'll just bet you goddamn could!"

I take a sip just to keep from shaming myself and immediately promise myself not to take another. I've never had a hole in my stomach but I'll bet drinking this shit is a good way to get one. "Jesus fucking Christ," I say and hand the jar to Earl. "That'll qualify as aviation fuel. I'll bet you money!" He takes it and hands it back to Buzz. "I'm not drinking any of that crap," Earl says. "You guys are dumber than mud."

"Hey," Buzz says, his eyes all lit up now like a tree on Christmas morning, "Come here. Something

I want to show you." He unlocks a metal locker and points to a black case, which he pulls out and sets on top of a workbench. He's grinning from ear to ear, now, and about to burst from excitement. "What do ya think this is?" He asks me. He's sweating from the moonshine and maybe the spice on Earl's barbecued ribs.

I take a look at Earl. "The suspense is killing me," I say.

"Take a look," he says and opens the case. "Bushmaster AR-15. My pride and joy."

For a moment I expect him to start talking to it like that little girl in the kitchen is talking to that weird horse. This, apparently, is his version of the My Little Pony Rainbow Power Pinkie Pie. He can barely contain himself. He takes it out and puts a blank clip in it—I think he likes the sound it makes—and sites down the barrel. He makes me nervous waving it around in the garage. One slip of the finger and he could take out half a wall, not to mention all of me. I make it a point to promise myself never to piss him off again. "You keep that thing locked up when show and tell is over don't you?" I ask.

"Course!" he says. "Them boys of mine would annihilate every small animal within a twenty mile radius of here. After that, I don't *know* what!" He winks and grins real big.

I'm supposed to be reassured, but somehow I'm not. We go back outside and I rack my brain trying to think what I'm supposed to say to sound impressed. "Awesome gun," I say, thinking that sounds good enough.

"You better believe it," he says.

The kids never come outside except to load up their plates and head back inside to the world of fake reality, what the teacher at the community college would call Plato's Cave. No wonder Jessie has trouble fitting in. When you're nine or ten going on forty something, life is hard. I picture her sitting in the movie theater with all that popcorn and candy, cheeks bulging, eating by the handful. To say she looked happy would be a stretch, but I think she was, at least a bit. Her little feet covered all over in pink kittens were swinging back and forth under her seat like crazy. That means happy, little kids swinging their feet, doesn't it? I always thought so.

"Hey dipshit," Buzz yells at me. "Where'd you go off to? You daydreaming again?"

"Sorry," I say. "I was thinking."

"Thinking?"

"Yeah. You know…uh…bout the look on Ray's face…when that coaster came down. Whoooooosh! Nothing left but a pile of wood and a big cloud of dust. But that look on Ray's face. Boy howdy! That was something, wasn't it? How 'bout that shit!"

I'm still quick on my feet, I guess, and fill with pride thinking how convincing that was.

"Here," he says, handing me another beer. "Have another Budweiser. Good for you and nourishing too. It's a meal in a can!"

That Buzz, I'm thinking. He's got a million of these Good Ole Boy one-liners and is proud to share them.

An hour later they start playing horseshoes and I'm done. When I tell Viola I have to leave she says, "Not yet you don't." She sits me down and puts a sheet around my neck. Next thing I know she's got her scissors and comb out and is making me lean my head back so she can wet my hair. Then she decides to wash it. I'm too buzzed on Moonshine and beer to resist and happy to be off my feet. Ellen supervises, as Viola is only half as capable at anything, as Ellen is. This is what she thinks, anyway, to hear Viola tell it. It's an old rivalry between them that they cherish and nurse like a newborn baby. She knows what she's doing and wastes no time. I'm about to fall asleep. When she's done I feel ten pounds lighter, and probably am, and fail to recognize myself in the mirror. "Who's that?" I say when they give me a look. "Might be you," Viola says. "Watch out! Women will be chasing you down the street now."

Ellen offers to give me a ride in their pickup so I don't have to ride my bike the seven miles back to Nowhere, where I live. While we head off into the afternoon haze she tells me all about raising a girl in today's society and how different it all is from when she was a child. I'm glad I have nothing to contribute because I wouldn't be able to get a word in, anyway. Which is good. Since I don't drink much anymore I'm feeling pretty loopy. "I could have done better," she says, then, looking at my hair as if she just noticed me sitting here, "but she got to you first." When we get to the edge of the field and I tell her she can let me out here, she takes a look around and says, "Wow! This really is nowhere isn't it?" I thank her and get out. Riding the bike is out, so I push it all the way. Walking is hard enough. I make my way through the grass and weeds and manage to stay on my feet.

At home in bed, finally, I'm halfway shit-faced and lying on top of my new sleeping bag. I'm out in two seconds and dream about birds. They're flying around the house and pecking at the windows. Then they stop and settle in the trees. I wake in the middle of the night and have to pee. Standing at the door and staring into the darkness I sees myself in all that nothingness and don't like the familiarity. This is not what I had in mind for myself way back when it was all just beginning. And now I'm not exactly sure what that was. I ease back to sleep thinking about what it was I did want and dream about it until morning, that and the nothingness I found so familiar outside my door. The light when it wakes me is small compensation. Now what, I wonder?

It's Sunday morning, so I lie in bed after waking, and doze for a while trying to remember the dream. Curious, I get up and go outside and around to the back to see if the crows are still there. There's one or two moving about but the rest of yesterday's crowd have gone elsewhere. I'm relieved and pee into the weeds thinking about how good Earl's ribs tasted. There's nothing like food that's bad for you. It's good for the soul, but bad for the heart, which sounds contradictory until you realize it's hard to mix poetry and science sometimes. Life is just always at odds with itself that way. As if it was meant to be. Maybe that's what all that philosophy's about, I tell myself. Things in opposition. Can there never be an answer?

After a while I peel and eat another orange. Then I look out the front door at the world in all its glory. The sun is where it's supposed to be and the day is just itself all over again; that much is probably intended and I'm glad it's so. Birds in the sky are flying about and occasionally sing out. The grass whispers and I strain to hear but only because I like the sound.

There's nothing to do again today.

So I do it.

Sixteen

"She's gone."

It's Mariela on the phone. "What d'you mean, she's gone?" I'm at work Monday morning and holding Ray's phone to my ear; the other hand's covering my other ear because of all the racket. We've got the chains saws out, cutting big pieces of framing into shorter pieces, trying to make sense out of this giant pile of wood that a few days ago was a roller coaster frame, doing our best reorganize it into cut lumber. I can't hear what she's saying. "Hold on a sec." I climb into Ray's truck and roll up the window. "Okay, I couldn't hear before. Who's gone?"

"Jessie. They took her yesterday."

"Who took her? Took her where?"

"Her aunt and uncle. Back to Alabama. Nobody told me about this. Nobody said a word. They waited until the weekend because they knew I was not wild about it. Came in when they knew I wouldn't be here and made all the arrangements. Then Sunday they took her and left. I just found out about it."

"........................."

"You still there?"

"Yeah. Yeah, I'm here. When was the last time you saw her?"

"Friday when they got here from Alabama. Charlene, that's her aunt. Her husband's name is Carl. I brought Jessie over to see them."

"How was she?"

"Jessie? The same as always, withdrawn, detached, not your normal child. But when they asked her how she'd like to come live with them the poor kid gave me the most heartbreaking look. I think she was afraid, but as usual she didn't say anything. Just looked at me, like, *can't you do something?* I thought I had a few days to figure it out but boom they went right into high gear and now they're gone. Said they had to get back because of their jobs so could they please expedite things. She seemed okay, but I didn't get a good feeling from Carl. Could just be me, but…"

In my mind I'm picturing all those crows up in the trees, and now Jessie's up there standing in the trees with them.

Naturally Ray and Buzz and Earl want to know what's going on. They take a break when I get off the phone. Can tell I'm angry, that something's not right.

"They took the girl," I say, so lost in thought about what's happened I don't think about what I'm saying.

"What girl?" Buzz says.

I look at Ray. Then I look at the pile of wood framing lying in a mess like a tornado just went through. It's how I feel—a tornado right after. "Just some kid I met."

Buzz says, "Someone took her? What does that mean?"

"I thought she was your kid," Ray says, "when you first showed up here."

"Yeah, well I made it seem that way so you'd let me work for you. I thought it was just for the day. I needed money to feed her."

"Well whose kid is she?" Earl asks. So I tell them about her and how I just sort of found her one day wandering around in an abandoned house and how she kind of attached herself to me and how I didn't have the heart to leave her all by herself.

Earl laughs and shakes his head. "Well this isn't *too* fuckin' weird, *is* it?" Spits in the grass.

"So who took her, then?" Ray wants to know, and I tell them the rest.

"That's how I know Mariela."

"Damn! This is a good one," Buzz says. "Like a fuckin' movie!"

"Yeah," I tell him. "It's a movie all right. Only I'm in it."

"Well," Earl says, "sometimes you just have to let go. If their related then what the hell. Why worry about it?"

But I'm not listening. I'm in my head far off somewhere. The one place you can't get rid of—the world inside your head. Even when you drink and do a lot of drugs. Every now and then you wake up sober, and that's almost worse.

A week later I'm still waiting to hear something. The drawing pad, and pencils, and crayons are still on the table where I left them. Her drawing on the grocery bag is still there and I stare at the two drawings. First the one of her family beside the car. Then I look at the one with the tree, the girl on one of the branches looking down. The dog seems friendly enough. The tail might be wagging. The man is tall. His face is not complete, though. He has eyes that are too far apart, but no mouth or nose. The tree in the background of the other picture has leaves on it. This new tree is bare, except for the girl. Who is this man and why is he standing there by himself looking in a different direction from the girl and the tree? Maybe she just didn't finish the tree, and had she spent more time there would have been a woman and little boy with the man, and the man would have a nose and a mouth. Then it would be a picture of her cut off from them, so they can no longer see her, like you'd expect. I have no way of knowing now. For some reason, though, the picture makes me uncomfortable. Like millions of crows sitting in a tree, it just doesn't look right—a little unnerving. Not what a kid would draw, either.

I have trouble sleeping and wait around hoping to hear something from Mariela. I count the cracks in the wall as though there might be a mathematical solution to this whole thing, wishing that the number of cracks could turn out to be a meaningful, significant number. It might represent a key to the answer, like Pi without all the decimals. The absurdity of it distracts me momentarily; then I'm thinking about the girl again. Remembering how she looked that first day. Pitiful. Then I tell myself it's not my problem, not my kid, and spend more sleepless minutes convincing myself of that.

THE GREAT MANDALA

Take your place now
on the Great Mandala
As it moves through your brief moment in time
- The Great Mandala by Peter Yarrow

Seventeen

After we haul all the wood framing away it's time to take down the Ferris wheel. It was a later addition to the park Ray says, or maybe the original one had to be replaced—he's not sure. It was made in the early sixties. Ray also informs us this will be an altogether different type of job. He shows up with a tractor trailer cab he'll be using. Like most Ferris wheels, these days, this one's portable, meant to be hauled around to different cities by traveling carnivals. Once upon a time it had its own set of tractor trailer cabs, three in fact, to pull the trailers that hold the four giant arms and all the extra pieces. The cabs were sold, probably, when they went out of business. The three trailers are the base for the whole thing, sitting side by side. Each of the two outside trailers has two gigantic hydraulic arms. The middle trailer has what will become the spokes of the two giant wheels lying flat in a stack between two more hydraulic arms. It can be assembled and disassembled in two days each way if you know what you're doing. We do not. Ray hires a guy from some place in Georgia who used to do that job for one of the many carnivals making the rounds back then—travel around with them and *put 'em up and take 'em down every two weeks*, depending on how long the carnival stayed in one location. This guy Ray hired, looking like Popeye minus the spinach and the muscles, shows up one day with the other tractor trailer cab. He does have a sailor hat, though, and tattoos on each arm, one actually of a Fisherman's anchor. Little guy, but solid. Isn't there five minutes when he starts in telling everyone about how he was in the Navy years ago and for how long and which ships he sailed on and where all they went, and what they did, until we drift away one by one to escape his yammering. Ray is left holding the bag at which point he becomes impatient.

"Okay," Ray says, "Let's get the wheel down before I fall asleep listening to this here memoir you're writing."

Popeye is miffed, but only slightly. From the way he looks and is acting now, he must have had that reaction already, once or twice in his lifetime. He's not one to take offense and hang on to it.

First the carriages come off, one by one. They are suspended between two giant wheels with spokes, like on a bicycle. Then the part of the two giant wheels where a bike's tires would be, the circumference part, separate and come off. It's made of pairs of struts between the spokes, which are taken off, one by one, like taking a tire off in pieces. This allows the adjacent spokes to come together like cards on a Rolodex. As each pair of struts comes off, another pair of spokes comes together and hangs down against the other spokes. Eventually they're all hanging straight down in a stack. "Ingenious!" Rays says. "Nothing like American ingenuity." As we continue, the spokes all wind up in a bunch at the bottom, leaving the two gigantic pairs of uprights, the hydraulic arms, forming an upside down V. These are lowered one by one. It'll take us at least three days to do all this.

When we break for lunch Popeye jumps up and says, "Just in case you gentlemen wanted to know, his name was George Washington Gale Ferris." He pauses and waits for our response like a comedian timing and pacing his act. He gets our response and looks disappointed.

"Okay, I'll bite," Ray says. Whose name?"

I'm thinking Popeye has perpetrated a clever way to launch into more of his horse shit storytelling, some kind of history lesson about the founding of this nation, from the sound of it. All I hear is George Washington. And I'm close. It *is* a history lesson. But it's not about the first President as we were all thinking.

"He's the man what designed and built the first Ferris wheel, in Chicago. 1893. George Washington Gale Ferris. It lasted thirteen glorious years. Caused quite a stir. You know how they took that one apart?"

"Were you involved?" Buzz says with a sideways glance at Earl.

Popeye ignores the comment and continues. "I'll tell you how. They blew the sonofabitch up! That's how. It was 264 feet high and took 300 pounds of dynamite to bring it down. George Ferris died three years later. If you ask me it was probably from heartbreak."

"Heartbreak?" Buzz says.

"That's a lot of powder!" Earl says.

"You better believe it! That thing was built to last—a regular Egyptian monument. The way they put it together, it would have lasted thousands of years."

"Why'd they blow it up, then?"

"I'll tell ya why, boys," Popeye says with a gleam in his eye. He's on a roll now and not to be stopped. "It's the answer to all questions, Gents, big and small."

"And that would be..?" Ray says trying to move him along.

"That would be money, my friends! Money!"

"Money?" Buzz and Earl say together.

"Yup! Money! They were building a whole little city around this thing. It was their brilliant new idea, a regular little industry. Shops, and hotels, and restaurants. Anything and everything. The wheel would draw them in and then once they were there they were curious to see what all was happening. They would get hungry waiting to get on the big wheel and after they took their ride they'd want to have a little something to eat and drink and then stroll among the shops and naturally couldn't resist buying something to take home with them. They sold bonds to finance it. Had quite a thriving business going for them. But then people stopped coming, eventually. I mean you can only go around in circles way up in the air for so long before it gets boring and you start to lose interest. They reached the saturation point of that market, as them college business types like to say, and then it was all over. No big surprise. It was bound to happen. It's what you're supposed to *learn* about if you are one of those college educated business types. So they took it all down and sold it as scrap. Just like this here Fun-0-Rama. It's disappearing before our very eyes. Is it not? It's an old story, boys, but that story has more lives than six hundred cats."

"Hunh," Buzz snorts.

"Tell me something, Mr.," Ray says to Popeye.

"Certainly. What's that?"

"You ever get tired of talking?"

Popeye takes a deep breath and folds his arms across his chest, puffs it out, looks defiant and says, "Nope! I don't!"

"Well, maybe you should give it a rest anyway."

Today we take the A frames down. They're supported by four hydraulic struts. Release the hydraulic fluid on one pair of struts, and the two massive arms come down on top of the trailer. Release the other two struts and down they come laying the opposite way. They sit side by side on top of the trailers, the spokes in a stack in between. Pull the bolts attaching the spokes to the arms and they sit in a stack by themselves on the middle trailer. The carriages are stored below in compartments along with all the struts and braces and whatever else we have to take off. Hook the tractor cabs up to the trailers and off you go. Ray has hired us all out to Southland Liquidators to drive the three truck caravan up to some outfit in Atlanta. We've all agreed to put the thing back up, again, when we get there since we now know the routine pretty much now and they're paying some good money to have it done. Only makes sense Ray tells us.

I use Ray's phone to see if Mariela has heard from Jessie. Nothing. Then I tell her we're going to be taking the Ferris wheel to Atlanta, so I'll be gone close to a week. It'll take at least a day to drive up there, then two days or more to put her up, then another day to get back. Buzz and Earl are voting for an extra day in Atlanta just to check the place out, which means to see what kind of bars they've got up there, which means bars with strippers.

"I've got Ray's phone number now," she says. "It's on my phone. I can let you know if I hear anything."

"Aren't they supposed to check in with you or the agency? At least for the first few weeks or months, or something?"

She answers, "That's the idea, sure, but things don't always happen the way they're supposed to. You know how it is."

I do know. It's the We've Got It Covered story, which always ends the same way: *not covered*. We leave early the next morning. I don't have a Class A Commercial Driver's License so I can't drive, but Buzz and Ray each have one and so does Popeye. "You ride with Buzz," Earl says, razzing me, but Ray quickly steps in and says I'm to ride with him. Buzz and Earl will go together, in their truck. I bring my sleeping bag and leave everything else at the cabin. I put most of my money in the tin can out back under the rock. Can't get a bank account without an address and that cabin might as well be a tent someone pitched in the wilderness and then went off and left for the bears to discover.

On the way up to Georgia Ray talks mostly about how hard it's been since the economy tanked. "Was a time," he says, "when we wanted something, we just went out and bought it. Nothing fancy ya know, but a new TV didn't need no big discussion with a calculator in my hand to figure it out. Just went and bought it. Is that so bad? To want a new TV? I worked as hard as any man in a suit sitting at a desk. Harder if you ask me." He drives a few miles stewing about it and then starts in again. "Now you got to watch every penny. And the kids just don't understand it. So the extra money from this little trip will come in handy." In an hour I'm fast asleep while Rays drives the truck wondering what the hell happened to the world.

Ray, Buzz, and Earl get a motel room near Sun Park South where we take the Ferris wheel, a proposed big new theme park in Lithonia, just east of Atlanta, almost complete but still in the building stages. Popeye will sleep in his truck, and I'll sleep in Ray's. I'm surprised at how big these cabs are. Popeye says that the expensive new trucks have regular little condos in the back. All the comforts of home. I daydream about getting a class A license and a truck and going on the road. I could live out of the truck and make $40,000 a year hauling whatever around the country. Without a house and family back home to pay for, that would be a lot of money. No one to bother you. Just drive around and live in the truck, save up my money and become a millionaire. They've got little kitchenettes like in a camper and showers and TVs and everything you could want. Do that for a few years, then retire to a little shack somewhere on a lake like the one I've got back in Florida, only with all the nice amenities, like water and electricity. This one I would own. Then I stop myself because I know this movie, too. It's a bad one. Over the road truck drivers have to take uppers all the time because the dispatchers nag their asses about turnaround times. So they don't get any sleep and the next thing you know your eighteen-wheeler's wrapped around a bridge abutment, and you're dead, or in a wheel chair holding your head in your lap.

We all go for a beer before hitting the hay, and find a little bar with food down the street. It's only half full, which is just fine with us. Mostly neighborhood folks playing Keno at the bar and putting the quarters they don't lose in the jukebox by the restroom. A few couples sit at the far end commiserating in low decibels. Who knows what their troubles are; there are plenty enough to go around. We take two adjacent booths by the window, a neon sign flashing **RED'S GOOD FOOD** outside in the parking lot, and a blue neon *COLD BEER* sign hangs in the window by our heads. Listen close and you can hear it hum.

"Tell ya what," Buzz says leaning back a bit to stretch and swivel the kinks out of his neck. "I'm glad to be outa that damn truck."

Popeye tells him, "Be glad we're not going all the way to California." Popeye's got his nose in the menu but that doesn't prevent him from commenting while checking out the entrees. I'm thinking he probably talks in his sleep. We order a pitcher of beer and see what looks good to eat.

"Where you boys heading to?" the waitress asks when she returns with our beer and four frosty mugs. She's not popping her chewing gum, but otherwise she's everybody's idea of a fifty year old waitress, with bleached hair dark at the roots, and too much makeup. I like her smile. Like most of these ladies, she's friendly and smart and makes us feel welcome.

"Right here," Ray says. "Supposed to deliver a Ferris wheel to this new water park they just built, Sun Park South, it's called." She looks at Ray like he had just said we were here to enter the Miss Teen Georgia contest. Then she says with a frown, "This one up the street here?" Sticks her thumb out toward where we left the trucks. "A Ferris wheel?"

"That's the place," Ray says. "Problem?"

"Guess not, but good luck getting your money. People been walking off the job from what I hear. Place isn't paying their bills. No one's getting paid. Electricians all left a week ago. No one's happy."

"Raaaaaaaaay?" Earl says.

"Don't know," Ray answers, concern breaking out like a big rash on his tired face.

Earl doesn't seem to like it and rightly so. "When was the last time you talked to the people we've been working for?" he asks.

"Oh…must have been a month ago."

"You boys want something to eat?" the waitress asks. Now that she's got our attention she wants to get down to real business and talking about Ferris wheels is not it.

We all get the same: cheeseburgers and fries and another pitcher of beer.

"Too late to call anyone tonight," Ray says. We still have our appetites but our spirits have dulled some. We all seem to be pondering the same thing—a long goddamn drive for nothing.

In the morning we're up and at the park early, looking for someone we're supposed to hand the

Ferris wheel over to, and make an effort to find out what's going on. Ray has a call into Southland Property Liquidators, the company that hired Ray to take FUN-O-RAMA all apart and clear the site. Now he's waiting on a call back. We track down what turns out to be a private security guard. Nobody else is around.

"Where is everyone?" Ray wants to know. The guard takes a deep breath and looks like he's bracing himself for yet another confrontation with pissed off contractors, which he's clearly expecting. He's a young guy, late twenties, maybe, and looks like he could use a plateful or two of Red's Good Food. Or a size smaller uniform, either one.

"I'm just the guard here," he says. "I don't work for the Meyerhoffs. I work for Johnson Security Service. So you'll have to contact these people for any questions." He hands Ray a business card. Ray holds it up to look at it, and squints.

"King, Slocomb, & Martin, Attorneys at Law, it says."

"What the fuck is going on?" Ray asks the guard.

The guard takes a step back, blinks and says, "My understanding is that they foreclosed on this place just yesterday. Anything else you'll have to talk to them people on the card. Just so you know you're at the back end of a long line of a whole lot of angry people."

"Well what the hell are we supposed to do with that, then?" Ray says, pointing to the Ferris wheel.

"What is it?" the guard asks.

"It's a goddamn Ferris wheel," Ray says, unhappy about the sudden turn of events and unsure what to do now.

"I don't know, but you can't leave it there. And there's no point in getting mad at me."

"Where am I supposed to leave it, then?"

"You'll have to ask someone else. I don't know anything about any of this. Sorry. I'm just a guard here. I don't even know the Meyerhoffs."

"And who are they again, these Meyerhoffs?"

"I think they're the people that were developing the park. The owners."

"Okay," Earl says. "We need to get a hold of Southland right away, but first I think you should call those lawyers and see what they say. Maybe they can tell you what to do with the wheel."

"Yeah, you're right. I suppose I should." Before he can call, Ray's phone rings. When he answers he looks even less happy. "It's for you," he says handing me the phone. "It's that woman. Make it quick. Or better yet have her call you back on Earl's phone."

"It's Mariela," the voice on the phone says. "How's it going?"

"Not good at the moment. I'll tell you later. Jessie all right?"

"As far as I know. What's going on there?"

" Ray's expecting an important call so I can't stay on his phone. I'll call you back in an hour?"

"Sorry, I thought it would be okay to call."

"It is okay. I'll call you back as soon as I can. Gotta go."

We stand around by the trucks waiting while Ray calls the number on the card. Buzz and Earl share a pack of smokes and spit tobacco everywhere. They spy a nice looking Harley across the road and go over to check it out. They get back in time to hear from Ray that everyone's in a meeting, *or just stepped out for a minute, or fell into a manhole, kidnapped by aliens, whatever, it's always the same thing; we can't talk to you right now. Take a number, get in line, have a seat, read a magazine.* They take Ray's cell number. "We'll get back to you," they say. So we wait some more. No one's holding their breath but getting a little impatient just the same. This is not what we had in mind coming all the way up here and now we don't even know now if we'll get paid.

At our new offices, Red's Good Food, we

have coffee and blueberry muffins, wait around, sit through a few of Popeye's stories, the Gulf of Tonkin, R & R in Singapore and Bangkok, and then go ahead and have the whole works, eggs, sausage, pancakes, hash browns, and mush with the usual token nod to our health, a tiny glass of orange juice. The day shift waitress is on so we get asked again if we're from around here and what we're doing in the area, are we staying long, blah, blah, blah.

"Looks like we're all gettin' haircuts," Ray says.

"How's that?" she says, perplexed but curious. She's not as snappy as the other waitress but does her best to please us.

"Figure of speech," Ray answers.

"Oh," she says.

Southland finally calls and has no idea what Ray's talking about. "Last they knew they had a deal with Sun Park," Ray says. He gives them the number on the card. "Sit tight, Southland says," he tells us with a big frown. It's looking worse and worse the longer we're here.

"I guess we're already sittin," Buzz says.

"Just like being in the Navy," Popeye adds.

"Don't start with that," Ray tells him. "Not in the mood."

We eat our food and drink our coffee until the

phone rings again. It's the attorneys' office returning our call. Ray talks, then listens, then hangs up.

"Says they're in foreclosure. We can leave the Ferris wheel, but to get our money we'll have to go through a settlement hearing."

"Fuck that!" Buzz says. "Southland's not gonna go for that deal."

"What'a we do?" Popeye wants to know.

"We wait," Ray says, "until we hear back from Southland.

"When's that?" Earl asks him, looking as glum as the rest of us.

"Damned if I know," Ray answers, completely stymied by the turn of events and feeling the full desperation of the day's failure upon him, done in now by life's recent history in general and now this, the day's events. "Is this whole country going to shit? Tell me if it has please because I'd just like to know."

I ask to borrow Earl's phone but he's getting no reception here. This means I have to wait some more to find out what Mariela wants. Ray won't want me tying up the phone. Not a good time to ask. Now I'm getting anxious wondering why she called. She sounded all right, but then again she wouldn't call for no reason.

We finish our breakfast, order more coffee and wait. "What's this do to our money?" Popeye asks.

"I don't know," Rays says. "But don't worry. You'll get paid even if I have to pay you myself."

"That's a bad deal!" Buzz announces, a certified confirmation of what we already know.

"This whole thing is a bad deal," Earl tells us. "I'll bet we're gonna have to take that damned thing all the way back to Florida."

"Well, if we do, we do. That's all there is to it. We have to go back anyway. Might as well take a Ferris wheel with us. We can set it up in Earl's front yard and sell us some tickets."

"That oughta make a nice addition to my electric bill."

"The city will love it too," Buzz says.

"Nope!" Popeye says. "Don't need electricity to run it."

"Come again."

"When I was in the Navy…"

"No you don't! No stories, please."

"Just listen. It's a good one. I promise. We were in Burma about thirty five years ago, now called Myanmar, don't ask me why, and there was a Ferris wheel there, but they had no electricity. What did they do? No problem. They're a resourceful people, used to improvising. There were lots of things they didn't have but they do have a lot of people. So they hired some boys to climb up into the spokes, being careful to stay in the center. Then once up top they redistributed their weight and began to rock the thing until they tipped it far enough to get the wheel moving. One by one they'd ride on the side that was going down until they could jump off and one by one they'd climb back up on the opposite side and then ride it back down again. The momentum kept it going around and around until it was time to make it stop using a big lever and a belt and pad brake system like the brakes on your car. The boys climbing all over the Ferris wheel were almost as big an attraction as the ride itself. I never rode on the thing, I just watched the boys climb up and hop around all over that wheel like a bunch of monkeys. Damn smart monkeys, though."

"You boys can climb," Ray says. "I'll operate the brake."

Around 11:00 AM Ray gets tired of waiting and calls Southland. Talks some more, listens some more, hangs up again. "He says he's still trying to figure something out and making phone calls to other potential buyers, but so far he's got nothing. He says we were going to have to stay another night, anyway, so he'll call us later tonight."

"Ain't this just something," Buzz says.

I get Ray's phone from him and call Mariela. "What's up?" I ask her.

"Well, I got a call from Jessie. Thought you'd

like to know."

"And…? What'd she say?"

"That's just it. She didn't say much of anything. She would barely tell me who it was that was calling. I guessed based on the area code. I think she must have used the phone when no one was around. Got off pretty quick after she called."

"She say anything at all?"

"Just that she didn't want to stay there. I had to drag that out of her. It's hard to tell what's up with her. She's so quiet, anyway. Never happy. Mopey, as you say. You know how she is. How can you tell if something's wrong? She *always* acts like something's wrong."

"What do we do then?"

"There's nothing we can do. I told her to call me if she needs to, anytime, day or night. Told her we'd help her if she needs help. What we can do way the hell down here, I'm not sure. But I wasn't going to tell *her* that."

"Where is she?"

"Near Birmingham, I believe they said."

"That's only about a 150 miles from here, where I am right now."

"Well, okay, but we can't do anything over one phone call."

"Okay," I say and tell her we're stuck for

another day. I hang up and try to keep from thinking the worst. I won't even let myself imagine what the worst could be. I just don't want to go there.

They're all looking at me. "Well…" they say.

"It's beer for lunch I think."

Ray shakes his head. "Not yet," he says. "We've got work to do."

Outside a dog wanders in the parking lot looking for scraps. It marks a car tire, drops its leg to trot a little ways, then stops to sniff something on the ground, marks again, then trots off again into the morning heat already rising fast and fat with the damp summer air. It's a good day—unless you're delivering Ferris wheels or speculating in real estate.

Eighteen

We take the tractor cabs to get fuel and check out the area, see what's around for tonight's possible entertainment. It looks like everywhere else I've ever been. Car dealers, Jiffy Lubes, Brake and Muffler shops, Home Depot, Winn Dixie, McDonalds, Motor Lodge, a Days Inn. Just pick a highway anywhere in the country, seems like, and drive down it, this is what you'll see. We stop at Ed's Beer & Wine and buy a thirty pack of Bud and a Jumbo Styrofoam cooler and a large bag of ice. We're like the people in Myanmar, we know how to make do; we improvise with ice and beer. When the movie gets too bad, you can always drink yourself blind. Booze is just a little down payment on the big sleep if you ask me, and by the time I get there I'll be goddamned ready for it.

They've got a big TV at the Motel 6 where the others are staying, so we all pile in there and watch football. The Colts are playing Green Bay. War, and its substitutes are always a popular pastime. Every now and then I remember to yell and holler when I'm supposed to. While pretending to follow the game, I can't help thinking we are so close to Birmingham I should be driving there tonight instead of sitting here in this motel room with all this testosterone floating around on the loose. Put some of it to good use, maybe. I don't know what I'd do when I got there, but I can't seem to get the idea out of my head. Next thing I know my eyes are closed. It's dark in here. What if she thinks we let her down.

It's morning and we have yet to hear back from Southland. We're back at Red's drinking coffee saying how we need to leave soon if we're going to go back today, otherwise we'll be driving half the night. Ray calls and gets no answer. We order another big breakfast and argue back and forth about what we should do. We finally take a vote. It's unanimous. We're leaving.

"About fucking time!" Buzz says through a mouthful of pancakes.

"Close your mouth," Earl says to him. "You're getting syrup on your shirt."

Buzz takes a look. "Crap!" he fumes. Tries to wipe it off. Smears it all around. Earl shakes his head and gives Buzz a little pop in the noggin while getting up. Popeye chuckles through his mouthful of Biscuits & Gravy looking content in spite of their predicament.

We hook the tractor cabs up to the trailers and head out. By the time Southland calls we're on the interstate heading south. They want us to bring the wheel back, which we're already doing. No one's happy. I can feel Birmingham burning a hole on the back of my neck. What we're going to do with the Ferris wheel once we're back is a big question. Southland says they're not sure yet.

By late evening we're pulling into FUN-O-RAMA. Popeye says he'll sleep here in one of the cabs. I get a ride with Buzz and I'm home by nine. We still don't know how the money's going to work out. Ray said we'll take a day off and start again the day after tomorrow. Next on the list are all the buildings and the big FUN-O-RAMA sign.

It seems quiet as hell at the cabin after three days of riding in the truck and hanging out with the crew. I light my Coleman lantern and stare at the ceiling. I think about three things: beer; where we're going to put the Ferris wheel; the girl. I wake up an hour later and the lantern is still on. I put it out and go back to sleep. The crickets are loud. After being away so long I'm not used to it. They're singing. They have their own rhythm, like a rapid heartbeat. Two syllables, like a name repeating over and over again.

I wake at the sound of a car. Unusual. Who could that be? The morning light is relentless and the birds are chirping and going full speed. I'm not.

I open the door to see a patrol car and two men. One's a cop. Young guy. The other's a man about ten years older than me, if not more, wearing slacks and a light tan jacket. Short hair, parted and combed. They're standing in front of the car. The cop has his hand resting on his holstered revolver. "Howdy," the cop says. "You want to step outside here a minute."

I step out in my underwear. The sun's warm on my bare chest. Be careful, I'm thinking. He's armed. Then again this could be a dream. "Anyone else in there with you?" the cop asks. He seems relaxed, but I'll feel better when he gets his hand off that gun. I shake my head no. "What are you doing here?" the cop asks.

"Sleeping," I say.

"Why are you sleeping here?"

I want to say because I'm tired but I know better and say, "I don't have anywhere else to go. The place looked abandoned to me, so I've just been staying here at night. I have a job I've been going to days."

"Not today?"

"No. Day off."

He nods.

"Well, this here is private property. Belongs to this man here. John Bingham. The sign says no trespassing."

"Oh," I say by way of explanation. It's clearly not enough. "I'm sorry. I'll get my things and clear out. I didn't hurt anything. Just needed a place to sleep."

"Where do you work?" the cop asks. John Bingham is still not talking.

"I work over at that FUN-O-RAMA for a guy named Ray."

"That place hasn't been open in years."

"We're tearing it down. Selling what we can for scrap. Ray works for Southland Property Liquidators. If you just give me a minute, I'll get out of here. Didn't mean any harm. Just…you know…"

They look at each other. John Bingham shrugs his shoulders. Then he looks at me and says, "Fifty dollars."

"What's that?" I ask.

"Rent," he says.

This has me peeved and I look at the cop. "Is that legal," I ask him. "I mean, how can I owe fifty dollars? I never signed a lease or anything. I thought the place was abandoned."

"No, no," John Bingham says. "Fifty bucks a month if you stay. I'll draw up a rental agreement right now. You sign it and you can stay here. No sense throwing you out if you have a job and just need a place to stay. You a drug addict or anything like that? Got any warrants?"

"No. None of that. Just a homeless man with a job. You know, there's lots of us these days."

"Well, now you're not homeless," he says. "All I ask is you don't burn the place down. I'll come by once a month and collect the rent. You don't have it, Officer Martin will come out and arrest you." He looks at the cop for confirmation and Officer Martin nods his head.

While he finds a piece of paper, I go get the money thinking: how can he arrest someone for not paying rent. Bingham writes out a short document for a rental on a monthly basis and has me sign it. We shake hands. He hands me a card with his phone number and address on it. "This place have an address?" I ask. He takes the card back and writes something on it. 17912 West County Road. He hands the card back to me.

"No cell phone?" he asks. I shake my head. "Well, like I said, don't burn the place down." They get in the car and leave. It's a relief to be legal, now, while I'm staying here, and it doesn't tie me down too much. I can leave anytime I want. Seems nice. Feels good to me all of a sudden. A place of my own. I look around and think maybe I'll plant some flowers. Grow some corn like a farmer. Get some chickens and have fresh eggs. I'm getting excited and carried away with all this and think, who knows; flower boxes on the front under the windows.

Or not! Fun to think about but not going to

happen.

I go back inside.

Later, I'm on my bike heading to the bank. I found all my money right where I left it in the tin can under the big rock out back behind the cabin. $1280.42. Now that I have an address, I can get a savings account. A checking account is too much. That's crossing the line. Paying rent is one thing. Paying rent and having a checking account is practically middle class. All that's missing is a car payment. Then you're cooked. Poor people are strictly cash only. It's easier. Technically, I'm still homeless. This is only temporary while I decide which edge of the earth I'm going to walk off of. That requires a lot of thinking and planning—days in fact.

I enter the bank and already don't like it. For starters the building is air conditioned, which I'm not longer used to. It's cold and it has that feeling of purification, like being inside a vacuum. Hard to breathe. But it's also the building, what it says. All buildings are stories. Banks, especially. The story of a bank is the story of Eternal Order. They have accountants to keep everything straight, so they want to emphasize the orderliness, eliminate any tension. Your money is safe, it says. Everything's been neutralized and sanitized and painted a pale gray blue except the trim, which is white. The architecture, equally stifling, is neoclassic if I remember right from my World History class in college. Order is the main feature of the day. To achieve this, every ounce and scintilla of life has been purged. Miss Ogleby asks how she can help me. Her name is pinned to her shirt. She's young and almost pretty but fresh as the summer air. She smiles pretty teeth and explains how it all works, handing me the folded brochures that give all the banking information. I open my savings account and thank her and leave as fast as I can.

The air outside smells good enough now to knock me over and even the noise of traffic moving past fills my head with joy and my lungs breathe in the air and I swoon. I'm like a man who has almost drowned and then at the last minute been saved, suddenly gasping to life again after being pulled from the water and given a few compressions to the chest and a lifesaving breath to the mouth. Air! If this seems excessive, I guess I'll have to plead guilty. I've been gone a long time. The ordinary world is hard to get used to when you've been absent from it and nowhere in particular except away from it all, out in the elements.

On the way home I'm struck with a thought. There is a problem with having this savings account. All this time I've been working off the books for Ray. He pays me in cash. Under The Table is the name of that story. But why not? As far as the government is concerned they've washed their hands of me and I've already walked off the edge of the earth, or died, and wherever I am, now, in this place there's no Adjusted Income on line 37. There is no line 37. When you're invisible like me, you no longer exist as a household member, have pets, and occupations for the annual census. You no longer have a name, beside which there is a box with a check mark inside it. Your box remains empty, an open space, and then it too disappears. You and all your check boxes have gone, evaporated, poof, forever, or so you thought. Now I'm reappearing, but ever so slightly. The faint outline of me can be seen in the fluorescent light of a bank, say, and that light—that makes the pale blue walls of the bank look slightly lavender, and the complexion slightly more pale, and like invisible ink that reappears under ultraviolet light, fluorescent light and pale blue walls make boxes reappear where none seemed to have existed before—and that light has pulled me out of nowhere like a reluctant ghost. And then suddenly here I am, again. It's a noticeable weight. Gravity once more makes its presence known on the surface of my skin. I feel heavier, now. Pulled down. Riding the bike is all of a sudden harder to do, and I'm regretting my decision to get a savings account. My money was fine where it was. Why, I ask myself, have I done this? I've entered the cyber space of data entry and retrieval, surveillance, crows sitting in trees, back in the world.

But I have done it, I decide, so I'm off to fulfill my next impulse of the day, a trip to K-Mart or Walmart, or someplace similar, a hardware store, one of those flat roofed boxes with a parking lot and a herd of shopping carts grazing in it, those places that have replaced life as we knew it in this country, with the mere remnants of a life we only once had long ago. My big plan is to buy one of those rural mailboxes with a red flag that swivels, and some sticky backed numbers for the house address, so I can nail it up to the wooden fence post out by the road and wait for the junk mail to arrive with my bank statement. Maybe I'm punishing myself. It's bound to be what it feels like when I open my first flyer from Winn Dixie full of coupons. I also have to buy a hammer and nails. Handy items if I ever decide to crucify myself. Could self-crucifixion be any worse than filling out a tax form after working an entire year for a paltry amount of money so you can give them so much of it?

Oh yes, and something to tie the damn mailbox to the bike with so I can get it home. There's no stopping this it seems. Like a virus. Once you get started resurrecting yourself it becomes an endless effort to fill the demands for more and more things. I draw the line at getting a tool box to keep the hammer and nails in. They do have a certain appeal. I'll admit it. I stop and look at them. They come in different colors and styles for the Do-It-Yourselfer. There's a movie right there. Look Honey! I'm redoing the kitchen. PLUMBING, a tragicomedy in one ridiculously long act, starring me. This week only. I'm exhausted from stress when I get back and decide to put the mailbox up some other time. This is all a mistake, I'm sure of it. I want my old life back. The one where I don't *have* a life.

Now that I have a few things and the would-be cabin is officially my personal and legal residence, I decide to get a padlock for the front door. The virus is running its full course, apparently. After work I get a ride with Buzz to the store and afterwards, back at home, I install the lock so my things will be safe. Buzz asks me what I have that anyone would want. I am unable to answer, but like thinking that I do and that whatever it is, it's protected.

We start in on taking down the buildings at FUN-O-RAMA today. We knock one over with the backhoe and then attack the pile of wood with crowbars and hammers. Then we toss the wooden boards into a trailer. FUN-O-RAMA is quickly disappearing. A once thriving hub of thrills and laughter is becoming an empty field. A bit desolate looking, it is now cleansed in a way, like the prairie after a fire. The Ferris wheel sits nearby in the lot all folded up like a big toy awaiting further instructions from Southland. They have no idea what to do with the damn thing. No one wants it. So here it sits, the formerly Great Mandala. There's a motor for the wheel if you have electricity, or you can hire a bunch of Burmese boys from Myanmar to climb your spokes and turn your world for you. Either way, we seem to require it.

Nineteen

I get myself a prepaid cell phone. It's against my better judgment but they're cheap and I want Mariela to be able to reach me, in case she wants to. Plus if I'm sick or attacked by a python I can call Ray and let him know I won't be there. To make sure it's working and to give Mariela my number, I call.

"I've been checking into the husband, Carl," she says. "Spoke with a former employer he gave us as a reference, and in the process I found out that Carl's not from Alabama, after all, he's from Pennsylvania. I'll be contacting authorities there today to see if there's anything on file we need to know about him."

"And if you find something?"

"If what we find is bad enough, we'll contact the police in Birmingham and have her picked up, then I'll go up there and get her. If it's just that he skipped out on some bills, or owes child support to some other woman, well, then that's a different story."

"I almost dread hearing what you find out. It'll be bad news either way. The bastard better not be doing anything to her."

"Well, let's not get ahead of ourselves, okay. Wait until we hear what they say."

I tell her about my new address and mailbox. I

hear her laugh. "You're becoming quite the regular citizen," she says like it was funny or something. "Aren't you?"

"Don't make fun of me. It's a fine line I'm walking here."

"Fine line?"

"Yes. Well, that's the problem. I'm not sure I know what it is I'm doing. I thought I did. Now I don't know anything."

"That gives me a lot to go on."

"I thought we were done analyzing me."

"That's not what I'm doing. Is that what you think I'm doing?"

"It sounds like analysis. Doesn't it?"

"How do you know? Have you been in therapy?"

"Detox."

"Oh, I see. Well..."

"So, no more games. Please."

"No games. Really. I promise. I'm just trying to get to know you better, that's all."

"Why? Why would you want that?"

"Now *you* sound like an analyst."

"Really? I didn't intend to."

"Well listen. I'm afraid I'm using up all your minutes."

"That's kind of abrupt, isn't it?"

"Sorry. I didn't mean to be. But, I'm just saying we could finish this conversation over a drink, if you want. Save your phone."

"Wait a minute. You're not asking me out are you?"

"No, no. Absolutely not. I'm just saying… finish our talk over a drink. In person."

"All right, fine, but I have to be in by eleven."

"That's real funny?"

"Sorry. Couldn't help it."

"This isn't a date."

"Okay, it's not a date. What is it then?"

"Just a chance to catch you up on what I find out."

"So it is a date."

"Don't push it. I'm trying to be nice."

She agrees to pick me up where my mailbox will go, if and when I'm motivated to put it up. I wash myself and change my clothes and brush my teeth with my new tooth brush and toothpaste. I even bought some floss and mouthwash. I'm remembering now how being a normal citizen is full of so much responsibility. It'll get worse if I let it. When she sees me standing out by the road she has this funny look on her face like she doesn't recognize me and is trying to decide who I am.

"Is that you?" she asks, dumfounded.

"No," I say. "I must be someone else."

"Wow! I'd never recognize you. You actually don't look half bad, you know that?"

I realize now she hasn't seen the haircut before. "Viola couldn't resist," I tell her. "She wanted to do my nails too but I wouldn't let her. I have a little bit of pride left."

"Who's Viola?" she says. I get in and we go. Every now and then I catch her looking at me and think I must've really looked bad before if she likes what she's seeing now.

"She's married to Buzz. My, uh…colleague."

I have to admit, now that I have a mailbox and a savings account I can't help noticing how nice she looks. When you crawl inside your head and shut the door behind you, you lose interest in lots of things. Now that I have the door open a little, it's all coming back to me.

We drive to a bar that doesn't say anything about cowboys out front, and only has one motorcycle in the parking lot. We get a table away from the bar. She orders wine, Pinot Grigio, I order beer in a bottle. We both fidget while I look around the room.

"You never married?" I ask, looking for something to say.

"Why do you want to know that?"

I can't tell if she's mad or not. Some attitude,

though. When am I going to learn? "Don't, really," I say. "Just making conversation."

"Sorry. People like to ask me that. It gets tiresome. Like I have to be married."

"Just curious. Didn't mean to pry."

"Think I might be an old spinster?" she asks with a laugh.

"No, no. Are you?"

"Well not exactly. I *was* married. He was a cop."

"Oh yeah?" Not exactly what I was expecting to hear. "What happened to him?"

"Killed. Drug dealer shot him."

"Oh," I say, taken aback by this unexpected response. "Sorry…I didn't…"

"It's all right. You didn't know."

This has taken a hard left and is going downhill quickly. I feel bad for bringing it up so I keep talking, hoping for an off ramp somewhere. Has to be a way out of this, I'm thinking. That must have been difficult. For you, I mean..."

I notice her face tightens. "It still is, if you want to know the truth about it."

"Yeah, of course. It would be."

"Think about it every day, really. Hard to get over." She now is looking down and not at me like before.

"Sorry. How long has it been…if you don't mind my asking?"

A crease forms in her brow as her lower lip stiffens then she says, "It's been a few years now."

Looks like I'm not the only one who would rather leave the past in the past but now that we're in it I don't want to appear uncaring. "So…no kids, I guess? Figure you would have mentioned it by now if there were."

Shakes her head. "No kids. Which is good, I guess given what happened. We tried. I can't have any, apparently. He'd already had a kid with someone else, so guess what? That makes me the culprit."

I feel bad for her, so I say, "Must help you then…working with kids and all, in spite of their circumstances."

"I suppose so, yeah. I try not to think about it that way. Why bring myself down."

"We don't have to talk about this," I say. I want this to be over, but don't know what to say. I don't want to seem disinterested. Then the waitress saves me by showing up with our drinks.

Mariela excuses herself now to go to the restroom. I'm glad for the break. I feel like a moron for asking all the questions. This is one of the reasons for staying inside your own head. Everything in there is crap you already know. There are no surprises.

Most of it you can just ignore. Old stories that don't cause as much trouble. They just bounce around inside and give you a headache. But you get used to it. You know what's there. It becomes automatic. Like breathing, or blinking your eyes. All my thoughts are like that. They're well worn—so well worn they can get by on their own. Don't need any help from me. I look out the window on the other side of the room and see a small bird flapping its wings on the tip of a bush. Not much of a life, but then it can fly. That's something special anyway. To them it's probably nothing. To me it seems like a lot. Easy to escape. Then again, where to?

When she returns, I look at her a moment while she studies the table. Whatever she's thinking about is not making her happy. Some part of her life is back to haunt her, I'm guessing. The dead husband; that she can't have kids. She slides her wine glass on the table top, back and forth, slowly, like the movie's rolling and she can't stop it, a time in her life so bad that everything after is thought of by her as just that —everything after. Then she straightens up in her seat and lifts her wine glass. "To all the people we miss and will never see again."

I clink my beer on her glass but find her toast too sad to repeat. "To them all," I say instead.

"How about you?" she says, after taking

another sip of her wine. I notice her hand is small and delicate, her nails polished. She has a nice face but getting a hardness when she doesn't smile. "You've been through a lot, yourself. I know you were married and have two kids. Homeless, prison, my God." She had been looking at her hands but now looks up at me. "What'll you do now?"

"Can't say," I offer after a moment to consider it. "It's hard to be ambitious with a prison record. Not that I didn't try at first." I say this because it's truer than even I like to think and because she expects at least some kind of an answer, even though it's not the one she wants to hear.

"So that's it? You're just going to give up?"

There's an edge to her voice I don't care for, like I'm being judged and about to be sentenced. I've been judged before by a real judge. Didn't care for it then; like it even less now. "Are we back in therapy again," I say.

"Sorry. I didn't mean that. Poor choice of words. It's been a while for me. I don't get out much. Sorry"

"We were doing better on the phone."

She smiles. "That's true. I suppose we were."

"So where's your boyfriend?" I say, taking a wild stab at inciting more trouble. "An attractive woman like you...you know, in spite of being a widow spinster and all, I'm thinking you must have a lot of men calling you up wanting to go out."

"Yeah, well. I get calls.There are lots of men out there, just not too many good ones. I know. I've been out with some of them. I could tell you stories. Assholes and creeps by the truckload."

"In that case why sit here having a drink with me, a convicted felon?"

"As far as I can tell you're not an asshole or a creep. I could be wrong about that but it seems like behind that messed up exterior of yours, you're probably not a bad guy. Seeing how Jessie was when she saw you that time told me a lot about you. About who you really are, that is. Or were before you fell off the edge. You're looking better now than when I first saw you, by the way. Someone just needed to run you through a car wash, was all."

"You and your sweet talk. You're going to make me all weak in the knees if you keep that up."

"I'm trying to be honest here. Don't go taking it the wrong way."

"Tell you what. Shall we get something to eat? I think we need to reset the game clock."

"Is that what this is, a game?"

"Everything's a game isn't it?"

"No. Everything isn't a game. You know that."

"Yeah. I guess I do."

"You say things you don't really mean." she says.

"My defenses kick in. When things get too hot I react."

"Why?" she says. "You think we're getting too hot?"

Well, I want to say, what is this? I never figured her to flirt with me. Must be the wine. I doubt if she figured it either. In fact, I think I'm getting way ahead of myself here. The beer must be going to my head. She's just jerkin my chain, anyway. Haven't I been in this movie once or twice before? You bet I have.

By the time we finish eating I'm feeling pretty good. There's nothing like drinking to knock all the edges off. And from the look on her face, she's not feeling any pain now either. It's all flowing nice and slow and easy. It's Friday so we don't have to worry about the time. We each have another drink, and talk about things that don't matter. To me, anyway. "Did you ever go to school?" she asks me at one point.

"School? Of course. Didn't everyone?"

"I mean college?"

"Oh yeah, college. Of course. I went at least a year or more. Had to drop out because of money. I got married. Took more courses off and on. Found out I'm not as dumb as I thought I was."

She smiles. "I never thought you were dumb."

"Well, let's just say it was kind of a secret for a long time."

"You're too modest, I think."

"Not when I'm drinking, I'm not. When I'm totally sauced I think I'm a genius and not half bad looking."

"You're not."

"Not what? A genius, or half bad looking?"

"Either, but that's better than that other kind of drunk."

"What kind is that?"

"You know, mean and nasty. Violent. But that's not you. I can tell."

"That's not me all right. Just the other day I was mistaken for Jesus."

"Oh Really? Not good, I have to say. Please don't tell me that."

"Sorry. I was only stating a fact."

"You're just making it worse."

"Sorry. I didn't say I *was* Jesus."

"Well that's a relief." She gives me a puzzled look. I'm guessing I disturbed her picture of me, whatever little story she was telling herself about who I am. But fuck it. Who does she want him to be?

When it's time to go she insists on paying, but I say no. We finally agree to split the bill. She's head strong, which I find appealing. We head back toward the cabin. On the way, she sees a package liquor store and wants me to stop so she can get a bottle of wine. "For later," she says. "I'm all out at home." This sounds promising until I realize she's headed straight for my place. When we get to the fence where the mailbox may or may not go, depending, she doesn't want to make me walk all the way through the field in the dark, which seems doable when you've had enough to drink. So we take her car through the gate and down along the curving remnants of dirt and gravel tire tracks, still just barely visible in the wiregrass and jimson weed. Everything's black except for where the car lights hit, cutting the world down to size, a narrow open path appearing directly in front of us. Everything else has disappeared. The little cabin lights up, too, when we get there. But all of a sudden, it seems like the loneliest place on earth. The weathered boards and tiny windows sag slightly, or is it my imagination? I don't have the nerve to invite her in, a dump like this, hardly a chair inside, but hate for the night to end, especially when I don't have anything inside to drink. It would be nice to open that bottle of wine.

"How do you sleep out here?" she says abruptly. "These crickets are so loud."

"After a year in prison you can sleep

anywhere," I say, and wish right away I hadn't said it. Why remind her.

She breathes out a long empathetic sigh. "That must have been awful," she says, looking at me in a way that has my attention because it's like she feels bad for me. The engine's still running, but she seems in no hurry to leave. I'm trying to figure out what's going on. "The truth is," I say in answer to her remark, "awful doesn't even come close to describing it." Now I'm the one watching the movie of my life rewind and replay itself in continuous short loops of the worst of numerous bad moments. "I better go in," I say. "You probably want to get home."

"Hey," she says, coming alive all of a sudden. "I have a better idea. You have a corkscrew?"

A corkscrew. Now, finally, my aversion to acquiring material possessions comes back to bite me on the ass. I don't have a lot of things, but why couldn't I at least have a corkscrew? They take up practically no space at all. They're inexpensive. They can be used for other things. They have that look—useful. I'm lost in thought because I'm stunned by this ridiculous impediment to the moment. She's waiting and looks beautiful now in the glow of red light from the dash board.

"Don't worry," she says. "There's another way. I saw somebody do this at a party once." She grabs the wine out of the back seat. "You have a knife?" she asks. I do have a little pocket knife and hand it to her. She cuts the wrapping and exposes the top of the cork. She asks me to take off one of my shoes, takes it from me, gets out of the car, and walks over to the corner of the building. Setting the bottom of the wine bottle inside my shoe she bangs the heel of the shoe against the house a bunch of times until the cork starts pushing out from the pressure. When enough cork is out to grab hold of she twists it until it pops the rest of the way out. I'm impressed. What's more, I'm wondering now if she didn't buy that bottle of wine just to take home for some other time but had this in mind all along. Intent is always the main thing in court; it always makes the difference between a first and second degree verdict. Guilty your Honor, I'm thinking. She planned this all along. I'm getting too hopeful.

Now she says, cheerfully, "You have any glasses?"

I jump from the car saying, "I'll be right back. Don't leave." I must be drunk. That's what I'm thinking now. I have the goddamn glasses, but not clean ones. I go inside and fire up the Coleman lantern. The only two glasses I have, bought for the girl when she was still here, are dirty, so I have to wash them with my bottle of drinking water from the well pump, kept in a re-commissioned milk jug in this sweat lodge I call a home. When I dry them off and turn around to go back outside, I see the car lights go out and hear the engine stop and the silence except for the crickets after. When I get to the door I see she is right there just outside. She's just a ghost in the darkness, like an apparition coming towards me with the bottle of wine floating on its own. She's tipsy and steadies herself. "That light's really bright," she says. "Can you turn it down?"

I turn it down as far as I can while she pours the wine. Taking mine, I clink our glasses together and she says, "To tonight."

"Tonight," I say, affirming her feelings of good things happening, and things about to happen, maybe, and stop there so as not to jinx it. She steps forward, then, and places a hand on my shoulder to steady herself. If music is the universal language, a hand on the shoulder is the universal gesture. It says, *Come into my heart. I invite you there*. Could I be this much of a fool? Yes. I kiss her. What else can I do? And now I know this story as well, it's the Inexplicable End Of All Things, part one. By *end* I mean, of course, purpose not death. Love, lust, eros. Whatever you want to call it. What else on this planet matters as much. Friendship, a different kind of love, then, but still. What else is more important? Even some animals seem attracted by it. After all, don't monkeys hold hands?

When I offer her the chair she sits on the bed. No translation needed there. I take a drink and set my glass on the floor. She does the same and so there's nothing else to do but take her in my arms. The luxuriant smell of a woman, known once before to me so long ago and so intoxicating, like nothing else in the world, paralyzes me with its power. Kissing her warm lips, lying back onto the bed and feeling the suppleness of her hips and neck, her arms and one of her legs encircle me. I can feel her heat and excitement enfolding me tighter and tighter as she pulls me towards her, and I wonder if I am only dreaming this, have been home for hours and dreamed it all. I feel as though maybe some giant Burmese Python has come for me, sought me out for the heat emanating from my pitiful heart, crawled into my bed, and has me in its fat coil like you see in pictures in National Geographic, me the hapless victim, like a chimpanzee, or a gazelle, a small zebra, thinking its last regretful thoughts: how could I be so stupid? How could I let my guard down like this, forget to hide, run fast, be careful? Survival! Did you forget about survival? *No. Well yes. Who knows?* But in the end I just relax, I have to, and give myself up to it. I'm unafraid. I'm ready for it, ready for that awful pain, and that final relief when it's all over, because it's always over, eventually—it's only a story after all, with its bright beginning, tragic middle, and pathetic end—when, after suffering all these thoughts, in an instant that seems like an hour, I come to a much better conclusion to this the unexpected. Why would a Burmese Python, I realize suddenly, be wearing perfume? Or am I just clinging to a different dream, one that I used to have?

I wake to an unfamiliar feeling. Is it the warmth of her beside me? A Burmese Python? Who knows? I'm not quite awake, but remembering that story, the one where you wake to see her in the kitchen—if I had a kitchen—with a pot of coffee on, still brewing and sending its no nonsense aroma around the room to entice me, her at the stove frying some eggs, sunny side up or over easy, whatever, just the sound of it crackling in the pan, so full of life and love, all the Time To Get Up Honey and Breakfast Is Almost Ready stories together in one dreamy thought. What I see instead is a half empty bottle of wine on the table and no one beside me. The only aroma is really a fragrance, actually, the remnants of her perfume lingering on the sleeping bag and me. If it was intoxicating last night, this morning it is just devastatingly sad. Why couldn't she be here? I understand why, of course, but why anyway. The why

I'm asking is really *why me* in the first place. Why would she or anyone else want to spend the night curled up on this crummy old bed and hot sleeping bag? Even the python's have so far taken a pass on it. And yet. Wasn't she here? Didn't we make love and didn't she moan and arch her back like she would if she liked it and cared? Yes and yes, so maybe I'm just too ready for the tragic ending. It's my specialty, after all: loss and all its side effects.

I get up to see if her car is gone. Why I do this, I don't know. I do, though, and it is. But gone is not the word for it. If you've ever been to North Dakota you'll know what the field outside my door looks like this morning without her car there. Two miles outside any town in that state is the physical rendition of the Spanish word that we have no word for in the English language. *Saudade:* the longing for that which can never be. In other words, me after the python has left. Not life after death but something like it. Like Adam and the rest of us after the snake—endless despair. I know the car won't be there, but I go and look anyway just to punish myself, and feel the unutterable, except in Spanish, feeling of despair, that longing for something that can never be. But it's our curse: hope, and I indulge it. Maybe she'll call.

Twenty

She doesn't. I wait all day Saturday for the phone to ring only to check it and find it needs to be charged. I ride my bike to the closest place I can find with an outlet where I can plug it in. For some reason there are Best Western motels down south here in Florida, which seems odd to me now that I'm thinking about it. This isn't even western Florida, but there you are. I see one just down the road a bit, so I go there and have a seat in the lobby by a lamp plugged into a wall. Luckily for me, there's an empty outlet, which I plug my phone into. While I'm waiting, I pick up a pamphlet for Stuckey's and look at all the pictures and read about their famous Peanut Log. Boredom, like water, seeks its own level. Stuckey's Peanut Log has got a creamy nougat center surrounded by peanuts, it says, which looks pretty good to me right now since I've had nothing to eat today except a bag of pretzels. I'm starving and decide to get something as soon as my phone has charged. I wrack my brain for what I might have said or done to upset Mariela. I don't know why I'm surprised but I would have thought she'd have stayed until morning or at least left a note or something. Wondering what I've done I try to remember what is only half there floating in my head from last night.

Desire, long dormant for me, and perhaps my looking at the Peanut Log, have made me anxious. I should know better.

There's a Roy's Burger Express down the street. I go there next and get a cheeseburger. It comes with fries and a Coke. The girl at the register is cute and smiles at me. I smile back. Then I pay and take a seat by the window. When my food is ready someone else brings it to me on a tray. I thank him and he says without a simple glance in my direction, "No problem."

I notice a small child is trying to get his mother's attention at the next table over, but she's busy with her cell phone trying to text someone. I assume this from the way she's pounding furiously at the little keypad with her thumbs and staring intently at it like that will make the little bit of difference needed. I could try texting Mariela if I knew how, *Hey Mariela*, but I don't, *S'up?* I can't stand waiting any longer so I call.

"Hi," is all she says.

"Somebody wasn't there when I woke up."

"Yeah…I…Listen. I don't know what to say. I guess I shouldn't drink so much. I don't know what I thought I was doing, but it was a mistake."

"Yeah, I had a great time, too."

"I'm sorry," she says, but doesn't sound as sorry as I want her to.

"Yeah, well..." I don't know what to say. "Heard anything?"

"Not yet. It's Saturday. Might be Monday before they get back to me. We'll just have to wait."

"Well let me know as soon as you hear anything," I say.

"I will. Soon as I hear. And I am sorry for leaving like that. It wasn't you. Really, it wasn't."

"Of course not. No problem. It must have been the other guy. I knew that."

"The other guy?"

"Skip it. I'll leave my phone on, just in case."

So it's like being swallowed by a Burmese Python, after all. Like Jonah and Pinocchio inside the whale's belly waiting to get out. It's dark in here so to light it up a little I picture the girl at the register smiling at me and bouncing on her heels while waiting for me to pay. It doesn't help. I want her say to something to me about how she thinks I have a nice smile, but what comes out instead is, *Napkins, salt & pepper, ketchup & mustard are all over there*. Another big smile as she points to the opposite counter.

As I walk out the door I find myself slipping downward, something that I thought I had under control. Now I'm back in the old shit. I picture myself jumping in front of a car but it's not a good idea and I know it. I'd live, but be crippled for life, wouldn't I? You bet! I get back on my bike and pedal. I'm heading home. Then I imagine myself yanking the phone out of that woman's hands and telling her to pay attention to her fucking kid, but she yanks her phone right back and calls the police. Then I'm arrested and back in the slammer waiting for trial and counting the seconds and the cracks in the wall and my many regrets. This is a good sign, I decide, this particular thought I'm having now. It shows that at least I'm thinking these things through to their realistic, logical conclusions. Long ago I would only think half way through something and that's exactly how you get into trouble. I find it a relief to be improving, but not much of one. Still. Baby steps! It's a good sign.

On the way home I stop and buy an avocado and some tooth picks and a plastic cup. I have reduced my original idea of raising chickens and becoming a farmer with a tractor and a cornfield, scaling it down to a more realistic project. This is another perfect example of thinking things through to their realistic conclusions. While waiting for my phone to charge I had watched the TV in the lobby. A man who called himself Mr. Nature was demonstrating how to grow an avocado tree from a seed. I thought, why not? I'll do it.

When I get home I wash and cut open my avocado, which I will eat on crackers later tonight. The seed—the size and shape of a small egg and looking, with its protective dried skin still on, like a single testicle from a three thousand year old mummy—I wash and place it suspended half in water by sticking three toothpicks around its sides so that it looks like a miniature sputnik floating in the top of the plastic cup, the toothpicks resting on and sticking out over the rim. I set this in the window where it will get sunlight all afternoon. This is another healthy sign of recovery, I tell myself, a constructive life affirming activity that will be uplifting if and when something happens, but really, deep down inside, I fear that I must be losing it. Who the fuck plants an avocado seed? Not an ex-convict. Not me. And yet I do it! I check it for signs of life every few minutes. Twenty minutes passes. Nothing happens.

I'm still obsessing over my avocado seed when the phone rings. It's Mariela. "Bingo!" she says. "They found something on our buddy Carl. Seems that he was once a registered level 2 sex offender in Harrisburg Pennsylvania. You're supposed to self-register wherever you are but they don't. Now he's in Alabama and nobody's the wiser—until now, that is."

"That sonofabitch! So can we pick her up

now?"

"Not so fast. Just slow down. I called the authorities in Birmingham and they're going to pay him a visit."

"The authorities? Pay him a visit? Are you kidding?"

"Hey, hey! Calm down. That's how you have to do it. Besides, they can be there within the hour. It would take us eight to ten hours to drive there and then we'd still have to find the place."

I'm trying to process this. I know she's right, but I'm like a dog who thinks he's heard something. It'll take me the rest of the night to calm down again. I pace the floor thinking only of what's been going on up there all this time? What he's probably done to her?

"That's why she called," I say. "She was asking for help and we didn't help her."

"Whoa. I beg your pardon. I *did* help her and that's why they're going out there to get her right now. Thank you very much."

"I'm sorry," I say. "I know that. You're right. You're right. I'm just worried. I'm afraid that bastard has hurt her. She's just a fucking little kid."

"I know that. Listen. Don't worry. Try not to get too worked up. She's going to be all right now. We'll see to it. They'll get her out of that house and then we'll go up there ourselves and get her. You, too. We'll go together. I know you're worried about her. We're all worried about her."

"Never should have let those people take her in the first place."

"Okay," she says. "I have to go. I'm waiting to hear back from them. I'll call you when I do."

Twenty One

Sunday.

I watch the dust float and sparkle in the bars of sunlight coming through the window. Silence washes across the space between me and the four walls. It can be louder than any real sound sometimes. Today my ears hurt from it. I listen for the phone to ring and hear it ringing but it's not. I take the chair outside and sit with the sun drenching my face and arms and think it will kill me to sit here like this another minute, and then more minutes pass and I'm still here. Then I think that not calling only means good news. It means they have the girl and are keeping her safe somewhere. They will call Mariela tomorrow and let her know what is happening, I think. She will call me, then, and tell me what they said, and we will leave the next day for Birmingham. We'll bring the girl back here and she'll come to visit me and I can show her the drawing paper and crayons and pencils that I bought for her. I still have them. I'm sure she will like them. I'm hoping she will.

Monday morning we take down another building. The Ferris wheel sits where we parked it, folded neatly into its contented self, waiting patiently for all the fun to begin again, the loud enthusiastic voices, the happy music floating in the night air while people laugh and part with their hard earned money. But for now, we're turning this place back into what it used to be. Not just an empty field, but a natural habitat for insects and rodents and birds, and somewhere also a handful or two of snakes, things that live in the soil, and things you can't see because they are so small. The natural world reclaims itself quickly when we get out of the way, looks like, now that we and all our neon fun are not here anymore. Compared to the planet we're ephemeral and a fairly recent event, the professor told us—and I can see it, a flimsy wish and a dream, it says of us, a forgotten cobweb on a fence post. The wind blows forever, nature thrives, but everything else is just make believe.

It's evening, and I'm sitting outside again with my eyes closed and hearing all the faint sounds in the distance, cars and trucks and a dog barking somewhere far away. The ring-ring of my phone wakes me from my terrible reverie and I run inside to answer it.

"Are you sitting down?"

"What is it?"

"You're not going to believe this." The tone of her voice tells me she's in a rage. "They can't find her. They said they can't find her. She's gone.

Charlene and Carl are saying they don't know where she is, that she must have run away again."

"The Police told you this?"

"Family Services. I don't believe it, but that's what they're saying. The police are holding Carl and questioning him but he keeps telling them the same thing. They don't know where she is. They got up and went to wake her in the morning, they said, and she wasn't there."

I'm listening to her say all this, standing here in silence, but feel like someone who has been set on fire, and now I'm wondering if this is really happening or I'm still asleep and dreaming the worst outcome to all this.

"I'm so mad," she is saying to me, "I can hardly sit still. What the fuck have those people done to her?"

"You people! You had to take her away." I hear myself saying, because I'm caught unprepared for this news, and if they hadn't taken her away from me for Christ sakes she'd still be okay. "She was fucking safe with me until you guys took her away. They put me in fucking jail and..."

"Are you at home?" she says.

"Yeah, I'm at home. Of course I'm at home." I say, this while trying to control myself so I don't slam the phone against the wall and break it into a million pieces. "I'll kill that motherfucker," I hear myself say, more to the empty room around me than to her. "If he's hurt her I'll kill that sonofabitch,"

"I'm coming over," she says. "Don't leave. I'm not far away. I was at Burger King waiting for an order when they called."

Waiting and pacing now. That is, I'm racing through each minute only to find myself at the end and starting over again at the next minute, which is just like the first one only it seems much longer. Then another one and another one and another one after that. I call Buzz because I can't just sit here with all this anger and yet when he answers I don't know what it is I want to say except I say, "Those fucking bastards have done something to Jessie."

"Who?" he says. And I'm so pissed off I don't answer him.

"Hey man. Take a deep breath. Tell me what's going on."

I stop, slow myself down and try to calm myself. I tell him what happened. "They say she's missing."

"Don't worry, buddy," he says. "We'll get her. We'll find her and bring her back. Just dial it back a little, man. Dial it way back. We'll take care of it. Don't you worry. We'll break that cocksucker's neck for him. And then we'll bring that girl back here."

Mariela finds me pacing in the weeds out front when she gets here. She hurries over to me and after a moment when we look each other in the eye she puts her arms around me in a hug and we hold on to our shared concern and fury. "I called them back on the way over," she says, keeping it calm, "to ask them more questions. Charlene told them Jessie's been gone for three days. When they asked her why she didn't call the police right away she said she was afraid they'd take her away from them when they found her. They didn't want that to happen because they need the money they get from the state for taking care of her. I can't believe those assholes. They need the money, she said. They need the money? And of course we know the real reason they didn't call. Because of Carl."

"Can't we go up there?" I ask. "Right now?"

"No. There's nothing we can do until they find her. We have to wait. We don't want to piss them off and then have them not want to give her back to us. You understand what I'm saying? You understand? We want to stay the good guys in their eyes."

"It could be weeks before they find her. That's *if* they find her. And we're just going to wait for a phone call?"

"What would we do up there? Go from house to house and ask if we can look inside for a missing girl?"

"Well…Jesus!" I can't even finish what I'm saying, whatever the hell that is.

We go inside while I mutter every foul thing I can think to say and run out of words and look around the room as though there's some sort of answer scurrying around like a mouse on the floor I'm trying to catch. She starts to pace, then stops and says, "I almost forgot. I brought you something to eat if you want it," she says. "It was for me but I can't eat it now. It's in the car."

I watch her walk out to her car and wonder if I'll be able to sleep tonight. Mariela opens the passenger door and bends down to grab something off the seat. I should be happy she's here but fuck that. She's back and hands me the bag with the food in it but I'm not feeling hungry either. I take the hamburger wrapped in paper out of the bag and stand there looking at it like I don't know what it is. "Where would she go?" I say, more to myself than a question for her.

"I have no idea. I hate to think about her out there wandering around." She sees me staring at the food. "Listen, you don't have to eat that. I just thought maybe you'd be hungry." She puts a hand on my shoulder. "We have to stay calm," she says. "Otherwise we'll go crazy with this. She could call, like she did before. Anything might happen."

"She doesn't have a phone."

"She's a smart kid. She'll find a way. I have to believe that."

"You don't believe that any more than I do."

"I don't want to hear that. Okay? I want to stay positive."

I sit on the bed with the hamburger still in my hand, trying to figure out what there is we could be doing. The bottle of wine is still on the table and she takes the cork out and looks for a glass. "What's this?" she asks, seeing the avocado seed in the window. She finds a glass, gives it a rinse and pours some wine.

"It's an avocado seed. With any luck something will grow there. For the record, I'm not holding my breath."

She looks again. "You're hard to figure. You know that?"

"What was the matter with you the other day, anyway?"

With a sigh she sits in the chair. "Don't know exactly. I just felt like I was being foolish. I don't even know you really." Then she stands abruptly and says, "Do we have to talk about that now?"

"You don't know me? That's not what you

said the other night."

"You're right. It's not. I can't really say what the problem is. I don't know exactly."

I take a bite out of the hamburger and find I'm hungrier than I thought. I chew and swallow and take another bite thinking it will distract me, but it doesn't.

"I'll call them again tomorrow first thing," she says, and sits down beside me. "Have another glass?" she asks. "I'll pour you some wine."

I get the glass and we sit on the bed drinking the wine, staring at the walls and imagining the phone call when we get it, hearing a ring tone and getting the news. Only…what news will it be.

"We need to get you another chair," she says.

"I'm trying not to think about her."

"I can't keep from it."

"I suppose I identified with her a little bit. Like you said. When I was fifteen, my parents divorced," I tell her. "It was like losing them both even though it was my father who left." I'm not sure why I'm telling her this. It has floated up from the bottom of an ocean of time, and telling it now is like a way of spitting it out, like something that comes up from the pit of your stomach you can't swallow back down and have to get rid of. Perhaps this memory is a substitute for what is going on, or because of it. I rinse my mouth with a swig of wine.

"Was that bad for you?" she asks, concerned that I'm mentioning this now, at this particular moment.

"I spent years hating him for her. Then one day she tells me he has cancer and he's going to die. I didn't try to see him until it was too late. That's how it goes isn't it? It's always too late, it seems. This was way before everything went haywire and I kind of died myself."

"How was it before the divorce? With your dad, I mean."

"I don't know, really. I loved him, I was terrified of him. He could be a bastard. Then again, I wasn't the best kid. He could be nice too sometimes, when he wanted to be."

"An old story, I guess. Isn't it?"

"Yeah, but when he took an interest…when he was nice…it was…"

"The best?"

"No. I wouldn't say that. Not exactly. It was all right. It was never the best. But it was okay."

"To be honest, I'm surprised you're telling me this. I thought you said you'd pretty well buried your past. Put it all away for good."

"I did. It was necessary, seemed like. I looked around me and said time to close up shop. I took everything in my life and put it in a box. Then I climbed up on top of a mountain and threw the box off. I watched it fall. I could see it getting smaller and smaller as it fell. It never made a sound, though. I waited. I heard nothing. For all I know it's still falling. You would think that somehow that box must have burned up, you know, from the speed of the fall, like from you know, acceleration due to gravity, or whatever it's called. The longer and farther you fall, the faster you fall. Eventually you should get combustion from all that friction. That's what it feels like anyway."

"And now?"

"And now…I'm still up here."

"Up here?"

"On top of the mountain." I go quiet for a long moment, wondering why I'm telling her this. My capacity for stupidity is endless, apparently.

"And..?"

"And…I don't know how to get back down. Guess I'm stuck up here." I look away and try to think it through. "Like, I just don't know how to do it." I look back again at her sitting beside me. She's wondering, I suppose, if there's more. "We've got to find her, Mariela. We're all she's got. And we fucked up. We let her down. We have to fix it."

"We'll find her," she says, trying to comfort me, but we both know how these things end. With some guy in a rundown trailer park that looks even worse-off than me. Some guy who didn't have the sense to throw his box away, but crawled inside instead with all that pain and garbage and pulled the lid shut over on top of him. Then one day he crawls back out again and snatches some little girl off the street and brings her home with him. I can't even let myself think about the rest."

She finishes her wine and sets the glass on the table, then walks over and looks at the seed suspended in the cup by the window. "How long is this supposed to take?" she asks. "Until it sprouts?"

"Oh, you know how it is. Like everything. Sometime between now and never."

We sit a while longer and then she stands and says she has to go. "My sister's just been released from the hospital. I need to stop and see how she is. Then tomorrow's another day sorting out other people's problems."

"Your sister? Really? She all right?" I ask, curious about this now and wishing I'd known. "Is it serious?"

"She will be. She had a lump removed from her breast. They got it early, but you know how it is; you never know."

"Well…I'm sorry. I hope she's going to be okay."

I watch her drive away and think how she should have been with her sister today, instead of being here with me. The sound of her car fades and the night air fills with crickets, and the wash of cars on the highway somewhere hums and whispers like waves breaking at the ocean, a faraway sound in my ear. I feel a single drop of rain on my arm. A few minutes later it's spitting, but can't quite seem to work itself into anything more substantial. A thunderhead forms loosely in the pink, yellow, and blue sky. I hear a faint rumble, half-hearted, disenchanted with itself—nothing that will keep me awake. Not that I'll be able to sleep tonight, anyway.

Twenty Two

At work, we're taking down more buildings, getting close to finishing the job. No news. No calls. Nothing about Jessie. Grass and a few weeds are already coming in. Rectangles of dirt and gravel mark traces of vanished sheds and semi-permanent concession stands, the spot where a giant clown once stood and then lain on its side. Nothing left but the ghost of what was. Nothing permanent, nothing stays the same. Things die; new things grow in their place. The field is erupting with natural life again. Earl points out all the wild flowers: violets, redbud, leatherwood, and larkspur lighting up the weed-heavy rough edges along the wire fence where a crow sits. Nearby, the Ferris wheel waits like a lost monument to a different time. A recent time, yes. A time in living memory. My memory. What's left of it. It's more of a feeling that you can glimpse but never quite get a hold of. Something that's gone now, but lingers still, seems like. In a word: yesterday.

Ray complains, saying we have to figure out what to do with the Ferris wheel and it's bugging him. They want it out of here, but where does it go? Nobody wants it. It's too big to just leave somewhere. It won't generate enough money these days to warrant its use. We would hate to take it apart for scrap. I know it sounds kind of stupid, but it would be kind of sacrilegious and we're all thinking that same thing.

At home, I take the mailbox off the other bed, Jessie's bed, what used to be her bed, and find the stick-on numbers where they've been sitting on the counter waiting to be used. After attaching them to the front of the mailbox I grab the hammer and nails and take a walk through the grass out to the road. I pick out a fence post close to the gate and play around with finding some way to attach it. Eventually I find a way that works, and hammer away, using more nails than necessary. The shed will never withstand a hurricane, I think, but this mailbox will be here forever. On the way back to the house I think about sending myself a postcard just to see if I'll get it. Maybe I'll get one at Stuckey's with a big picture of their famous Peanut Log on the front. "Eat this, you dipshit!" the postcard will say. A little joke to myself.

I empty the water from the cup with the avocado seed in it. Then I put fresh water in. The man on the TV had said that the water will get moldy and dirty and generate bacteria that could kill the seedling if I don't change it. I inspect the seed but know it will be a while before anything happens. I'm not expecting this to work, anyway. I don't even know why I'm doing it. Am I really going to get avocados off this thing even if it sprouts and grows leaves? At best it'll be a house plant. I can't imagine planting something as exotic looking as this seed that eventually grows, becomes bountiful, produces fruit, and feeds and sustains me. Might as well plant a dollar bill and expect an income for life.

So far, Mariela's been telling me, there's no news on the girl. "I'm trying to find out just exactly what it was he did to get the sex offender record in Pennsylvania, but so far I don't have anything. My understanding is that if they don't find something to charge Carl with, they'll have to release him. Right now they can't prove he's done anything to Jessie."

I want to argue with her about it, but don't. She's telling me what they're telling her. Another day goes by and then another. I go to Stuckey's and get my postcard. I write a message to myself on the back and mail it to "Occupant" at my new address. We're done at FUN-O-RAMA—the place that used to be FUN-O-RAMA, that is. Ray tells us he has no work for us right now, but will try to find something as soon as possible. Another demo job, maybe. Whatever he can scare up.

Sitting around with nothing to do is getting to me. Mariela comes by one night after she gets off work and brings me another chair she found in a junk shop for cheap money. It's pretty scuffed up, but works. It's sturdy enough. We sit at the table and eat a pizza she brought, along with a bottle of wine we pour and drink, trying not to get worked up into a big tizzy over Jessie. "I think you should know I went out with a guy the other night," she says, out of the blue. "Just want to be up front about it."

She's acting as if it's nothing so I do too. "Hey," I say. "It's your life." I'm trying not to show the disappointment I feel. The thing is, she doesn't owe me anything. So why not go out with someone? Still…it bothers me. Naturally.

"It's nothing, really. Someone I used to work with a few years back and he just found my number and called me up. He's been out of town; now he's back. So I went. It was just a night out. Nothing special."

"Whatever," I say, with a little too much fake nonchalance attached to it. I get up and pretend to do something because my face is like a movie, sometimes, like when I'm pissed off or bothered by something. ACTS I, II & III unravel on my face and credits play at the end. As if there wasn't enough unspoken tension in the air over the missing girl, and no word on her, and all this waiting around to hear from the Birmingham Police, her little disclosure has kind of killed the evening and she leaves not too long after we finish eating. "Thanks for the chair," I tell her. "And the pizza." She leaves the rest of the wine, which I quickly slug down. Might as well mellow out if I can.

I pay Buzz a visit in the morning. We discuss taking a little trip to Birmingham to ring Carl's neck for him. "Maybe we can squeeze something out of him," Buzz says with a grin. He seems too fond of this idea. And I worry I won't be able to control myself, either, and we'll hurt the guy a little too much. A guy like Buzz could kill him. Then what? Going back to prison doesn't appeal to me. Once was bad enough. Better to get the sonofabitch convicted and sent to prison himself. They'll take care of his ass in there for sure. They hate child molesters. His ass'll be so sore he'll never sit down again and then they'll kill him.

But then Mariela comes by with an old chest of drawers. "My neighbor was throwing it out," she says. I don't know how to read her. Who is she, anyway? What does she want from me?

When I tell her I don't really have anything to put in the drawers, she says, "You need to go shopping, then. Get more underwear, for starters. Socks, T shirts, a few more long-sleeve shirts. You can't keep wearing the same clothes every day. It's… unpleasant."

I don't say anything. I know what she's

getting at. I guess I got used to it. I was living like an animal, and eventually you don't care anymore and by then you don't know the difference.

"There's something else," she says.

I'm not sure I want to hear it.

"I found out more about Carl." She says this while busying herself with the drawers, as though not wanting to make a big deal out of it. "He had been found guilty of touching a young child that Charlene was babysitting back in Pennsylvania."

"Touching a child. A *child*?" I'm looking her straight in the face, now. "You mean a girl, don't you? By child you mean girl!"

She's reluctant to say it, but she does. "Yes. A girl."

I'm surprised at how calm I am. It's bad news, but in a way I welcome it; it removes a barrier, the line is erased, so in a way it's a relief, permission to act. "Touching a child?"

"But that doesn't mean he's done anything to Jessie," she adds when she sees the look on my face. I think my being calm scares her more than if I'd gone into a rage.

"We both know what it means," I say. "These guys don't change. They can't. Their brains are fucked up. Something's happened to her, no matter how you want to look at it. Something bad's happened."

The time for waiting is over. Buzz finds Carl's address on the internet. He gives Viola a hug and we jump into the pickup, tear off into the hot morning as though we are about to right the world from a tilted axis. On the way to Birmingham he doesn't say much, just eyes on the road looking intent. Then out of the blue he says, "My brother Bobby didn't die in Iraq so some peckerwood from Pennsylvania could go around here molesting little girls. Game over, Dude. We're comin to getcha!"

I'm hoping that the long drive will take some of the edge off. Who knows how dangerous Buzz could be when he's pissed off.

We reach Birmingham by late evening the following day. We stop at a Wendy's and get something to eat, decide how we're going to do this. Once upon a time, he informs me, Buzz had worked for one of the bounty hunter outfits in Louisiana doing jobs for bail bondsmen. He knows the drill, he says—how to sneak up on a house, how to gain access, all that stuff. First we have to find the place. When it's good and dark we'll plug the address into his GPS. We get to the neighborhood and follow the directions. Once we find the house we sit a long while and watch what's going on up and down the street, see what activity there is at Carl's house and at the others. He's got this camouflage goop for our faces that he uses when he's hunting. "This way it'll be hard as hell to identify us later," he says when I look at him funny and stare at the can of camo paint like, "are you fucking serious?" We've got knitted watch caps on and gloves, dark clothing. He's got a revolver, a forty caliber Beretta. I made him promise not to use it. "Only for visual effects," I had said. "As a persuader." He wouldn't go unless he could take it. "For my own protection just in case," he said. Now we're here and on our way and I'm worried about the gun all over again.

We wait about an hour. It's a quiet street, not too many houses, just crappy little cabins and bungalows, a few trailers, spaced far apart with lots of brush, overgrown fields and wooded areas in between. Buzz removes the plates from his truck and puts them behind the seat. The house is a dumpy gray-shingled shoebox with weathered Christmas decals on the front picture window—Rudolph with his nose so bright and Frosty. We make our way around toward the back and sit where we can see in the kitchen window. A metal trash can waits patiently by the back door. Before long a guy we assume is Carl comes into view and heads for the refrigerator. He stands there with the door open looking for something to eat, yawning like a prick who couldn't care less that the girl is missing. I'm relieved to see he's not a particularly big guy. Buzz finds a good sized rock that fits in the palm of his hand. This gets my attention. What's he going to do with that? He puts the rock in his pocket and we head for the corner of the house. A moment later Buzz sneaks over and drags the trash can farther out into the yard, then he returns to where I'm waiting and wishing we weren't doing this. But then I feel the rage build all over again in my chest and stomach from the sight of Carl in the window, yawning some more and scratching his belly. Ray takes the rock out and hurls it at the trash can, which makes a loud banging sound when it hits. He must have been good at baseball when he was a kid because he nails it dead center. Pretty soon the door opens and right on cue Carl comes outside and walks over to see what the noise was and why his trash can is way out in the yard. Before we can say, "maybe we shouldn't do this," we are across the yard and dragging Carl off into the woods. Buzz has his hand over Carl's mouth and has Carl's arm in a hammerlock behind his back. I have him by the legs and we carry him like he was a big duffel bag with a six man tent stuffed inside. He's squirming and trying to make noise with his mouth until we stop and Buzz puts the gun to his head. This calms him down quick.

We stick a piece of duct tape over his mouth, and wrap tape around his hands behind his back, and tell him if he makes the least little peep we'll put a bullet in his brain. It's just like in a fucking movie and my adrenalin is pumping so bad I'm glad it's not *my* finger on that trigger. When we get him to the car Buzz drives away while I sit in the backseat with Carl, holding the gun in my hand, careful to keep my finger off to the side where it can't slip and take us in a whole new direction. We didn't bring shovels to bury a body with. The last thing I'm going to do is shoot the bastard but he doesn't know that. I get a good look at him now and see he's got a weird face. Or something. I don't know. Big eyes, or maybe just too far apart. The rest is nondescript. The nose and mouth kind of small. Not much of a chin. It's the eyes you notice right off.

We find a secluded spot and Buzz pulls over. He gets out and opens the back door and drags Carl out onto the ground. Carl is sweating and shaking like the scared little shit he is. Buzz rips the tape off his mouth with such a loud tearing sound it makes *my* mouth hurt. He says, "Do all the little girls shake and piss their pants like this when you molest 'em? Eh, Carl?"

"Who are you?" he manages to say through a lot of sobbing and blubbering out of panic and fear.

He's terrified and I have to remind myself why we're here to overcome my natural distaste for this kind of thing.

"Where is she Carl? What did you do with Jessie?"

"Nothing," he blubbers. "I told them. I told them I didn't do *anything*. She ran away. She wasn't happy. Please. She just ran away."

"We're not buying it, Carl. Why wasn't she happy? Tell us that." Buzz pulls a hunting knife out of a sheath that I now see is hanging off his belt. "And if you don't tell us something right now we're going to fix you so you can't harm any more little girls. You get my drift, Carl. It's a surgical technique. I've done a few of these, before, so I know what to do, but some of them don't come out quite right, the patients don't make it. They bleed out before the ambulance arrives."

"I don't know why she ran away," he says. "I'm telling you the truth. Who are you guys, anyway?" he's whining like a four year old, which only makes things worse. Makes you want to hurt him more for some reason. "This is a mistake," he continues blubbering. "I didn't do anything to her. Please, don't hurt me. Please!" And then he cries for real. Real big tears pouring out of his eyes that are closed so tight it's making me feel bad. The girl! I have to tell myself. The girl! “Who are you?” he says again.

“We’re cops, Carl. This is how we get information when we can’t get it any other way.” I wouldn’t have figured Buzz for such a crafty sly fellow, but it sounds too much like a half assed movie script for me. Plus I’m getting the feeling now that this piece of shit Carl may not know where she is after all. What then? Continuing would just be pointless, so now what?

“Unbutton his trousers,” Buzz says to me with a wink. I play along and pull them open and start yanking them down. The guy is squirming like a baby pig. I can’t stand the sight of this guy in his underwear and the whole thought of it, even though we’re only trying to scare him is creeping me out. The thought of castrating him has me picturing one of us grabbing a testicle, seat of his desire, his entire ego in a shriveled little bag. I imagine putting the knife to it, which now makes me think of the mummy’s testicle floating in water in a cup on my window sill, and I start to falter. Maybe he was falsely accused back in Pennsylvania, like I was by my ex. I could just as easily have wound up on some sex offender list. And I really was innocent.

Carl is really terrified now and thrashing and blubbering, saying, “No. Please no. I didn’t do anything, I didn't do anything. And I don't know anything. I don't. Oh God…Please, please…" the words are coming out with the rhythm of his sobbing but getting lost in all the drooling, his face wet and shiny with tears. I've had enough and grab Buzz by the arm. I shrug my shoulders and hold out my hands like, what the fuck, let's let him go. He seems to have come to the same conclusion, so we drag Carl back to the truck and tape his mouth shut again. He's still shaking but crying less, realizing, I suppose, that we didn't cut his balls off after all and probably are not going to. We drive him back to his house and see Charlene walking around toward the back from the side, looking for her missing hubby. Carl gets antsy at the sight of her; his eyes bulge and dart back and forth. He starts to whimper. When she's out of sight we tell Carl if he says anything to anyone about this we'll be back and next time we will castrate him and then we'll kill him, and then we shove him out of the truck. He lands with a thud and waits a second to see what's next then makes a quick dash for his house where he can wait for the shaking to stop and decide what to tell Charlene. Before we get too far away and around the corner, Buzz stops and puts the plates back on. Then we head for the interstate, decompressing, like astronauts back from a trip to Mars. I feel awful, kind of sick to my stomach kind of like I *had* been to

Mars. It's a good hour before either one of us says anything. My heart won't stop racing and my stomach has a knot in it now that's like something a Boy Scout would tie to win a merit badge. I could throw up, but don't, just swallow a few dozen times and hope we get back without getting caught.

"What a dumb fucking idea, coming up here," I say. I have to picture the girl out there, scared and alone, just to calm myself down.

"Guess I don't know what the hell we accomplished," Buzz says. He sounds mad still but worn out.

"Wasn't too bright, was it? Guess we were wrong about him. You'd think if he knew something he'd have told us."

"Don't know, but maybe he thought if he admitted doing something to her we'd have killed him for sure anyway once we had found her."

"I suppose."

"Fact is he might've been right."

"Yeah? Think so?"

Buzz nods his head. "I think so."

I glance over to see his face.

"You ever kill anyone?" He asks.

"Nope. Have you?"

"I came close a couple of times. When you're in the middle of a bar fight you don't know what the hell you're doin'. You're just tryin' to keep from getting killed yourself. I've relocated a few jawbones though. Broke a man's arm for him once. I put the hurt on more than a few sons'a bitches who thought they wanted to mess with me. Don't make me proud. Just a fact is all. I don't fuck around. You can get hurt that way."

"Well, I don't know what to think about our buddy Carl. He does give me the creeps, though. I'll say that about him. He's a strange dude and looks weird as shit."

Lights wink on and off in the distance as we fly along and the trees and buildings come between them and us. I'm still going over the night's endeavor in my head watching the cone of our headlights bathe the weeds and tree trunks when a pair of eyes stares at us from beside the road up ahead. They appear out of nowhere, hover near the ground, then turn away and are gone just as fast as they came. Don't know what it was. In the dark everything but the loneliness of a distant porch light is beyond comprehension, seems like. A guy like Carl, like something crawling around at night, is hard to figure out. A thing beyond knowing.

"He was a wiggly son of a bitch, I'll say that," Buzz observes. "Didn't like him neither. Not one damn bit. Cryin' like a fuckin' little baby."

Twenty Three

We do another day's work with Ray. He's all excited. "Popeye's coming back," he says. "There's a deal going down. We have to set the wheel up and get her working soon as we can. Has a guy wants to buy her, but he wants to check her out first."

We wait a few days for Popeye, then we get the show rolling. It goes back up in the reverse order we took it down, but it's more of a job than we thought. Takes time to figure out what goes where, and in what order. As I said, It's always easier to take something apart than it is to put it together in the first place. A life for instance, or a country, I guess. I'm just sayin'.

We start by raising the two arms on the front. Then we have to install the hub and axle and other various parts on the rear arms. All this takes most of a day. Then we have to unload the smaller pieces and get them ready for attachment. As it begins to take shape we find ourselves getting kind of excited. The spokes extend, making pie wedges that create the two wheels when they're all on. On the second day we connect the cross bracing on all the spokes. We have to set the carriages in place before it begins to look like something. It's hard work and we're feeling pretty tired by the end of each day, but it'll be worth it if we can sell it. The Great Mandala's almost all together when Popeye says he has to get back to his job in Georgia. Once the guy's ready to come check everything out, we'll finish her up and rent a big ass generator for power, Ray says.

At the end of the last day Ray hauls out a cooler full of beer for us. We sit in the bottom gondolas, and drink and tell lies until it's almost dark when everyone goes home. I stay where I am, sitting in the dark, and thinking about life and Mariela, wondering what if. I imagine the wheel going around and around, but I'm having a hard time telling myself the Ferris wheel story. Sometimes stories are just not enough.

In the morning I wake and check my avocado seed and change the water. For breakfast I look at the picture of the Peanut Log. This just makes me hungry so I'm thinking I'll take the bike and go somewhere and have a real breakfast with pancakes and eggs and all that good stuff that's so bad for you. I can stop at Stuckey's after for dessert. I hear a car so I go outside to have a look and see John Bingham standing beside his car staring up at the Ferris wheel. He has a look of disbelief on his face, as though he thought maybe he'd accidently driven off the edge of the real world into Area 51, or straight into an episode of Twilight Zone and found what the Air Force has been hiding all these years. I step out onto the grass. He looks at me now like I'm from another planet. Then he shakes his head.

"I don't know why," he says, "that I didn't think to put something in the rental agreement about Ferris wheels. I guess it just slipped my mind."

"I can explain," I say.

"I'll bet," he says. "Can't wait to hear it."

After I tell him what's going on and he collects next month's rent, I go back inside and try to recapture my earlier dream of eating pancakes. I even say out loud to my dead mother, "I'll have pancakes, Ma." No answer, of course. There's another movie I'll never be in again.

Then I'm sure I hear another car and go outside to find Mariela standing there with the door open. She too is looking up at the Ferris wheel. I wait for her to ask and then say, "What Ferris wheel?"

She isn't laughing. "I'm on my way to Birmingham," she says. "Are you coming or not?"

"They found her?"

"Yes."

On the highway, she's all revved up and so is the car. She's driving way too fast. The roadside is flying by my window turning the world into a smeary blur. "You'd better slow down a little," I warn her.

"It's a long way up there and you don't want to get pulled over. They like to drag things out, make you wait a long time even if it's just a ticket. Then who knows what they'll put us through if they ask to see my ID and get a look at what I've got for a record." She sighs a whole mornings worth of sighs and lets up a little. It takes her a few but eventually she calms down to a reasonable speed.

"I've only got bits of the story," she says. "Carl didn't have her stashed away somewhere, after all. She ran away on her own. Now, here's the hard part. The old woman they found her with was dead. Been dead a while, they said. Jessie was hiding in a closet in the back bedroom. The house was a mess and overrun with stray cats, some of them practically feral, two litters of kittens in the basement. They don't know how Jessie came to be with her. I guess, big surprise, she's not saying much."

I'm relieved but having a hard time taking this in. "Dead?" I say.

"Yeah, dead. No foul play suspected. The woman was old. I mean *old*, old. Probably died of natural causes. So far there's no reason to think anything else."

"And Carl?"

"They don't know yet. That's one reason why I brought you. We need to help them with getting her to talk. They want to know what the hell happened. With the old lady and with Carl."

"And the other reason?"

"I thought it would help her to see you."

"Yeah?"

"I also thought it would be a nice thing for you. You know, not to have to sit in that little shack waiting for us to get back."

"So they'll let us take her?"

"I think so. That is I hope so. Once they finish checking her out. They have to evaluate her condition, they said. But only because I'm with Child Protective. They wouldn't give her to anyone else. I sure as hell won't let them give her back to Carl and Charlene."

There's no talk about us, and I know better than to bring it up. She's got this other guy now and I don't really want to make a fool out of myself. There's more than one way to skin a cat, they say, but this one's already done been skinned—and hanging on the wall, apparently.

In Birmingham, we stop first at the Sheriff's Department. Mariela hands them an envelope with some forms for them to sign transferring temporary custody to Mariela and Florida Child Protective Services. Then we head for the hospital where they're holding her. There's an officer sitting in a chair outside her room. Jessie's sitting up in bed watching

TV when we enter. You can tell she hasn't eaten in a while. She looks like she did when I first saw her. They've given her a bath and washed her hair, but she's thin and tired; there's a vacant look to her eyes. I see a book lying on the bed. Lemony Snicket, the Wide Window, but she's not reading it. She seems surprised to see us but doesn't speak. Her face doesn't light up and she seems confused by our presence. She looks at Mariela, then at me. Mariela runs over and hugs her. I take her hand and try to give her a reassuring smile.

"As soon as they'll let us," Mariela says to her, softly, "we're taking you back with us."

I'm not sure what we were expecting but there's no reaction at all. Not even a glimmer of a smile. It's clear now that she's been severely traumatized, from before probably and this latest thing only the final straw. And we have no idea what really happened.

A woman wearing glasses enters the room and identifies herself as Dr. Harris, a child psychologist. She wants to speak with us in another room, she says. We assure Jessie that we're just going to visit with the doctor for a little bit and we'll be right back. She looks down at her book and pokes at it with her finger, pushing it away, gently and slowly, an eighth of an inch at a time. Disturbed is how it strikes me.

She's in her own little world, I guess. God knows what she's thinking. I see tears glisten in the rims of her eyes—still blue, but…what can I say? Sad doesn't tell you what's in there. It's somewhere way beyond that.

We're led to an office down the hall and sit facing a desk where Dr. Harris sits. She has a pair of half glasses that sit low on the bridge of her nose giving her an extra air of credibility. She appears competent, and has a warm personality that puts us more at ease. "I want to thank you for coming all the way up here," she begins. "This whole thing is disturbing, and I have to say, not a little strange. Little by little we're getting the story out of her, but she's not a talker." Mariela and I exchange a smile at this, of course, but brace ourselves for what's to come. "It's not clear yet why she ran away, but probably has something to do with Carl. That's my guess based on experience. She doesn't like him, and he, of course, has a history, as we've come to find out. How she wound up in that house with Mrs. Holloway we're not sure. According to a neighbor, the girl, Jessie, was standing in Mrs. Holloway's backyard and a bit later the neighbor saw the girl picking up pieces of the bread that Mrs. Holloway had thrown out there earlier for the birds to eat like she did every day. The girl was eating the bread, apparently. Must have been starving, the poor thing. The neighbor went to get her husband so he could see what the girl was doing and when they got back she was gone.

"Mrs. Holloway was a shut in, kind of a recluse, and not all there for a few years, now, due to Alzheimer's or perhaps it was just ordinary dementia. Her family had sort of abandoned her and yet she got by somehow. People checked on her from time to time; someone paid her bills, family I suppose, but otherwise she was all alone in there with her cats. I guess she had dozens of them. The house reeked of cat pee and they'd started doing their business everywhere. The litter boxes hadn't been emptied in weeks. The cats were half starved and some of them half wild, the police said. She was a bit of a hoarder, I guess. Junk piled everywhere. They'll do an autopsy, but it looks like she died of natural causes. She was in her early nineties from what we've been able to figure out. We're getting her records from the census department. In any case, she was just lying there, in the living room on her recliner in front of the TV with a blanket pulled up to her chin.

"I think Mrs. Holloway must have seen Jessie in the yard and opened the back door. She probably smiled and said Hi or something and being senile had no idea who the girl was and what she was doing in her backyard but was glad to see her. Maybe she thought she knew her. Jessie was hungry and all alone, and probably felt safe with this old woman who looked like anyone's grandmother, and so went into the house and let the woman feed her. Seeing all the cats might have been an attraction. What little girl doesn't like cats? Seeing all the food in the house she had good reason to stay. She had nowhere else to go and it was safe. The grocer's apparently sent a boy over on a regular basis with a box of groceries and was paid by whoever was managing her money. Not sure how long she'd been dead, but several days at least, they said. The neighbor finally called when the delivery boy left the box of groceries on the front stoop because no one answered the door. She knew something was up when it was still there the next day and went to investigate. When she opened the door, the smell alone was enough to make her call the police, she said. They found Jessie hiding in the closet with a kitten in her lap.

"As to why Jessie ran away in the first place, that will take more time. She's been through a lot, poor kid. From what I understand this is just part two or three of a much longer story. The first night she was here, I guess that was two nights ago, I tucked her in and together we said a little prayer. Afterwards she said to me, 'He's not coming back, is he?' and I asked her, 'who's not coming back, dear, who's not coming back?' thinking she meant Carl, and she looked at me and said, 'Jesus.' I have no idea why she would ask me a thing like that. Because of the prayer, I guess."

They are, of course, anxious to find out if Carl did anything to make her run away. But before they can drag him back in for more questioning, they want to get something concrete from Jessie. That's where we come in, helping them do that, Dr. Harris says. We can't drive back tonight, anyway, so Mariela asks Dr. Harris if she can stay in Jessie's room with her tonight. I find a room down the street and grab something to eat at a diner next door, then I get a beer in this bar I find a few doors down. There's a game on the TV. Baseball. I try to watch but it's been so long since I did that and these are not teams I've ever cared about, anyway. I drink my beer and picture the girl in that house alone with all those cats and that dead woman in her recliner. She's curled up in the closet with a kitten, for Christ's sake. That's what should be on the TV. A picture of Jessie in that closet. Not a goddamn baseball game.

Later, I lie in bed wondering what they did with all those cats. I'm in high gear now going over all of it. Where are they? I wonder. How many did she say there were? And what would you do with that many cats? Where do they take them? And the kitten.

Where's the fucking kitten? What did they do with that? Is it with the rest of the cats? Is it? And what the fuck did he do to Jessie? What did that piece of shit Carl do to Jessie?

In the morning, the police are back with their own Psychologist. He looks like a Sunday school teacher, but not exactly born in a manger, if you know what I mean. I make an effort to like him and finally give up. They take Jessie into a room with anatomically correct dolls and try to get her to play with them. She won't take the dolls and after fifteen or twenty minutes of making nice and gently pushing they get her to cry. You can't tell at first, but then you see the tears dripping off her chin. They back off and Mariela suggests leaving her alone with some crayons and paper. We also ask if, after she settles down, we can sit in the room with her. Reluctant, and with a snooty arch of his eyebrows, the Sunday school teacher says okay.

It's getting late in the morning and we want to get started, if we have to drive all the way back today, but after a bit, we busy ourselves with something else, discussing how to get to the interstate and the weather forecast, and eventually Jessie starts scribbling on the paper out of boredom. Then we notice that she's beginning to draw something. We try to ignore her but are curious and want to know what the picture's going to be. Mariela has to stop me from leaning forward and looking over Jessie's shoulder. There's a knock on the door and the police want back in, but we nix it. Mariela nods her head towards the girl busy with her crayons. They seem to understand and back off. Jessie keeps drawing, pausing to look around the room and think about whatever's going on in her head, bored, maybe, and then looking at the paper again, monkeying around with the crayons, the way all kids do. She brushes the hair from her eyes and starts to draw some more. Then she gets frustrated, makes a face, and scribbles violently in the corner of the picture. This goes on for a while until she stops and tells us she's thirsty and has to use the bathroom. While Dr. Harris takes Jessie down the hall, we all crowd around the table for a look at the drawing. There's a girl standing in a doorway with what looks like a cat. On the other side of the paper there's a bed and a man standing beside the bed. There are more cats near the bed. She had started to color the cats with a black crayon. The cat in the doorway by the little girl is pink. This hits a nerve with me. The title of the story now is Lump In My Throat. Then I notice something about the man that makes me cringe. I notice how far apart his eyes are. It could be my imagination, but I can't help thinking of Carl. Maybe it's just the power of suggestion. I want somebody to pay for what's happened to her. But I can't help but notice the resemblance.

This, of course, on its own—my thinking the drawing looks like Carl—will not be sufficient enough to cause the police to arrest him. They need for her to accuse him of something. Maybe in time she'll be able to tell them, or us, but right now it seems unlikely. I tell this to Mariela and she agrees. We ask Jessie who that is in the picture with her, but she just shrugs her shoulders. "I don't know," she says. Of course, you can't suggest anyone, offer a name. That would nullify it as evidence. Besides, the fact that she puts someone she knows in a picture doesn't mean anything. We have a talk with Dr. Harris, and the psychologist with the police department. "We'll keep working with her and try to get her to open up some more," Mariela tells them. They seem to accept this so we make arrangements to take custody of Jessie and have her dismissed from the hospital.

In the car, she sits quietly in the back seat. An hour into the drive she's sound asleep and slumped over. Her drawing, rolled up and held in place with a rubber band, is on the seat beside her. I doze off for a while, but wake when Mariela stops so we can use the bathroom and get something to eat if anyone is hungry. Jessie has no trouble putting away her burger and fries but still doesn't say anything. We ask her how she's doing and she just says, "Fine," and reaches for more French Fries. Mariela is quiet, as well. At one point her cell phone rings and she steps away from the table. I hear her say she'll call later. I'm wondering now what it will do to Jessie to be sent off with a new family once we're back and things have settled down for her. How is that going to be? At least Carl won't be there, I tell myself to make me feel better. Maybe that will be a relief to her, but it's going to be hard just the same. How could it not?

Mariela drops me off and takes Jessie home with her. She's asleep again in the backseat when I shut the car door. Inside I light the Coleman lantern and sit at the table feeling glad to be back home, but unsure how to feel about Mariela or why I bother thinking about her. Mostly, I'm unsure how she feels about me. Forget it, Bucko, I tell myself. It's a lost cause. I tell myself I need to change the water in the cup with the avocado seed and make a mental note to do it in the morning. I check and see that there's water in my milk carton then put out the lantern. Lying in bed I think how glad I am that Jessie is safe now. These things don't always turn out this way. But safe or not we don't know what happened when she was alone with Carl. I hear a little "tick" in the darkness as the shack settles itself into the downward drift of all things and I too drift off into sweet oblivion, for a while anyhow. Just a little while. I'm glad to be drifting into the invisible nothing of sleep. It's…

Twenty Four

In the morning I get a call from Ray. Says he has an idea. Says Southland is getting pressure from his client. They want the area cleared of everything so they can sign off and be done with the job. "I told the guy at Southland we'd take the wheel off his hands for scrap," he says. "We'll move it at our own expense and he'll be done with it. Nobody wants the damn thing. 'We'll take it off your hands for you,' is what I told him."

"That's great!" I say. "What'll we do with it?"

"We sell it ourselves. That thing's worth something."

"Okay, what am I missing, here? I thought nobody wanted it."

"Nobody wants it *now*. But when the economy comes back it'll be worth some good money to someone. Fun never goes out of style, Bucko. Kids will always want to ride on a Ferris wheel, and young guys will always take their girlfriends to a carnival and up in the wheel where they can hold hands and make out a little. It's as American as baseball and the 4th of July. We just have to hold onto it and wait. My grandfather told me once that the people who made out okay in the Great Depression were the people who didn't sell their property. They stuck it out and eventually it came back."

I see his point, but he's about fifty years behind on the kissing your girlfriend in a Ferris wheel. I wouldn't want to tell him what they'd be doing now, and probably on the school bus on the way to school, too, even. "So where do we put it while we're waiting for America to resurrect itself? That could be years."

"It won't take no *years*, I don't think. But that's why I called."

My first thought is, what if the economy *doesn't* come back? I mean at all. I heard a guy on TV talking about this. *This isn't 1941*, he said. *This is now! Things have changed. It won't be like 1945 when we were the only horse left in the race. This is different. Those jobs are never coming back. Manufacturing? Forget it.*

"You and Earl and Buzz and I are going to spend the rest of our lives doing demo work," I say. "Taking it all apart, not putting it together. There'll be no more union wages and contracts for us. Have you seen an auto plant lately? Full of robots! Don't need people and people's wages, anymore, or benefits and payroll tax expense. They're done with that. We're in the salvage business now, buddy. Scavengers living off the bones of the past. The trickle down is just that: a trickle and it's done trickled out."

"Christ! Is that what they taught you in school?"

"Well yeah, it is. And I heard it on TV when I was in Alabama."

"Baloney!" Ray says to me. "You're a dick, ya know it? I never saw such a pessimistic sonofabitch in all my life."

"Well thanks," I say back. "I appreciate that."

"Don't mention it," he says.

I hear them coming when they're still a half mile away. The big diesels growl, then exhale like wooly mammoths taking their last breaths. Then they growl again in the down shift. I see the plumes of black smoke belching out, floating up and into thin air. And then the big red cab comes into sight and starts to make the turn but stops midway. I hike on out there and find them reconnoitering as though making battle plans. The enemy it turns out is the fence and, specifically, the one fence post my mailbox is on.

"Have to pull it," Ray is saying when I get there.

"Wait a minute," I tell him. "That's my mailbox on that post."

"Well," he says, "it'll still be your mailbox and it'll still be on that post. Just be layin' on the ground now, is all."

"Well, fuck!" I say and stick my chin out and spread my arms and open hands in a silent plea that makes me look a little pathetic.

"Hey relax, hotshot," he says. "Don't get yer panties in a bunch. We'll put it back when we're done. No problemo!"

"Shit," Earl says. "No one's gonna send you any mail, anyway. What the hell!"

They pull the fence post and lay it aside, with the wire fence still attached, so there's room to make the turn. Then they climb aboard their trucks and belch some more black smoke and head toward the little house. We pick a spot about twenty yards away and park the three trailers side by side. They dwarf the house and seem an odd addition to the place. This metal contraption is everything the field of wiregrass and jimson weed is not. The crickets have stopped their racket and a crow circles overhead on a desperate gliding reconnaissance to grasp its meaning. The concept of a Ferris wheel and its purpose, especially in this, it's more or less dormant state, are beyond the bird's simple brain to fathom, much less the notion of escape into fantasy and imagination when it's brought to life and goes around and around up in the air, a hopeless attempt at flight—a charade, to be honest about it! If you ask me, the world is the world, from the crow's point of view. And it can fly. What more could you want?

"It might be a while," Ray says, "but we'll sell it, you'll see. Now all I need to do is find us some work."

They unhook the trucks and leave as fast as they came, stopping first to put the fence back in order, the mailbox with it, and then I climb up onto the metal contraption and survey the world from up there. Things look and seem a little different high up compared to my chair in the grass. No bugs or snakes to worry about. Such a contrast to everything around it, the trees and dirt and grass and weeds of the natural world. It's an object other, completely devoid of life. Until you unfold it, that is. Then it comes to life, in a way, when you think about it, like a big metal flower with people all over it shouting pure happiness. That Mr. Ferris knew his shit. He knew what people wanted. Whether they needed it or not, is something else again. That's a question for the psychologists. It makes people happy, though. How can that be bad? But here it sits, a monument to what seemed like a good idea, the American Dream. You can buy it a piece at a time, little stories made of plastic and metal and wood that say: Happy!

No visit from the Birmingham Police. Carl

used his head apparently and kept his mouth shut. He's had enough of them and us, too, I'm sure. My guess is he wants to be left alone, probably forever. Something I can certainly understand. He's got Charlene, what else does he need? Unless he's guilty, and then he's got that craving. I don't know how you'd live with something like that. You'd have to hate yourself for giving in to it, or die of frustration if you didn't.

I go with Buzz to visit his brother's grave. The sun's out. It's a beautiful day. A faint breeze keeps the heat from cooking us, and keeps the mosquitoes away. The place is manicured like a golf course and gives you a pleasant feeling of wellbeing. Except for all the dead people it might be the Garden of Eden. The gravestone sits in front of a huge willow tree. Buzz looks at it and goes somewhere else in his mind, no doubt reliving a day years ago when they were still just brothers, boys doing whatever boys do on a long, lazy summer afternoon, and now it's all gone. I read the inscription: OUR FALLEN HERO. It's Robert Hanson's new story, now. Now and forever. A bird's song comes to us from somewhere inside the branches of the willow tree imploring us to listen and then it is gone. Buzz is slowly shaking his head now, walking up and dropping bits of grass he's picked, one by one onto the grave. "Sometimes I wonder," he says in a softer than normal voice, "what he ever died for. If he'd had the damn body armor he should've had, and the Humvees had the extra armor on them, he'd still be alive today, maybe. All the money in this country and they couldn't give them boys the proper equipment? How can that be? Huh? This country's falling apart at the seams, and over there…hell. They'll never get their damn shit together. They're happy to stay living in the twelfth century or whenever. They don't want what we have. They've got their own way of living. Only way to get rid of Al Qaeda and the damn Taliban is to nuke the bastards. There's no winning that war, otherwise. That's a lost cause. Ten years from now they'll still be goin at it. So tell me, what did he fuckin die for? I want to know. What'd he die for? Those Wall Street motherfuckers? They don't give a shit about us!

I have to agree with him, but instead I say the one other thing that I'm sure is true about it. As well as I can figure it. I tell him, "He died for you Buzz. Whatever else was going on at the time. He was there for you, and your family, your parents and the people he cared about. Everything else is beside the point. He died for you, buzz."

"Fuck that," he says. "I'd rather have him back."

Mariela seems to have cooled off on the two of us being whatever it is we were—friends I guess. I'm thinking that she's been out with the old co-worker, the guy from her past with a good job and clean shirts. I check the mailbox every day and find nothing. Then the next day it starts. Flyers from house painters, those college kids who show up high on ganja, with their loud radios and *fuck you* attitudes, that stay high all day dripping paint everywhere. There are numerous ads from grocery stores with pictures of different cuts of meat and all the prices per pound. Real Estate agents send glossy postcards with lists of foreclosed properties and snazzy photos of themselves with big smiles. In my situation it's actually nice to have their company but only in a picture. You get the friendliness without all the drama that comes with real live people. The Cancer Center of Florida wants a donation of $50, $100, $200, $350, or $500. Each comes with its own corresponding thank you gift. I study each gift because I'm out of work and have nothing better to do the rest of the day once I'm done studying, contemplating, admiring, and filing all the junk mail in the "No Thanks, Up Yours" file. Then it happens. I open the door to the mailbox and find among the piles of paper crap, my postcard from Stuckey's. I could almost cry, but I don't of course; it's just an expression. It's addressed to me by hand. My own hand, but hey! I'm strongly considering a $500 donation to Stuckey's just to see how many Peanut Logs I can get for the money as a thank you. I leave the card face up on the table all day, as though I'm going to have the Peanut Log for lunch or maybe for dinner. I don't have a lunch or a dinner, but it's not a real Peanut Log anyway, it's just a picture of one.

Ray finds a few days' work for us, and then afterwards I call Mariela to ask about Jessie. She says she doing as well as can be expected.

"You must be busy?" I say. I'm not very subtle.

"Well, to be honest, I have been busy, and also I've been out a few more times with that guy I told you about."

I don't know what to think. The voice doesn't quite match the words. But it's so direct.

"Okay. I get the picture," I say. "By the way, does Children's Protective Services have a mailing list? I thought maybe you could put me on it. I have a new past time, sort of a hobby, now that I'm out of work. Maybe they could mail me out a pamphlet or something. You know, for me to occupy my time with."

"This is why," she says, nothing ambiguous about her tone of voice now. "This is exactly why.

You say things like that. I need someone with a life. You don't have one, and you don't seem to want one, either. All you have is your pain, which you're in love with. You have a big hole in your heart, which is sad, but it's not a life. And I can't fix it. I can't give you one. I can't fill that hole in your heart for you, either."

I'm so stunned by this I just hang up. What can you say to that? I mean it's true. I am in love with my pain. And I don't have a life. How can I? Not without some other people in it, anyway. I don't have any people—her, for instance. Of course, I know what she'd say to that. I have to have a life first, for her to want to be in it. But crap! That's the part I don't know about. How do you have a life without a fucking job? Tell me that. That's how I lost my life in the first place. I lost the job. Then everything else disappeared with it. Then I disappeared. Simple as that. Once you're gone it's hard to come back and recreate yourself. There's a saying: Nothing Comes From Nothing. But I thought the mailbox was a good start. After that I might buy more T shirts, get a job, a checking account, a credit card, electricity, running water, a TV, and season tickets. Is that what it would take for her to want me? That's what the avocado seed was supposed to be for. A demonstration of my good faith.

A TIME WITHIN A TIME

Just a time within a time
Just a scheme within a scheme
A little world within a world
Yes, just a dream, within a dream
Once you said goodbye to me
Now I say goodbye to you.
- Say Goodbye by Lindsay Buckingham

Twenty Five

Ray calls and says he has a job for us roofing a barn. Well, hey! I think, why not. Work is work. We climb up the ladders and start ripping the old shingles off with metal bars made for the task that have a wide, flat, claw-like end to them. You ram them up under the shingles and it pops the nails and pulls them loose. It's hard work and messy. The sweat rolls off my forehead into my eyes where it stings if I don't keep wiping my brow so I tie a rag around my head to make it stop. I have to be careful not to get the grit from the shingles in my eyes when I toss them off the roof onto tarps draped from under the soffit, where they slide to the ground. We'll have to pick all that up later and get it into the back of a truck. They ask about the girl and I tell them she's okay. She's not okay, but I have to say something and she's safe for now, anyway.

The avocado seed has done exactly nothing, but they said on the video it would take a while. A while is precisely what I seem to have, a long while, so I sit at home after we finish roofing the barn and watch my seed do nothing. I change the water every day, or so, and make sure it gets plenty of sun. I move it around from window to window. Give it little pep talks. Nothing happens. I hope it appreciates my efforts. In lieu of success and satisfaction one would at least want appreciation.

Mariela finally calls and says Jessie is doing better. Then she tells me she's applied for permanent custody, which means she'll be Jessie's new foster family. Just before getting off she tells me there is one other thing. Her friend, Hank is his name—like I want to know his fucking name—has asked her to move in with him. "I haven't given him an answer yet," she says. "He said for me to take my time and think about it. I wasn't expecting it, of course. It was kind of out of the blue."

I'm not sure what to think about this. I wasn't expecting it either. Don't know what I'm supposed to say. It isn't what I want to hear. Not that I thought things would change, but this seems so sudden. I liked having at least the impression that it might turn around, a false hope, not even a hope but a possibility, nonetheless. Like the Lottery. You know you're not going to win but Hey! This news is too abrupt and final. I feel like I am hurtling through space, now, as it sinks in; like I'm falling at a rapid rate of speed towards earth. Waiting to hit I'm oddly suspended in free fall. "Are you there?" she says. "No," I say, "I'm not here," and hang up. It's like I've boarded the wrong train and can't get off. I sit and wonder why I care. But I know why. I want my story back, what little there was of it and this feels too much like before when I lost everything. There's a cumulative effect now that's just not cool.

When we're done with the roof Ray gets us a job painting a house. I'll be there, I say. The other day I was a roofer; now I'm a house painter. Earl and Buzz hate painting houses and bitch and moan all day. "Don't do it," Ray says. "Have to," they say. "Need the money." We wait for the guy Popeye knows who wants to see the Ferris wheel. We scrape at clapboards, soffits and fascia boards, nasty little islands of old paint hanging on tenaciously while other bigger pieces peel off like onion skins. It's the worst part of the job. You wire brush it and the flakes fly in the air and stick to your skin, and your arms and neck get tired, and your shin bone hurts where you press into the ladder to keep your balance, but you have to get the old paint off so you scrape away. No sense putting new paint on old peeling paint. And I'll be honest. It makes me nervous to be forty feet in the air on those ladders that sag up and down in the middle when you climb too fast. I'm tired when I get home and fall asleep sitting in the bottom carriage of the Ferris wheel. Then I wake at midnight in the dark with a stiff neck and wonder where the fuck I am and then eventually I remember. Oh yeah. I'm here. Nowhere.

One morning I wake and go outside to pee and right there, sitting on its haunches, is a dog. At least, I think it's a dog. It might be an amateur's first attempt at taxidermy gone awry then dumped here to biodegrade with the rest of the natural world. Only thing is, it's still moving. If it's a dog, it might be the saddest dog I've ever seen. You can count its ribs and he's got some kind of skin rash. I can see it's a male, some type of mongrel, a cross between a hound and I don't know what else. He might have a cute face if it wasn't so glum looking and emaciated. The look in his eyes might kill you it's so sad. Tears are matted in the corners and weeping still, so right away I'm thinking it's the I'm Hungry *and* I'm Pitiful story. I tell him to beat it but he doesn't know that particular command. What do I do? The last thing I need is a dog hanging around wanting to eat all my food. I go ahead and take my pee and he watches and seems to appreciate what's going on. In his head he's probably thinking: Okay, I do that; I guess we should be friends. He thinks I'm marking my territory and I don't discourage him from it because I suppose in a way I am. "Go get your own place," I say, but he might be from a Hispanic home or something, and might not know a word of English. "Vete!" I yell, but he doesn't speak Spanish either, apparently. He lies down instead. I pretend to throw things at him, but he only moves aside, barks at me, and lies down again. "Okay," I say. "Stay if you want, but I'm not feeding you."

Later, the dog is still here. I've been inside watching my avocado seed motivating itself to sprout. It's trying, I'm sure of it. This is what I tell myself. Once I thought I saw it move, but I may have been mistaken. Now it is very still, as if in contemplation of something profound. Spiritual enlightenment, perhaps, as in Buddhism. It's perfect for that. It clearly has no ego. It lacks all attachment to desire, I can tell. Otherwise it would have sprouted by now. Maybe Buddha sat under an Avocado tree.

The dog, on the other hand, is a flea ridden bag of desire with legs. It plies me with its look of pathos, which perhaps is the answer after all—resignation. It has those watery eyes, ink black shiny jewels, settings in a ring that lure you in. The face is distinctive and almost noble in a way. Then I realize the trap that's being set for me. There is a story on this dog's face, and the story is a Trap. The bait is in his eyes. In the story I am giving him something to eat. All dogs love to eat. If the story had a name it would be the name of another story I once knew: Sausages and Tomato Paste. What dog wouldn't love that? I almost fall for it, but now I'm merely upset.

"You fucking bag of fleas! Get out of here!" I

say, and wave my arms at it. Now he's whining. And of course I know what this is, too. It's the Whining Story. It's only a chapter in a much bigger one called the I Get My Way With People story. I run back inside and slam the door.

In the morning, the dog is still here. I pee in his direction again and he just hangs his tongue out the side of his mouth and pants and drools. His eyes this morning are even more pathetic than the day before and say, Please! In several languages because the eyes speak the same in every language.

I'm not heartless, but I'm no fool either. I know there's no such thing as feeding him once. I know for a fact that he doesn't have a home somewhere else and he's just out scavenging for the fun of it and will go back where he came from if I just relent and give him a little something to eat. He's as alone in this world as I am and he knows it. And this, of course, is my undoing. As soon as this thought enters my mind, as soon as it registers on that part of the brain that's connected to my heart that we are the same he and I, I know I've lost the great battle for my independence. I'm stuck with this bag of fur and bones, a dog that would probably disappear altogether if all those fleas jumped off him at the same time, and he knows this too. "Okay, you pathetic excuse for a canine. You win. But you're not getting in this house until you're fumigated. I don't care if it rains all night."

He answers by scratching his ear with his hind leg then wetting himself.

I ride the bike to Buzz's house and have him drive me to a pet supply store.

"A hunting dog?" he asks when I tell him I found a stray hound hanging around the house.

"Might be a coon hound," I say to get his interest. We get some Frontline Flea and Tick Control and a Triple Action Flea and Tick shampoo. The dog food section is a little more difficult. Blue Seal dog food has at least twenty-two different formulas. I narrow it down by half, right away, by eliminating the wet formulas. I go for the Adult formula dry food, but then have to decide between Krunchies and Natural 26. A quick check of the prices decides that one for me and we get the cheaper, big bag of Krunchies. Finally, I pick out a collar, one of those orange nylon jobs that'll keep the dog from getting shot by a hunter. My plan is, if I spend enough money on him today, he'll be gone by tomorrow. That's how it works. It's the Can't Win For Losing story. Never fails.

"You got a name for this dog?" Buzz wants to know on the way back to my place.

"I thought about calling him Buzz."

"That name's already taken," he says. "How about one of those indian names like, Walks Home From Store With Forty Pound Bag Of Dog Food Over His Shoulder? That's a good one."

"All right, calm down. It was just a joke."

"Now Earl would be a good name for a dog. You like that one?"

"I've got enough enemies. I think I'll call him Blue."

"Blue? Why Blue?"

"Do I have to have a reason?"

"I think so."

"Okay, for the color of the sky like in that story."

"What story?"

"You know, Blue Skies, like in 'there'll be blue skies forever for you and me'." Of course the sky isn't really blue, any more than the ocean, but we like to pretend it is.

"That's a song, I think, not a story."

"Whatever. Songs are stories, aren't they?"

"You're a weird sonofabitch you know that?"

"I'm beginning to."

The dog's still here when I get back and Buzz looks him over with a quick glance. One look and Buzz gets back in the truck.

"Where you goin? I haven't got my stuff out

of the back?"

"We're going back to the store. You should get your money back on the dog food and flea and tick stuff. Keep the collar and wear it yourself. You're the one that oughta be on a leash."

"That's my dog you're talking about, Buster."

"That ain't no dog!"

"Hey c'mon. Don't be a dick. You're pissing me off now."

"You sure that's a dog?"

"Not a hundred percent."

"Maybe after you feed it awhile it'll look like one."

"Hope so. He's one sorry looking dog right now, isn't he?"

Twenty Six

We paint another house and then Ray tells us Popeye called. He's bringing his potential buyer down the day after tomorrow. Ray shows up the next day with the generator and we finish getting the wheel ready for the big demonstration. I keep feeding him so Blue starts to look more like a dog and doesn't scratch so much. He smells like a Vet's office, now, but it's better than the way he smelled before. He quits doing that thing where he jerks and snaps his head around, teeth bared with a low growl, looking at his hind quarters, like, what the hell was that? Of course it's when some flea takes a big bite out of his ass, then lays low to drive the dog crazy—the small tragedy that is a dog's life. Blue seems to like people okay. He jumps all over Buzz, like maybe they'd had a past life together. I've always figured Buzz for being a dog in a previous life. He's practically one now.

I teach Blue to fetch and so far we have the first part down real good. I throw the stick and he goes after it, but he doesn't seem to grasp the second part where he's supposed to bring the stick back. He just runs around with it in his mouth, while I holler his name and pretend he's going to obey. Or else he comes back right away, but without the stick. When I let him in the house for the first time he trots all around sniffing and sticking his wet nose on everything as though he's never seen furniture before, then he pees on the floor.

I try to shame him into behaving. I make elaborate heart felt pleas to his sense of decency, and moral responsibility. But then I remember that he doesn't speak English or Spanish, or any other languages except with his eyes, which are cross cultural in their epic despair and dolefulness. I resort to something more direct and kick him in the haunch, but it's just like with fetching, he gets the first part, but not the second—the ouch, but not the *sorry, I'll do better next time.*

Mariela calls and for an instant my spirits pick up, but quickly settle down when I hear her voice saying, "She's starting to tell me things." I brace myself, not sure I want to hear. "She's having bad dreams," Mariela says, "and waking up afraid and crying. I sit up with her until she goes back to sleep. She tells me about the dreams and it's mostly something or someone trying to get her while she's asleep. Then finally she tells me that Carl used to bother her when she knew him before. Before, when she lived with her parents. When her Aunt Charlene and Uncle Carl would come visit them. After she went to Alabama with them, he started coming into her room at night. She'd wake up and feel his hand on her. At first he pretended to just be checking on her. He'd fuss with her blanket and would tell her to go back to sleep. Then he'd leave. Then, of course, he got more brazen and it got worse; she'd wake up with his hand under the covers, on her stomach or reaching up her leg. That's when she just took off. She said she hid out at the library for a day or two but when she got really hungry she went looking for food. She just happened to see the old lady, Mrs. Holloway, throwing bread in her yard. I've contacted the Sheriff's office in Birmingham. They said we'll have to have an attorney so she can take a deposition."

"Can they do that down here?"

"We'll have to go to the courthouse in Tallahassee."

There's a pause on the other end of the line.

"How have you been?" I ask.

"I'm fine." Another pause. Neither one of us says anything. Then she says, "I've become engaged to Hank."

"Well…" I'm reluctant to say it. I have to force it out. "Congratulations."

"Just thought you should know. Listen, she wants to see you."

"Well, you know where to find me." I hear dust settling around me, the air sliding about the room, sunshine pouring through the window at the speed of light.

"Okay," she says after a slight pause, maybe, to consider how upset I might be.

"Thanks for letting me know."

"I'll let you know before bringing her over."

"Sure." I hang up and look at the wall across the room. No answers there. None expected. I contemplate the detachment of the avocado sitting in the window. It's a lesson I need to learn. Existence is suffering I read when I was in school. So I welcome it, I guess, but realize also that I'm probably not supposed to be wallowing in it. Now I have to start over and turn my attention back to the avocado.

I sit and throw sticks for Blue to chase and not bring back. Then he lies at my feet and sighs, like life is terribly difficult for him. But I have no sympathy. I watch my avocado seed, still in deep meditation or possibly inert, and drink water from my water jug. There's no TV here so I watch flies for entertainment. It's always the same, over and over. Fly around then sit. Fly around then sit. Two days pass before they show up to look at the wheel. There's an accident on the highway so they don't make it down until evening. Earl and Ray and Buzz are here. The man gets out of his truck and looks up at the Great Mandala and nods his head affirmatively. "Don't look too bad," he says. He's a healthy looking man with a big belly and a red face. When he laughs it sounds like loose change in someone's pocket.

"If we wait a bit you'll be able to see the lights real good," Popeye tells him.

"Anyone want a beer?" Earl says, and pulls a cold one out of a big cooler, filled with ice and Budweiser, he's brought for the occasion. The sun's down. Popeye and the man from Atlanta, George Reevis, sit by the base of the big wheel and enjoy a moment's respite after the long drive. Blue makes the rounds leaving a consolation prize of wet nose and slobber on everyone's hands, knees, and feet. Nobody seems to mind. Dogs seem to have two effects on people. They either quiet the ego or enrage it, depending.

The phone rings and Mariela says they're on their way back from Birmingham. The deposition went well she tells me. They used it as sufficient cause to arrest Carl. Jessie still asks to see me so she wants to know when a good time to come over would be. "Come over now," I say. "I can finally give her the drawing paper and crayons I've been hanging on to all this time."

"Are you sure it's okay?"

"Sure, why not?"

There's a pause. "Hank's with us," she says.

"Oh." I look at the sky for something to say. No clouds, even fewer words. I look at Blue and think of my Avocado. "Well, that's all right, I s'pose. C'mon over." I'm not happy about it, but I'm anxious to see both of them, Mariela and Jessie.

It's getting dark now so we run the wheel and turn on the lights and it all seems to work, eventually. It takes a while to get it going, fiddling with wires and cables, but once it does, it works pretty good. The generator motor is louder than hell causing Blue to bark and pace before settling back down. "Sixteen gondolas," Popeye says, throwing a little spin on the sales pitch. "Look at all those lights. Listen to that music." A calliope sounding thing is belting out The Blue Danube Waltz. George Reevis is happy enough so it's just a matter of working out the price. He naturally doesn't want to pay what we're asking. He low balls us at ten thousand dollars. Ray makes a face and says he wants twenty. After dicking around a while and making this or that objection and parry, we shake hands at fifteen thousand. "Good enough," Ray says with a grin. We pass the beer around and talk nonsense while George Reevis writes out a check. He seems happy. We're happy. Blue's happy.

By the time Mariela and Jessie get here, it's pitch black out, and the Great Mandala is all shut down, the crickets in full cry. I see their headlights flash as they ride up over the hump at the gate and then settle again as they make their way along the path. I walk out to meet them halfway, and get them to stop the car. Hank is driving. I nod at him and then tell Mariela I want to get in the back seat with Jessie. She's been asleep and just waking up when I get in. "I've got a surprise for her," I tell them in a whisper.

I shake Hank's hand and turn to Jessie. She has about as much of a smile on her face as she ever gets, which is only what you'd think of as a smile to me. I know she's glad to see me but is still a little groggy. "Do me a favor," I say to her. "Put your hands over your eyes like this." I demonstrate with my own hands, putting them over my face. She looks at me and seems unsure at first but then she does it, she covers her eyes. "Now don't take them off until I tell you."

"Maybe we shouldn't," Mariela says. "All this has been hard on her."

"Don't worry," I say. "It's all right."

When we get to the house, I have Hank leave the car lights on, and tell him to kill the lights when I give him the signal. They're pointing off at the trees away from the Ferris wheel. I get out of the car and go around to Jessie's side and open the door and help her out. "Keep your eyes covered," I say. Then I stand behind her and put my hands over her hands. I remove one hand long enough to wave it at Hank and he cuts the head lights. I remove my hands and her hands and before our eyes can adjust the Ferris wheel starts up and the lights come flashing on and winking in different colors and the music comes alive filling the air above the field with a booming melodious song, like it's all magic and she's still asleep and dreaming, and the gondolas start turning, and go around and around. Her mouth opens in a wide gasp for breath, and her eyes are shining. I take her by the hand and walk her over to the wheel and there she sees all the men who have waited around for this moment. Buzz, who's been holding Blue by the collar all this time, lets him go and Blue puts his big wet nose on her arm and wags his tail and wiggles his butt. She squeals and pulls back until someone grabs him. We stop the wheel and I ask if she's ready to get on with me and go for a ride. She has that stunned look of disbelief on her face, and doesn't know how to respond. "C'mon," I say, and take her hand and we walk up the metal stairs to the platform. I help her into one of the gondolas and get in beside her. She's got a hold of my hand now and she's squeezing tight. Her little body pushes up next to mine so I put my arm around her and say not to be afraid. They lock us in and start it up. We move backwards, and then we're going up and up, higher, and higher, slowly, and then up and around and about to go over, and at the very top she is staring out into the darkness, bugs winding wildly in frantic circles all around us in that glaring brilliance of color, her eyes as wide as she can get them, the reds and blues and pinks and greens from the neon lights sliding across her face as though she is swimming through a rainbow. There's this big smile on her now face now, and tears brimming in her eyes, tears the colors of all the lights. She looks at me and back out into the darkness as we come down, and then glide backwards, and then up and up again and over and over and down again and back and up again and over. The story on her face now is the Happy story and I think if nothing else ever happens to me the whole rest of my life I've been in the one movie that matters most to me—this one.

"Shall we stop," I ask her over the music, and she yells back, "No! No! Don't stop! Don't stop!"

As we go around again I look down and see Mariela standing beside Hank. He has his arm around her and her head is on his shoulder and I think they look happy. They make a nice couple, I suppose. Jessie should be happy with them. I hope so. Then I have to look away.

When they're leaving Jessie gives me a big hug and says she missed me. I forget to give her the drawing pad and crayons and pencils and, of course, the doll. When they're gone the crew drinks another beer together to close the deal and we make plans to take the wheel down the next day and help deliver it to Atlanta. Then everyone is gone and I sit with Blue in the dark and hear the echo of the Blue Danube fading in my mind, but not the look on her face; I see it clearly and know it's the truest thing I've ever seen, a pureness that is worth believing in. Later in bed I can't sleep and lie here thinking how good it felt to make her smile. And how I wish the night could have lasted longer, as in forever, but know in my heart that nothing ever does.

In the morning the wheel is somber and solemn-like sitting in the hazy, amber light. The magic has fled into the ether like the music and that feeling of something, whatever it was. The neon tubes are dull and faded looking, now. I see all the rust along the metal bracing and girders and the dirt in every corner. Paint is chipping on the gondolas, the colors fading. I feel sluggish from all the beer. Blue waits by my side for something to happen. It's going to be a long wait I fear. I tell that to Blue and he rolls onto his side. A snuffle of air blows through his jowls in a quick aspirated half-hearted snort. I'm guessing he probably feels the same way I do. We're not, either one of us, too different from one another I'm afraid, or too hard to figure out, although Blue is a much better Buddhist than I am. He has detachment down cold.

Twenty Seven

The day comes when we have to take the big wheel down. It is slow going and we work and watch as it folds back into itself, as if without the music and lights life is not worth living. It is not enough to just sit here and devolve into rust; it has to go around. It was such a sight, too, turning round and round and round. The world in a colored wheel. The great mandala. It has a purpose, be it only pretend. Necessary, I suppose, for the well-being of the spirit.

We finally finish two days later and on the third day head out onto the highway. Blue rides up in the cab with me. Buzz is driving. I tell him about Carl. His face goes red. "We should have wasted that motherfucker when we had the chance." He snarls when he says this so I'll know he truly means it.

"No," I say. "This way's better. You wouldn't like prison, Buzz. Trust me on that."

It takes a day to get there. We park the wheel and head for a motel. We eat and drink beer and feed pizza to the dog. Blue seems to like life on the road. He couldn't be happier. Who would ever have figured him for an over the road truck driver. Maybe in the next life, I tell him.

Back at the house I fall into my old routine. Mornings I pee out the front door, then I make coffee with a little camp stove I finally bought. Blue snorts and rolls in the dirt and makes those growly noises dogs make, and the sun comes up and then it goes down again. Every day I check the avocado seed and every day I wonder why. It starts to develop a crack around its top and bottom like it's supposed to do, but otherwise nothing more happens. Sometimes Blue paces back and forth and whines and then I pet him and he's okay.

Blue walks with me every day out to the mailbox. I show him all the pictures of the food on the flyers from the grocery stores. He tries to lick and smell the pictures of grilled steak but is always disappointed. It's mean, but I want to include him in whatever I do. Sometimes I take the avocado seed out of the window and show it to him so he can see how futile life can be. He declines to comment. Avocados and their seeds are a whole other universe to him. They don't seem to register.

I call Mariela to see how Jessie's doing and tell her I have the doll and the drawing materials to give her. She says she'll get them sometime when they come by for a visit. I don't know when or even if that will ever be. Meanwhile the doll sits in the chair, eyes open, looking hopeful through the blue in her eyes, though I doubt much of anything is going to happen to us.

At night Blue and I sit outside under the stars and watch the universe unfolding before us. It's an awesome thing to see. There are a million stars when you start looking. But it's a very old story, the stars. What you're seeing is really the past, mostly. That's how long it takes the light from them to get here. A lot of the stars you're seeing aren't there anymore. They burnt themselves out a long time ago. Sad when you think about it. What you can't see, though, are the new stars that actually are there. The light from them just hasn't reached us yet. So we look at the past, instead. It's all we can see—and a whole lot of now. Once I lit the candle in protest, but who am I kidding. The universe is a big place. No one will ever see it.

One evening Blue and I are sitting outside waiting for the darkness to come, and with it the stars in the night sky. I look up and I see what looks like a small girl coming towards us through the wiregrass and Jimson weed. I watch as the girl gets bigger and bigger, head bobbing, her body bouncing with a lilt that could only be one person I know.

But then I look at Blue to see if he's watching, and when I look back again she is gone. It's only the light still coming from her, I tell myself; she isn't really there anymore.

A week later I'm putting air in my tire at the gas station and wondering where my life is going now. Riding this bike everywhere is getting old. I'm thinking now it might be time to buy an old four cylinder beater and hit the road. It will give me something to get around in. Then I realize I'll have to get a driver's license and of course I'll have to get insurance for the car and so I decide it's maybe not such a great idea after all. Buzz calls then and asks me where I am. He says the police stopped by his place and they're looking for me. "Carl's attorney is telling stories," he says, "about an abduction, his, and an assault by cops with a gun, threatening to kill him. The police are saying they don't know what the hell he's talking about, but Carl insists the guys that took him told him they were cops. They were pretty well skunked until they got the idea to call Mariela and found out from her that you had come up there with her to get Jessie."

The rest seems clear enough; he doesn't even have to say it. After running my name on the computer my record popped up and made me a person of interest. Assault and battery seemed just about right for a guy like me. This would be bad enough in itself, but to have had possession of a firearm, which was used in the assault, violates my parole. I'm going back to jail for sure if I stay around here, I say, but

Buzz says not to worry, "there's no way they can identify us." I'm not so sure. Buzz has never done time. Once you've had that experience you know how quickly you can go from born free to locked up.

The air compressor is on the side of the building by the restrooms where I'm squatting beside my back tire half in a daze, reeling with fear and confusion. There's a tire gauge built into the handle of the air hose that actually works so I check the pressure and decide it's okay. While I'm putting the little black cap back on the valve the door to the rest room opens and a young woman steps out. She's wearing jeans and a tank top and has a bit of a strut. Giving me a curt look she walks right past but then stops and turns around as if to say something. When I look to see why she's stopped she has a questioning look on her face, like she wants to ask me something and says, "Hey you're that guy, aren't you?"

"What guy?" I reply wondering what the hell this is.

"The guy they threw out of Chicklets a while back. It's you."

I have only a vague memory of the last half of that night but now she is looking kind of familiar. I vaguely remember my unfortunate exit involving a dancer who was not so exotic but somehow more appealing to me than the other one, the hot one with the attitude. The one I didn't like for some reason. I remember being pissed off and buying the drink that's supposed to be for that bitchy, pushy dancer but then giving it to the other one I kind of felt sorry for.

"That would be me all right," I say. I stand up and put the air hose back on the pump and look over my shoulder at her. She's still standing there looking at me with an expression halfway between what looks like bitterness and something else, I'm not sure what, and underneath it all I see what might be a lurking epic pain. Could be real sadness I see behind that smirk. I know that look because I've seen it before—complicated. There's a lot of hostility that stands out above whatever else is going on. It's the look they get when they've been shit on by more than a few guys and knocked around some for good measure. I knew this one girl in particular who had been strung out on something or other but was still ready for life somehow, in spite of everything, still thinking life's got something for her, after all, that things just might get better yet, a little spunk left in spite of how it's been. It's hard to know what life has in store for this one, but she has that same look, lots of pain but still on her feet, shoulders back.

"Well, you were right about her," she says to me, still wearing that scowl on her face but wanting to talk for some reason, and then she turns and heads for her car.

"Right about who?" I say back.

She turns and stops to look at me again before answering. In the daylight I can see that she's still no beauty but tries to make herself look good, anyway. Has her hair fixed and she's not shy with the makeup. "That other dancer. Britney," she says. "The one who got your ass kicked for you."

"Yeah…what about her?"

"You were right, that's all."

"Oh, yeah? How's that?"

"She *is* a cunt!" Then just the slightest hint of a smile appears on her face before disappearing again behind the hardness and the pain and the smirk as she turns to go to her car.

"So," I say not really knowing what I'm going to ask her but wanting her to wait, not ready to be done with this. "Are you still working there?" I say this as I take a step forward and wait.

She stops again and turns. "Yeah. Why?"

"Just curious."

"Yeah, well, you know. Until I can find something better I am."

"Don't like it?"

"Would you?"

"Why stay there then?"

"Because," she says with her chin in the air.

"The pay's too good."

"Well that's a good reason I guess. So…uh… you off today, then?"

"I am."

Cars are lining up behind her so she says she has to go. "So long. I hope they didn't hurt you too much."

When she pulls away from the pump I'm still standing there looking at her, watching her as she's about to drive off into the afternoon traffic, right out of my life and into the rest of hers. She looks back at me once briefly and sees me staring then pulls out into the street. I turn back to my bike and wheel it around to leave and take one more look up the street even though she's blocks away by now. Remembering my current situation and slipping into a comfortable dread I try to think what to do. Then I see coming down the street in my direction a familiar car that's now signaling left and turning into Papa John's next door and heads right back towards where I'm standing and stops just in front of me. The sun is out and all I see in her windshield is the glare of a blue sky and the ragged edge of a cloud and nothing else. I wouldn't even know she was in there if I hadn't just been talking to her. Then the clouds pass in front of the sun and everything turns a little darker in the shade of the cloud and suddenly her face appears in front of me framed by the car window. What I notice so much that has my attention is the clarity in her eyes. She's not smiling only staring back at me. And then the clouds pass, the sun's out again and I see nothing except the blue sky and the whiteness of the clouds floating where her face should be. But I know it's only a reflection. Inside, in front of me, is the person in the car looking back. She's still not smiling. Inside she's just sitting there, waiting. She's waiting for me to do something, I suppose.

"Hey!" I say and she looks at me while I walk toward the back of the car. "Pop the trunk," I tell her, and she does. I stow my bike and slide in on the passenger side. I look at her and then lean an elbow out the open window and look off into the distance at the sky and the clouds. She puts the car in drive but the car doesn't move yet. I feel her looking at me as if to say, *now what?* But I'm still not looking at her because I'm remembering something out of the blue that has all of a sudden popped into my head, seeing myself when I was a child, some day long ago when I had gone to the corner store like I often did and come out with a frozen popsicle in my hand. I began peeling back the stuck paper and holding the popsicle in the bright sunlight while walking home with a friend. The popsicle was orange on one side and raspberry on the other side, my favorite flavors. I'm remembering the way the two colors looked together and how it made me feel. I just liked the way they looked in the sunlight. The moment has stayed with me, for some reason, and I feel it now, fully, the pureness of the colors and the way they glowed in the morning light as though lit from inside, the way they tasted in my mouth.

"Hey," she says still looking at me. "Where're we going?"

I'm still looking across at the horizon and thinking now about the police and what's coming my way if I don't leave. "I don't know," I say, seeing the clouds drift, the sun peeking in and out, the memory slipping away now back into the past, a past that's no longer here but still remains somehow, just a time within a time, a long time ago.

"Somewhere," I say. "Somewhere else, I guess."

Twenty-Eight

They had stopped for the night at a Motel somewhere a few miles outside Mobile, Alabama. He gave Buzz a call to have him look after Blue, saying he'd be gone a while but would let him know when he was coming back. They were feeling hungry and looked around for somewhere to eat, seeing instead what looked like a carnival just down the road. He couldn't help noticing they had a Ferris wheel. She seemed excited at the thought of it, like she'd never in her life been on one before. So after getting a room and finding a Taco Bell they drove down to see it up close. "Look at the Ferris wheel," she said. "Hey! Let's ride on that. You want to?" They bought tickets and were let onto the blue gondola at the bottom of the wheel and waited while they were locked in by the attendant. A moment later the wheel lurched backward with a jolt, stopped a second, and then kept moving back and up a short distance until the next gondola in front of them was at the bottom where it stopped and more people were let on. They watched as the next couple took their seat and were locked in and waited for the lurch and movement so that every few minutes they went a little higher until eventually they were all the way up at the top of the circle looking out at the world and waiting for a few more customers to show up. From there they could see for quite a distance all the way around—a view of the world entire. The night sky was a streak of purple and pink fading into dusky evening, the landscape unfolding in a spray of twinkling lights as far as the edge of the horizon. The town and surrounding houses lit one by one in each window, and the streetlights lit along the streets and bright colored signs appeared along the major thoroughfares. He wondered how many of those houses would be empty soon. On the way there, in the car, they heard stories on the news about collapsing markets and dire predictions. To hear them tell it the country was on the edge of a cliff and about to go over. Banks would need bailouts or they were doomed and that meant the rest of us too. The world was upside down, or at least the houses were, which can be the same thing if you're living in them. Where was all the money now, he wondered? Was it all pretend? And then he thought that's it: it's all just an idea, this whole goddamned country. None of it is real. We're all like those boys in Burma making the wheel turn by climbing up to the top and riding it down again, over and over and over. It is just a dream. It looks real enough when he sees it, but so do the stars in the night sky. Only some stars are real; some not. The lights of the Ferris wheel flickered then and became more intense as daylight faded. She placed her hand on his thigh above his knee and left it there. Eventually he placed his hand on hers.

"Look at that," she said, her mouth a'gape in wonder. "The world looks pretty from way up here, doesn't it?"

"Different, for sure," he said.

"I wish I could stay up here like this forever."

He was trying to imagine it. The way it was for her, the way it looked like something you could believe in, though to him everything in life was only a dream. He pictured it in his mind as his thoughts unfolded in that myriad expanse. It was an idea that he worked on with sudden keen interest as they sat looking out at the horizon.

"Plato had a theory about that," he said.

"Plato?"

"The philosopher."

"Oh," she said. "About what?"

"About ideas."

"Yeah? What ideas?"

"You know, things that can go on forever—because they're real."

"Nothing's forever," she said, as though it was just a fact and he should know it too.

"How could you stay up here forever then?"

"You can't. I just said it, because I'd like to."

"Well," he said, considering it. "I guess maybe you're right."

And then the wheel began to turn and for a second he felt like it was the world below that was turning, and he had the crazy idea again that all the people down there were scrambling up in the spokes of that great wheel that was the world itself and the people were doing their best to keep it going in spite of there not being any power left anymore. Then he saw it was their gondola that was moving and not the world, and they had started and they went round and round with it, over and over, up and around, over and over.

Real or not, they were moving.

"Look," she said, pointing up into the night sky, her younger self sitting there with him now and looking out at the sky in wonder.

And while they watched, and like the lights, coming on one by one in the town all around them, the stars came out.

CPSIA information can be obtained
at www.ICGtesting.com
Printed in the USA
BVOW03s2248040118
504520BV00001B/1/P